THE
Butterfly HOUSE

THE
Butterfly HOUSE

MARCIA PRESTON

MIRA is a registered trademark of Harlequin Enterprises Limited, used under licence.

First published in Great Britain 2006.
MIRA Books, Eton House, 18-24 Paradise Road,
Richmond, Surrey, TW9 1SR

© Marcia Preston 2005

ISBN 0 7783 0103 6

57-0106

Printed in Great Britain
by Clays Ltd, St Ives plc

ACKNOWLEDGEMENTS

My fascination with butterflies and moths began in childhood and never waned. This book was seven years in the making, and along the way I'm sure some of the names that should be included on this page have been lost. I ask forgiveness for any such omission.

I am indebted to author and lepidopterist Robert Michael Pyle of Washington State for his patient advice and expertise, and to Kent Wilson, a fellow Oklahoman. Any scientific inaccuracies in this book are due to my own failings in understanding the intricacies of science, or to intentional licences taken in the name of a better story.

For advice and consultation, my thanks to Stephen J Cribari, Esquire, University of Denver College of Law; Doug Carr of the Spokane County Public Defender's Office; and novelist Debra Purdy Kong of British Columbia.

Love and gratitude to trusted readers Robyn Conley, Patti Dickinson and Bette Ward Widney, and also to editor Miranda Stecyk, who's been a dream to work with, and to my intrepid agent, Elaine English.

For Paul – husband, lover and best friend.
I love you more.

CHAPTER 1

Alberta, Canada, March 1990

From the window of my husband's house, I see the stranger stop beside our gate at the bottom of the snow-covered hill. He steps from his black Chevy Blazer, leaving the door open, and peers at the name on our mailbox. His down jacket hangs unzipped despite the cold overcast of the morning, and he's wearing cowboy boots. Even from this distance I am struck by the contrast of his black hair against the snow.

"You have the wrong house," I whisper, hoping he'll turn around and go back the way he came. Instead he gets back in the car and drives slowly up the slope. *Damn.*

I switch off the single lamp on the sunporch and lay aside the pillowtop I'm embroidering, a gift for someone I love. This one is a yellow-and-black anise swallowtail, scientifically correct. A dozen other pairs of silent wings lie stacked on a closet shelf—my butterfly collection, David calls it. Each time he says the words I feel the wings inside my chest. He has no idea.

From the cool shadows of the house, I watch the stranger park his car and walk up the snow-packed sidewalk to the front door. He is surefooted and somber. I guess him to be about fifty, nearly twice my age, and for some reason this makes me even more uneasy. I stand motionless, holding my breath as he rings the bell and waits.

Go away. It's the wrong house.

He rings again. He doesn't look like a robber or rapist, but I'm too tired to open the door and pretend to be amiable while I give him directions to whatever he's seeking. I need my solitude, especially today. I realize I'm pressing one palm flat against my abdomen and jerk the hand away, clenching my fist. My breathing clots in my chest.

The bell chimes again, and I jump when the doorjamb rattles under his knock.

Go away, for heaven's sake! Nobody's home. Whoever you're looking for isn't here.

And then the stranger calls my name.

Not Roberta Dutreau, my married name, but my childhood name.

"Roberta Lee? Bobbie?"

His voice sounds deep and somehow muffled. "I saw your light. Please open the door."

My heart pounds. I don't know this man; how does he know me? David is at work—I don't know what to do.

"Please," he calls out. "It's about Lenora."

My breath sucks in. I hurry to the door and jerk it open, sending small tufts of snow onto the hallway floor. No one ever uses this door.

The stranger stands bareheaded, his weight on one leg with both knees bowing outward like a cowboy's. But he isn't a cowboy. He's Indian. His dark eyes meet mine and there's something familiar there—something I cannot name. He's stocky and muscular, a full head taller than I am.

I haven't spoken aloud all morning and my voice sounds hoarse. "Is something wrong with Lenora?"

The stranger keeps one hand in his jacket pocket and the other hooked by the thumb through the belt loop of his jeans. When he finally speaks, his bass voice is flat and expressionless. "You mean besides ten years of prison life?"

I grip the edge of the door with both hands. "Who *are* you?"

He meets my eyes again. "I'm Harley Jaines."

The name echoes in my head, bounces through the empty rooms. *Harley Jaines Harley Jaines Harley Jaines...*

"You *bastard*." I grip the door tighter. "Harley Jaines is dead."

"Sorry to contradict you, but I'm not." A muscle in his jaw twitches.

I remember a photograph from years ago, a young man in uniform with the same black eyes—my best friend's missing father. How I envied Cynthia the heroic status of that photo.

And now he stands at my door.

When my knees sag, the stranger reaches a hand toward my elbow, but I shrink away. He drops his hand to his side. "You'd better sit down. May I come in?"

I turn without answering and weave my way back to the sunporch, my hands touching each chair back and door frame as if I'm walking on a moving train. I hear the door close behind me and his quiet footsteps as he follows.

Sinking into the flowered chair beside the lamp, I pull the afghan over my legs and hug my knees tightly to my chest. He stands in the center of the room, waiting, and finally sits on the sofa without being invited.

His voice is so low-pitched it's hard to distinguish the words above the buzzing in my ears. "I'm sorry to surprise you like this. I need to talk to you about Lenora."

"Have you been to see her?" I ask.

He nods. "Regularly, for several months. Ever since I found out where she was."

"How is she?"

"She says she's all right, but she isn't. I can see it in her eyes."

"We thought…she said you were killed in Vietnam."

His eyes look away. "It's a long story."

He leans back, gazing out the wide windows toward the endless vista of snow-covered pines. "What I came about," Harley Jaines says finally. "Lenora needs your help."

He looks at me as if waiting for a reaction. But my mind has flown a dozen years away from here, to a house called Rockhaven that overlooks the Columbia River. I'm seeing Lenora the way she was then.

"I talked to the lawyer who represented her, if you can call it that," the stranger says. "He's convinced there was more to what happened than Lenora told him."

The wings rise to the back of my mouth. I wonder if he can see them beating behind my eyes as I regard him blankly. "And what does Lenora say?"

"She's told me about most of her life, a little at a time. She talks about you a lot. But she won't talk about that night."

He waits. A patient man. But my heart is like the permafrost beneath the northern Canadian soil. Resistant, enduring. I face him with silence.

"The attorney thinks you know the whole story. Says that when you were in the hospital, you told him Lenora was innocent."

My mouth twists. "Which hospital? Which time?" But I know exactly what he means.

"Lenora has a parole hearing in two weeks. I want you to come and testify. I've hired an attorney, a good one this time, and we're going to ask for more than parole. We're going to try for a pardon."

Harley Jaines watches my face. "She shouldn't have gone to prison," he says. "You know that, and I know it. I believe you have the power to set her free, if you come to the hearing and tell the truth."

I shake my head. "You're wrong. I have no power."

Outside, it has begun to snow again. I watch the air thicken. From the windows of our sunporch the world is a Christmas card, the pines stacked deep with snow. Despite the warmth of the house, I feel winter in my limbs.

"She's dying in that prison," he says. "When the spirit dies, the body follows."

Wrong again. I'm living proof. How can he be so naive? He's twice my age, a war veteran, a Cherokee, as I remember. But I don't bother to contradict him.

"Bobbie," says this man I've never met before, using the nickname he has no right to use, the nickname his daughter gave me. "Do you know where Cynthia is?"

The question catches me unprepared. I stammer. "I hear from her now and then."

"Why hasn't she visited her mother?"

My eyes cloud and I tighten my mouth to keep my face blank. "You'd have to ask her that."

"I'd like to," he says. "I'd like to see my daughter. She doesn't even know I'm alive."

Cynthia Jaines's husky, anguished voice on the phone six months ago echoes in my head. I picture the thin ghost who came to see me at Green Gables—a euphemism for the mental health facility where I lived for five years before I married David. Would seeing Harley Jaines save Cynthia, or push her, too, over the edge?

"She never gives me an address. I have the impression she moves around a lot. I don't know where she is." This is all true, so I meet his eyes when I say it. I've never been a good liar.

He nods, his face impassive. I can't tell if he believes me. *Where were you all those years,* I wonder. *Why did you let Lenora think you were dead?*

But I don't want to know his secrets. I don't even want to know mine.

My mind flutters to the appointment I've made at the women's clinic tomorrow morning and my stomach contracts. Will I be able to drive myself home afterward? What if I'm ill, or bleeding? What can I tell David that he will believe?

If Cynthia were here, she'd go with me. She'd take care of me, lie for me. Or talk me out of the decision I've made. I pull the afghan around my arms and take a deep breath. When Harley Jaines stands up, it startles me.

"I'll let you know when the hearing is scheduled," he says. "May I have your phone number?"

Perhaps if he can call me, he won't come here again. I rise slowly, untangling myself from the afghan, and scribble the number on a pad by the phone. I hand him the paper without meeting his eyes. "Please don't call in the evenings."

He accepts it with cigar-shaped fingers that bear no rings. "Lenora doesn't know I'm here," he says, and pauses. "You tried to tell the truth once, but no one would listen. I'm asking you to try again."

Suddenly I'm weary of his childish assumptions. My voice tightens. "Truth doesn't set people free. Didn't you learn that in the war? You have no idea what you're asking."

This time his dark eyes register some emotion, and I see them take note of the scars that snake down my jawline and flood my throat. He has no right to come here and ask me to rake those scars raw again.

A thought comes to me that his sudden appearance might be some cosmic punishment for the procedure I've consented to tomorrow.

But no. That decision is merciful. I'm sane enough, at least, to know that. If I never know another thing for certain, I know I have neither the right nor the skills to mother a child.

I lead Harley Jaines to the door, close and lock it behind him. But with my back pressed against the door, my eyes closed, I see a vision of Lenora as a young woman—Lenora, with the ocean-colored eyes, the person I've loved most in all my life.

This isn't fair.

Then I remember Lenora seven years ago, in a cold room floored in cheap tile. Her face looked ashen against the orange prison garb, her long chestnut hair already dulled and streaked with gray. And I hear the prison guard's comment behind my back as I stepped into the visiting room: "Ain't *she* something? Come to visit her mother's killer."

Outside, the black Blazer's engine bursts into life. I lean against the door until I hear the SUV drive away, then make my way back to the sunporch. Without turning on the lamp, I stand at the window and watch the snow.

Harley Jaines is wrong.

No one knows the truth about Lenora and Cynthia Jaines, Ruth and Bobbie Lee. Least of all me.

Chapter 2

Cynthia Jaines's mother kept butterflies in the house. Summer afternoons, from grade school to high school, I pedaled my bike up the steep, winding road to Rockhaven, where my best friend and her mother lived in an enchanted world of color and light.

The house clung like determined lichen to a forested slope above the Columbia River. Sweating my way up the incline, my leg muscles stripped and zinging, I would tilt my face toward the glassed-in porch winking above me and picture the kaleidoscopic flutter of wings inside. A Swedish immigrant named Olsen had built the house half a century before, but in the years I frequented its stuccoed rooms, Rockhaven cocooned a female existence—its single resemblance to the bleak frame cottage my mother and I shared in the village below.

Rockhaven loomed large and beautiful to me then, although now I realize it was neither of those things. Tunneled partway into the hillside, it had two windowless bedrooms that stayed cool in summer, warm throughout the winter blows. Dining and living rooms faced off in the center of the house, unremarkable except for their respective views of sunrise and sunset. The cockpit kitchen pooched out on the sunrise side in a bay of miniature windows. But the ordinariness of those rooms escaped notice, overshadowed by two distinctive features: a native-stone fireplace whose chimney rose like a lighthouse above the river, and the stilted, glass sunporch jutting from the hillside into green air. Below its windows, the teal-blue Columbia looked placid and motionless, except when flood season churned it to cappuccino.

After the fire, only the stone chimney of the house remained. Blackened and naked, it towered above the leafy riverbank, a monument to Rockhaven's history.

Cynthia and I were fatherless. During the long, pajamaed nights of prepubescence, we lay wide-eyed in the darkness inventing romantic histories around the shadowy figures who'd shaped us and then disappeared. But when we first met, at age seven, neither of us had any idea of such commonality. I was the new kid in school, a lost puppy, and Cynthia was the matriarch of second grade.

During my first week at Shady River Elementary, Petey Small and his band of apostles approached me at the lunch table. I was sitting alone, considering whether it was safe to eat the taupe-colored pig in my pig-in-a-blanket without any mustard to sterilize it. Petey plopped onto the seat across the table from me, rattling the plastic "spork" on my tray. The others hovered close, watching. This couldn't be good, I decided, and chomped a semicircle from my peanut butter cookie to discourage theft.

Petey twirled a black-and-white checkered ball in his hands. "Did you play soccer in Oklahoma?" he demanded.

Undoubtedly a trick question. I wasn't falling for anything that sounded like "sock-her." I shook my head vigorously.

That morning Mrs. Hanson had asked me to tell the class about my background, a ploy I recognized even then as an attempt to integrate the new girl into the fixed social structure of hometown kids. They'd all hushed to hear my voice, the first time I'd spoken aloud inside the classroom. I confessed, my face steaming, that I had lived in four different states: Atlanta, Oklahoma, New Mexico and now Shady River. Mrs. Hanson was tactful enough not to correct my geography.

Thus Petey's interest in me. "We need one more player for the other team," he said.

Still suspecting a prank, I shook my head again. Was *sock-her* the Shady River version of dodgeball? I'd played that before, and wanted no part of a rerun.

Petey and the boys didn't leave, and I realized he expected more of an answer.

"They play football in Oklahoma," I whispered. Then added, "But not the girls." Actually, in Oklahoma, I'd played running back during a touch football game organized by one of my first-grade teachers. I was small but evasive, swiveling through a gauntlet of classmates to the goal line, my frizzy braids flying free. The moment illuminated my memory with a freeze-frame of rare joy.

But I wasn't inclined to share that recollection with Petey Small.

He twirled the ball and watched me with blank eyes, his mouth hanging open. Petey's mouth always hung open.

At that moment, salvation appeared. A crescent of dark hair swung into the corner of my vision, followed by Cynthia Jaines's oval face.

"Wanna jump rope with us?" She eyed my plate. "After you eat?"

I hadn't had so much attention in my entire life. My cheeks burned, and I could feel my freckles standing out like Cheerios in a bowl of milk.

"Yeah!" I popped from my chair, grabbing the cookie and a celery stick. "I'm finished."

Cynthia turned to Petey Small with a smile that showed two missing front teeth, one dimpled cheek, and mischief sparking in dark-
chocolate eyes. Already she knew how to wield her charm like a
weapon. I watched her, wide-eyed.

"Petey's such a *mensch,* he'll take your tray," she said. "Won't you,
Petey?"

Neither Petey, nor I, nor his merry men had any idea whether
he'd been flattered or insulted, but the strength of Cynthia's superior knowledge struck the boys silent.

"Thanks," I said to Petey, and shrugged.

As I hurried away from the table with Cynthia, aware of the
stares that followed us, our eyes met in a moment of feminine col-
lusion. We burst into giggles.

Cynthia's patronage saved me from a miserable school year. At
Shady River Elementary, every child among the eighteen in my
class had spent not only first grade but kindergarten together. I
hadn't attended kindergarten. And after switching schools twice
during first grade, I struggled to catch up. Because of Cynthia, the
other children accepted me with tolerant indifference, in my view
the perfect response. Left alone, I navigated safely within my three-
cornered universe: the fantasy land of books, the reality of the
shabby rented house I shared with my often-absent mother, and the
exotic world of Cynthia Jaines.

The first time Cynthia took me home with her after school and
we approached the strange rock house on the hill, I thought it
looked like something from the *Aesop's Fables* our teacher sometimes
read aloud. I'd never heard of a *real* house that had a name.

The door to Rockhaven stood open to an October breeze, and
Cynthia bounded in. Before my eyes could adjust from bright sunshine to the interior darkness, something huge and fluttery brushed
past my head, chilling me to stone. I strangled a scream, and Cynthia's laughter bubbled.

"That's Zoroaster," she said, holding up a finger as if the wild-winged thing might alight on her hand. "Isn't he beautiful?"

He was indeed. My mouth stretched open as I watched an iridescent-blue butterfly waft toward the light of the sunporch. Wide as a dinner plate, its wings beat as if in slow motion. "Wow," I said, while goose bumps tickled my skin.

"It's actually a blue *Morpho* from South America," she said, "but Mom gives pet names to her special ones. We have lots more. Come on, I'll show you."

I followed her toward the light.

The green aroma enveloped us even before I stepped onto the tiled floor and gaped at the ceiling of vines, backlit by diffused sunlight. Plants tangled at our feet and sprouted like fountains from massive pots. Along the glass walls, table planters of dark soil nourished a jungle of spiky fronds and lacy ferns. Occasional bright flowers glowed like Christmas lights among the greenery. And weaving through the maze, multicolored butterflies flapped and floated, random and slow as the river beyond the glass.

Cynthia's mother separated from the forest and spoke to her, startling me.

"Hello, sweetie. Oh, good! You've brought a friend."

Her voice was the forerunner of Cynthia's, low-pitched and slightly sandy. Lenora Jaines smiled at me, her temples crinkling around sea-green eyes. I'd never seen eyes quite that color before.

"This is Bobbie," Cynthia said, shortening Roberta into the nickname we'd agreed on after much consideration. I'd never had a nickname before, and to me it represented acceptance in my new world. For her, we'd picked Cincy, *Cindy* being far too common.

Lenora Jaines's dark hair was swept back into a low ponytail, and loamy soil clung to her hands. Her skin was moon-colored against the backdrop of leaves. She said, "Hello, Bobbie," and I knew then that Bobbie was my real name.

"Her mom works at the River Inn and isn't home yet," Cincy said. "What can we eat? Can we make rock cookies?"

Lenora appeared to think that over. "I'll wash up and we'll see what we can find in the kitchen." She brushed off her hands and followed Cincy into the main house, but I lingered a moment on the sunporch, unwilling to leave the mysteries of that indoor Eden.

Once alone, I stood stock-still, my head thrown back in wonder, and inhaled the chaos around me. A zebra-striped butterfly flitted from bloom to bloom. In all four states, I'd never seen anyplace so beautiful. I wanted to take it all inside me—to sip nectar and float above the world on psychedelic wings.

"Bobbie? Come on!" Cincy called. "We're going to bake rocks!"

I hesitated a moment longer, then turned and skipped toward the kitchen.

Lenora Jaines occupied her house with the same airy freedom as the butterflies. Mundane things like grocery shopping rarely occurred to her. In the midst of putting together supper for the three of us, she'd discover with genuine surprise an absence of milk, or cooking oil, or bread. This delighted Cincy and me, because then we'd be sent on a mission to the market.

Rockhaven sat on the Washington side of the Columbia, but the village of Shady River spread along the Oregon bank. Riding double on Cincy's silver bike, we flew down the winding road at terrifying speeds and crossed the wide river bridge, arriving at the grocery store breathless and giddy. After making our purchase and storing our booty in the bike's wicker basket, we walked the bike back up the incline, chewing licorice whips or sucking on sour mints—whatever dime treasure we'd chosen as our reward. In winter we rode Cincy's homemade sled down the hill.

One balmy spring evening, we arrived back at Rockhaven bearing a dozen eggs and found a car in the driveway.

"Company!" Cincy shouted. Her mom seldom had visitors.

My neck prickled. "That's my mom's car," I whispered.

Cincy clutched my arm, the aroma of jawbreaker warm on her breath. Her black eyes were caverns in the twilight. "Are you in trouble?"

"Who knows?"

She stowed the bike and we hurried inside.

Mom and Lenora sat at the scrubbed pine table in the dining room. Lenora cradled a coffee mug in her hands, and her smile looked slightly too cheerful. A wineglass stood before my mother, a remnant of dark red seeking its stem.

Would you like some coffee, Mrs. Lee?

Thanks, but do you have something stronger? Long day at work, you know?

"Hi, Mom. What are you doing here?"

Both mothers laughed, in that *kids-what-are-you-going-to-do-with-them* way parents have when they get together. I glanced at the clock. Mom had gotten off work only twenty minutes ago, but she'd taken time to change out of her pink hotel uniform into a pair of jeans before coming up the hill. She hated that housekeeper's uniform.

"It was getting dark, so I came to pick you up," she said. "Besides, I thought it was time I met Cynthia's mother."

She was using her kind voice. My muscles relaxed, but only a degree. I looked from her face to Lenora's, then back again. "I'm spending the night, remember? You said it was okay."

Cincy stood beside me still holding the eggs in their paper bag, a half smile on her face, her eyes curious as she watched my mother.

Mom shrugged and another mat of cinnamon hair escaped from its plastic clamp. "You must have asked me when I was half asleep." She turned to Lenora. "Which I often am, after these ten-hour shifts. I'm supposed to get three days off that way, but they're short-handed at the hotel and I wind up working five or six days anyway."

Lenora shook her head. "That's grueling."

"Yeah, but anything over forty hours is time and a half." She straightened in the chair and pressed both hands to the small of her back. "Thank God I'm off tomorrow."

"Bobbie's welcome to stay tonight," Lenora said. "You could sleep late."

Mom looked at me. *"Bobbie?"*

I hadn't told her my nickname and the stamp of her disapproval was clear.

"Please, can she stay?" Cincy said. "Two of our cecropia moths are supposed to hatch tomorrow."

I knew the verdict before she answered. Begging would only bring trouble later.

"Maybe next weekend," my mother said. "I haven't had a Saturday off in a long time. Roberta and I need to do some shopping."

"Of course." Lenora's voice was open and friendly. "But please know that Bobbie's always welcome. Any weekend you have to work, send her up. I'm always home."

The slightest stiffening of my mother's neck sent me into action. "I'll get my bag."

I ran to Cincy's room, snatched my pillowcase satchel from the debris on her bed and flew back to the kitchen, afraid to let something happen in my absence. Cincy stood where I'd left her, still watching my mom with intense interest. I wondered what she saw. They had met once before, at my house, but only for a few minutes when Cincy and I had gone by after school to leave Mom a note and found her home unexpectedly. That day, she'd taken off work with one of her headaches and was glad enough for us to leave her alone.

"I'll call you tomorrow to see if they hatched," I said to Cincy.

"Okay. If they have, maybe you can come up and see them after you get back."

"Get back?"

Cincy looked at me. "From shopping." Her voice sounded envious.

"Oh. Okay."

With sudden understanding, I realized Cincy was picturing a mother-daughter day out, perhaps trying on clothes as she loved to do. I wondered if Lenora thought that, too. She gave me a smile but I couldn't read her eyes.

On the short drive down the hill, my mother and I didn't talk. A pale amber moon had risen in the southeast, glittering the wide surface of the Columbia as our tires rumbled onto the bridge. This bridge was the last wooden structure on the entire river, my teacher had said. I rolled down the window, but I couldn't feel the magical pull of the river the way I did when I crossed the bridge alone. Tonight the river was only a deep-slumbering giant, distant from the lives of little girls.

Mom began to sing, her voice silvery and clear as the light off the river. *"I see the moon, the moon sees me, down through the leaves of the old oak tree. Please let the light that shines on me, shine on the one I love."*

The tires rumbled off the bridge and onto the blacktop beyond. "So I guess now you're mad at me," she said.

I didn't answer. I stared ahead toward the sparse lights of Shady River.

"I was lonesome for you, honey." Her voice was soft now, conciliatory. "Seems like we're never home at the same time. At least, not *awake.*"

The knot in my chest softened, but I still had nothing to say. I took in a deep breath that smelled of the river.

My mother sighed and changed tactics. "What in the world is a *see-crap-ya* moth?"

I burst into giggles, knowing I'd been tricked but grateful to give up the painful anger. "Not *crap*-ya! Ce*crop*ia. It's a huge moth that doesn't have a mouth. It can't eat so it doesn't live very long."

I linked my thumbs and pressed the fingers of each hand together, like wings. Moonlight animated my hands with shadows. "The caterpillar spins a silk cocoon that's brown and hairy, like a coconut. But smaller, of course. Lenora counts the days and knows when it's supposed to hatch."

Caught up in the mystery of metamorphosis, I watched my hands act out the drama. "When it's ready, it gives off some kind of juice that makes a hole in the cocoon, and it crawls out. Its wings are all wet and crinkled up on its back. As they dry out they expand, like a bud opening into a flower."

"Lenora told you all this?"

"Uh-huh. She's seen it happen."

"Yuk," Mom said, and shuddered. "Sounds disgusting."

She began to sing again. *"Through thick and through thin, all out or all in, but we'll muddle through...."*

She paused, waiting for me to join in, but I wasn't in the mood. *"To-geth-er,"* she finished.

It was her traveling song. She'd sung it as we drove the miles from Atlanta to Oklahoma City, from Oklahoma City to Albuquerque, from there to Shady River. Bored on the long drives, I added my unmusical voice to her firm, resonant one, a kazoo accompanying a violin. Somewhere along the miles, listening to my mother's voice, I came to believe that everyone in the world has at least one gift. I wondered what mine might be. Maybe I'd be a scientist, like Lenora. Once I'd caught up with my classmates, I turned out to be smart at school. Maybe I'd win the no-bell prize for science that my teacher had mentioned, though I couldn't figure out what bells had to do with it.

Mom parked the old Ford Fairlane in the beat-out track beneath the carport. She'd stopped singing now, her mind on other diversions. I recognized that quietness.

Inside the house, I queried the darkness for Rathbone, the stray cat who'd adopted us part-time. "Kitty, kitty?"

No answer. Somehow Rathbone managed to come and go from the house as he pleased. Mom probably forgot to close one of the windows.

She switched on the small light over the kitchen stove and made bologna sandwiches, pouring milk for me, wine for her. I ate my sandwich and left the milk. She left half her sandwich but drank the wine and refilled her glass.

"Get ready for bed, honey. It's getting late," she said.

In my tiny bedroom, hardly larger than Cincy's walk-in closet, I donned the oversize T-shirt I used for a nightgown, then went into the bathroom and brushed my teeth over the stained sink. When I came back to say good-night, Mom was sitting on one end of the sofa in the darkened living room, her feet curled beneath her. She offered a one-armed, halfhearted hug.

The faint disinfectant scent she always carried from her job mingled with the stronger odor of wine. I knew that, in the darkness, the wine bottle sat on the end table next to her.

"You ought to go to bed now, too," I said, resting my head against her soft breast. "You're always tired."

"I will, honey. Pretty quick. Sleep tight, now." She kissed my hair, dismissing me.

In my dream I was a cecropia larva, trapped inside my cocoon. I chewed and clawed but I couldn't rend the tough silk fiber I'd spun around myself. I awoke in a panic, the sheet twisted around my legs. Kicking free, I lay in the darkness with my eyes open, waiting for my thudding heart to return to normal.

A dim light still glowed through the open bedroom door. I gathered up the chenille spread from the foot of my bed and carried it into the living room.

My mother was asleep on the couch, snoring lightly, the empty wine bottle on the floor beneath her outstretched arm. A shaft of moonlight whitened the hourglass-shaped scar on the inside of her arm, a mark she would never explain. Her breathing didn't change as I covered her legs and pulled the spread up to her chin.

My feet were cold when I crawled back in bed, and the knot behind my breastbone had returned. But this time I was angry at myself. For a moment that evening, driving home with my mother and the moonlight on my hands, I'd actually believed we might go shopping tomorrow.

CHAPTER 3

Shady River, 1974

Three, six, nine, the moose drank wine,
The monkey chewed tobacco on the streetcar line.
Line broke. Monkey got choked.
All went to heaven in a little blue boat.

I was pretty good at jumping rope, Cincy was better, but Samantha never missed. Never. We had to make a new rule for her, or else it would have been her turn the entire recess. Lean and tall, with long red curls that thrashed about her head in rhythm to her pounding feet, Sam called out her own cadence without even panting. She said that after high school she was going to play ice hockey for a pro team in Canada.

Sam's best friend was Patty Johnson. Patty had no coordination, but she had a wide, freckled face that laughed at everything, and besides, she brought the rope. The four of us met on the playground every recess of fifth grade. We'd chant the cadence, then count each rope-skip until the jumper missed—or Samantha reached a hundred. We knew half a dozen rhymes, but the moose one sounded so sophisticated and subversive it was our favorite. Years later, in college, I heard a jazz musician sing the same words and felt a thrill of kinship.

Occasionally, other girls joined us. When six or more of us stood in the circle, sounding off in unison like an army cadre, our blended voices drew a crowd of watchers. Those times were exciting, like having company. But I loved it best when it was just the four of us, carefree and comfortable together.

On the rare days I couldn't go home with Cincy after school, my stomach began a queasy rolling as soon as the dismissal bell rang, as I wondered if my mother would be home yet, and in what condition. Usually she drank wine, which made her mellow and affectionate. If I targeted my requests for the third glass, I could do pretty much whatever I wanted. Waiting past the third was successful but risky; the next day she'd deny giving permission. But on the rare occasions she drank whiskey, she got mean. Later on, as a budding high school scientist, I deduced that the different effects of wine and whiskey must be psychosomatic; alcohol was alcohol once it entered the bloodstream. Probably she drank wine when she was feeling gentle and whiskey when she felt mean. But in grade school, all I knew was that the only times Mom struck me were accompanied by the yeasty aroma of bourbon.

In the seventies, nobody thought a parental palm across the mouth of a sassy child constituted child abuse. Not even the child. Nevertheless, by age ten I'd learned to search the house when she wasn't home and pour any hard liquor down the drain. I washed away the odor with plenty of water and replaced the empty bottle where I found it, so she'd think she drank it all the night before.

I left the wine alone. She was rather cheerless when she was sober, and she worried too much.

Even the wine didn't help during the holidays. Mom began to get irritable around Thanksgiving and by Christmas she'd progress to morose. I had one hazy memory of a merry Christmas—Mom, Dad and me beside a sparkling tree; their laughter as I careened back and forth on a spring-mounted rocking horse necklaced with a red bow. The last Christmas we spent together, I was three. Every year, when the first tinsel and fake snow appeared in department store windows, I called up that memory and turned it over and over in my mind to keep it alive.

Mom always feigned good cheer as we opened our gifts, but there was no light in her eyes and they sagged at the corners like the cushions on our secondhand sofa. The only sparkle came when she opened my handmade gift.

Since I never had money to shop, I'd continued the tradition initiated by my first grade teacher, who helped us make a felt-wrapped, glitter-spangled pencil holder from an orange juice can. Mom had made a fuss over it—after I explained what it was—and her fate was sealed. In second grade, the homeroom mother provided red-and-green strips of polyester which I dutifully wove into a pot holder, perhaps the single ugliest handicraft ever committed. In third, we framed our school photos in plaster of paris, painted gold, and in fourth grade Mr. Burns helped us tie-dye T-shirts and print them with autumn leaves. Our fifth-grade teacher, an unartistic sort, abandoned us to our own devices. I panicked.

Cincy, as usual, provided the answer. From a high shelf in her cluttered closet, she produced a sand bucket full of tiny seashells. "I picked them up at the beach one summer when Mom and I went to the ocean," Cincy told me. She dumped them onto the bedspread, sand and all.

In her mother's sewing box, Cincy found a gold metallic string left over from the sixties when Lenora strung love beads. Cincy often wore them to school. Digging deeper in the box, I claimed a piece of thin black cord, soft and shiny like satin. It was the perfect contrast to the delicate chalkiness of the shells.

Every day that autumn, as the afternoons shortened and the evenings chilled, we sat cross-legged on Cincy's bed and strung the scrolled, pastel treasures into necklaces for our moms. The project went slowly. Most shells required tiny holes bored with the tip of a screw before we could string them. Lenora accepted her banishment from the room with good humor, and I saw her only when we arrived after school or when she called us out for supper. It was that December, when we were almost eleven, that Cincy told me about her father.

Accustomed to an all-female world, I hadn't thought to wonder about the missing male in her family. At my house, fathers were a taboo subject. But one evening as we prepared to work on the shell necklaces, Cincy moved a pile of rumpled clothes on her dresser and knocked over a picture of a man in camouflage clothes.

The picture bore an inscription at the lower right: "To Lenora, with love. PFC Harley Jaines." I picked it up. "Who's that?"

"That's my dad," Cincy said matter-of-factly. "He was killed in the Vietnam war."

The young man in the photo was dark-complexioned, and even with his military haircut, I could tell his hair was ink-black. He stood against a backdrop of foliage as dense as the wilderness on Lenora's sunporch.

"He kind of looks like you," I said.

"He was half Cherokee. Which makes me one-quarter."

"How did he get killed? I mean, was he shot?"

"Nobody knows," she said. "He was reported missing in action. His body was never found."

She laid the picture on the bed beside us while we bored and strung the tiny shells. PFC Harley Jaines smiled up at me, proud and straight, and I wished my father had been killed in a war, instead of deserting us. I had no photo of him.

"They went to college together, in California," Cincy told me. "Mom's parents divorced when she was in high school, and she got a job and lived by herself. She had a scholarship for college but she had to work, too. She was a waitress in the Student Union."

I'd never heard of a Student Union, but I could hear the echo of Lenora's words in the story Cincy told, so I kept quiet, craving this glimpse into her past.

"My dad worked there, too," Cincy said, "only he wasn't my dad then. He worked in a big room where they had pool tables. He'd come over to the café and talk to Mom and drink Cokes, and they fell in love."

In my mind, the image rose up in black and white, like an old movie. "Then what happened?"

Cincy slipped a shell on her string and reached for another. "Harley didn't like school, so he dropped out and got a job building houses. Then he got drafted."

"What's *drafted?*"

"Called into the Army, to fight in the war. Mom didn't believe in it—the war, I mean—and she tried to get him to run away to Canada. But he wouldn't. He went away to get trained, then came back for three days. Then he got on a ship and went to Vietnam." Her voice turned confidential. "She never saw him again."

"Oooh. That's so sad. But if she never saw him again, how—"

"Pretty soon she found out she was pregnant." Cincy's eyes flashed up at me, mischievously. "So guess what they'd been doing those three days!"

My face turned hot and Cincy giggled, bouncing the bed. "She wrote to him and they were going to get married when he came home. But Harley was reported missing in 1963, the year I was born."

My mouth fell open. She seemed pleased that I was properly impressed.

She leaned forward, whispering. "I'm *illegitimate*. A love child. Mom says not to tell anyone because some people wouldn't understand."

"I'll never tell anybody," I promised.

"The same year I was born," Cincy said, "Mom's father—my grandfather—committed suicide. Shot himself right in the ear! He left her some money, so she loaded me and all her stuff in the old Volkswagen—the same one we have now—and started driving."

I pictured the two of them, alone on the road—just like my mom and me. Only Cincy had been just a baby.

"When she came to Shady River, she bought this house with the money my grandfather left. People thought she was a war widow and they were real nice to us, so she used Harley's last name and pretended they'd been married."

My chest ached with a sweet, sad longing. Haltingly, I explained that my mother and I, too, had come to Shady River alone, looking for a place to settle.

Cincy grasped the parallel at once and embraced it with characteristic vocabulary. "Fate brought us both here!" she said, her dark eyes shining. "We were destined to be best friends forever."

The power of my emotions embarrassed me, and I averted my eyes.

"Yeah," I said. "Forever." And concentrated on boring a hole into the peach-colored shell in my trembling hands.

On the Thursday before Christmas we had snow. Cincy left school early to visit her grandmother in Seattle. She wouldn't be back until Sunday, the day before Christmas Eve.

My mom had to work Saturday and Sunday, so I spent the long, gray days home alone, wrapped up in a blanket with my Laura Ingalls Wilder books. The evenings were even lonelier, with Mom at the lowest ebb of her holiday funk.

On Sunday evening Cincy phoned. "I'm back!" Her voice was bubbly, full of adventure and holiday spirit.

Mine was envious. "Did you have fun?"

"The airplane ride was cool. Grandma's kind of a pain—she's always nagging at Mom. But she gave me lots of stuff. Some of it's weird, but there's this hood with a long muffler attached, and it's lined with *fur*. Wait'll you see it."

She paused, as if noticing my silence. "So what've you been doing?"

"Absolutely nothing."

"Is your mom home?"

I had no secrets from Cincy. *"Three, six, nine..."*

"Your mom drank wine," she finished, giggling. "Good! Then she'll let you come up! Ask her and call me back. I'll meet you at the bridge."

The night was crystalline, with diamond-nugget stars and a crescent moon bright enough to illuminate the snow. Bursting from the oppressive bungalow into the sharp beauty of the night, I felt like a prisoner set free in a fantasy land. I couldn't keep from running.

I had stuffed my pajamas in one pocket of my blue car coat and my toothbrush and hairbrush in the other. With the hood buttoned under my chin and Mom's black boots over my tennies, I felt snug and insulated from the cold. The air bit my lungs as I whooped and howled huge puffs of steam toward the moon.

After a block I slowed to a walk, tired out by the extra baggage of boots and padding. On a rise I turned and looked back at the lights of the village. Red and green dotted the edges of scattered rooflines; a church steeple ascended in tiny white sparkles. All was silent. As I stood panting warm air onto tingling fingers, a carillon began its wistful chime: *"O come, all ye faithful, joyful and triumphant..."*

Somewhere far off a dog barked, and my vision shimmered as I turned toward the river again, my boots crunching through the snow.

The steel arches above the bridge framed it in a latticework of white. From my end, I could see Cincy entering the other, a dark red blotch against the snowy rise beyond. On the darkened hillside, Rockhaven's sunporch glittered with holiday lights like a jewel nestled in black velvet.

"Merry Christmas! Ho, ho, ho!" Cincy shouted. Her husky voice echoed from one riverbank to the other.

I laughed aloud, delight welling up until I thought I'd explode in a shower of stars.

Neither of us ran to the center of the bridge. Instead, we paced off the distance like graduates, or soldiers bearing the casket of a fallen friend. At the center of the bridge Cincy opened her padded arms and mitten-clad hands and we bear-hugged, two snowmen giggling with the secret of life. She was wearing the fur-lined hood her grandmother had given her and she looked like a snow princess.

We turned and looked out across the slow-moving water. It was too beautiful to talk about, and too cold, so we leaned on the railing in silence.

Finally, Cincy clapped me on the back with her red wool paw. "Let's go home before we freeze, Gwendolyn. Your teeth are chattering."

She was always making up dramatic names to call me. "Quite so, Alexandra," I said.

"Follow me, Rapunzel."

"Lead on, Sarsaparilla!"

Holding our sides, we laughed and stumbled all the way up the hill to Rockhaven.

When my mother opened the tissue-wrapped box and saw the pale swirls of salmon and ivory nestled on their bed of cotton, her mouth dropped open. After so many crude and childish gifts, this one was a shock. She glanced at me quickly.

"I made it. Cincy gave me the seashells."

Her fingers lifted the necklace slowly, touching each unique link. "It's beautiful, Roberta! Like something from an expensive jewelry store."

I beamed, my ego bursting. This must be what people meant when they said it was better to give than to receive.

Mom slipped the necklace over her head, lifting her frizzy hair so the shells wreathed her neck and hung down over the sweatshirt she wore for pajamas.

It was Christmas Eve, our traditional time for exchanging gifts. We had eaten supper, put on our pajamas and made hot chocolate, then come to the tree. We never did play the Santa game. After the rocking horse year, Mom always put my gifts under the tree early. Maybe our ritual let her avoid memories of Christmas mornings with my father. Whatever the reason, I liked opening gifts after dark much better than in the cold light of morning, when the tree lights looked pale and hungover.

As usual, three gifts waited under the tree for me, only one for Mom. Before we moved to Shady River, she used to get something in the mail from her sister Olivia, the only relative she ever admitted to having. But we hadn't heard from Aunt Olivia in years.

The Christmas of the shell necklace was special for another reason, too. After I'd opened my two boxes of clothes and one containing a new mystery book, Mom told me to put on my shoes and coat.

"What for?"

She smiled and leaned toward me, her eyes wide. "You have one more present, and it was too big to get in the house." She seemed excited while we scrambled into our wraps.

Cold wind sneaked under the tail of my nightgown, molesting

my bare legs as my mother led me out through the carport to the backyard. It was a small area, unfenced, that bordered an alley used by garbage trucks. I never went out there in wintertime. In the snow-lit night I saw next to the house a large shape covered with a sheet of plastic and an old quilt. I gasped, hoping beyond hope that it was what I thought it was.

Mom helped me pull away the covering. There in the moonlight stood a bicycle. Even in the darkness I could tell it was metallic red.

"I can't believe it! This is so cool!"

"It's not new, but it doesn't have a scratch on it," she said. "Look." She reached over and squeezed the rubber bulb on an old-fashioned horn attached to the handlebars. It made a sound like a lost Canada goose.

The horn would have to go, but I didn't say so then. Stamping my feet in the snow, my teeth chattering, I ran my hands over the silver handlebars, the red fenders. I still couldn't believe it was real.

I never asked for specific Christmas presents because we were always short on money, but I wasn't above hinting. For three years I'd dropped hints about a bike and finally given up. This year I'd started on contact lenses, though the eye doctor said there was no sense getting them until I was fifteen. I figured a four-year head start was none too soon. The bike proved my theory.

"Are you sure we can't get it in the house?" I said.

Mom shrugged. "Maybe the two of us can."

She brought the quilt while I rolled my new bike through the carport. We hefted it up the two steps and into the kitchen, where it left wet marks on the linoleum. The kickstand was missing, so I leaned the handlebar against the kitchen cabinet and inspected every gleaming inch of my incredible gift. Mom watched me, smiling.

I didn't know how she'd managed the money, and I didn't care. I didn't want to know anything that might diminish my joy.

"Thanks, Mom. I love it."

I hugged her, still looking at the red bike and thinking I could hardly wait to show Cincy. I'd learned how to ride on her bike.

But I couldn't do that tonight, so we popped corn and Mom opened a bottle of wine while I wiped the bike tracks from the floor. We curled up in blankets on the sofa and watched television together until we fell asleep.

When I awoke it was light and a church program was on TV. Mom's blanket lay empty at the other end of the sofa. I smelled bacon and waffles, and then I remembered the bike.

I wrapped my blanket around me and shuffled into the kitchen. "Merry Christmas," she said. "Breakfast's ready." She ate her waffle dry, like toast, and had wine instead of apple juice.

By midmorning, Mom was beyond caring when I put on my coat and rode my new bike through quiet streets toward the river. Left-over snow lay in brownish-gray heaps along the roadside. Not a car was stirring, the children still inside playing with their Christmas toys.

O little town of Bethlehem, how still we see thee lie, the church bells played. *The hopes and fears of all the years are met in thee tonight.*

On my new bike, in the crystalline morning with my friends' house in view, I couldn't have said why I was crying.

CHAPTER 4

Alberta, Canada, 1990

On Wednesday morning, the day of my appointment at the clinic in Calgary, I awake at 7:00 a.m. feeling nauseated. David's side of the bed is rumpled and already cold. My limbs feel like pine logs and a dull ache pulses behind my eyes. I remember watching the clock's red numerals flick to 2:00 a.m., then three, and four.

From beneath the warmth of my down comforter, I sense a coldness in the house and know that it's snowing outside. Winter here is heartless and beautiful, and it lasts most of the year. David grew up in Canada and he inherited this house, his father's summer place, in recompense for years of neglect. But David loves the house and these mountains; his few happy memories from childhood are here. After college he wanted to move back to the mountains, and I didn't object. I had nowhere else to go.

I pull on my robe and fleece-lined slippers and squeeze behind

David's weight machine to look out the tall, narrow window of our upstairs bedroom.

A world of white assails my eyes. There's no horizon, no sky or land or trees. Nothing but a blur of blinding whiteness.

The icy knot in my stomach expands. Calgary is a forty-minute drive in good weather, the first part over two-lane mountain roads. David will take his four-wheel-drive to work, thinking I'll stay home as usual. I have a vision of my silver Honda sliding over a steep edge, nosing down into free fall with me gripping the wheel in stony horror.

At least I wouldn't be pregnant anymore.

Downstairs, in our warm, country-style kitchen, I realize that once again I've calculated wrong. David is humming about in his navy sweat suit, obviously not ready for work. Even the baggy suit doesn't camouflage his lean fitness. Surely he won't run this morning, in all this snow.

Coffee gurgles into its glass carafe and I smell bagels in the toaster. The radio plays softly from a cluttered shelf opposite the white square of window. David looks up, brown hair askew and a shadow of stubble on his cheeks. He grins. "The pass is closed!"

The shine in his brown eyes makes me think of the first time I met them across a worktable at school. He was smiling then, too, and I felt something like an electrical shock, a buzzing in my fingertips. His major was history and mine biology. We might never have met if we hadn't been assigned to the same practicum at the Museum of Natural History in Tacoma, where we were students at Puget Sound University. The first time I saw him he asked me on a coffee date. I said yes without even thinking. I was nineteen and had never been on an actual date before.

I smile back at him now. "Lucky you." I look away quickly to hide the glaze of panic that stiffens my face.

I'll have to cancel my appointment. How can I phone without his knowing?

David is a curator of exhibits at the Glenbow Museum in Calgary and he loves his work. Still, he's as happy with his snow day as a kid out of school. He hums around the kitchen, pouring orange juice into a glass, which he sets at my place on the wooden table.

"What would you like with your bagel, ma'am, besides creamed cheese? An omelet? Fruit?"

I slide into the wooden chair, feel the coldness of its carved spindles against my back. "Just coffee, thanks."

David looks disappointed. The toaster ejects two sliced bagel halves and he stacks them on a small plate and inserts two more. He sets the plate before me along with two cartons of creamed cheese from the refrigerator—strawberry and maple pecan.

I look at the food with a mixture of hunger and nausea, thinking *only a pregnant person could have both sensations at once.* I take a moment to wonder at this phenomenon and a niggling regret etches through my chest. Some primordial part of me wants to experience pregnancy, some part that's genetically programmed to preserve the species. I picture a small, warm body in my arms. I imagine telling David he's going to be a father, and seeing the innocent joy on his face.

It can't happen. I'd mess up the child for life, leave it an emotional cripple like its mother.

My fingernails rake the scars on my forearms. After all these years, they still itch every morning. Tears have welled at the corners of my eyes and to hide this from David I rise and pour coffee into two oversize mugs. Coffee slops over the edges.

"Be right back," I say, and head for the bathroom.

During breakfast, with no newspaper today, David wants to talk. "This omelet tastes great."

I glance over at his eggs, speckled with bell pepper and mushrooms, and my stomach rolls.

"Want to share?" he says.

"Um. I'm not that hungry."

He wolfs down another forkful. "So what are you up to today?"

A bite of bagel clogs my throat. I cough, take a sip of scalding coffee to wash it down. "Nothing really. Just my needlework, I guess."

"Want to put on snowshoes and go for a walk? The mountain will be *spectacular* in all this snow." He lifts his eyebrows hopefully.

"Um. Maybe later, if it lets up. Right now we could get lost, it's so heavy."

"Nonsense," he says heartily. "I'll drop bread crumbs."

When I don't respond, he leans his arms on the table. "You ought to get out of the house more," he says, his levity gone.

I don't want to have this conversation again this morning. Finally he shrugs and turns the radio up a notch. The news is mostly about the weather. They expect the snow to keep up until early afternoon. The snowplows won't bother trying to clear the pass until it stops.

David will be home all day. *What if I don't call, and simply don't show up for my appointment?* They must be used to that—young women having second thoughts, changing their minds. I don't know this doctor and will never see him again afterward. His name and the number of the Calgary clinic were given to me by a women's hotline. They promised me anonymity. If his nurse won't let me reschedule, I can always get another name. But I can't wait too long.

Another thought freezes me: if I don't show up, will someone from the clinic call here? I try to remember if I gave them my number. I think I did. Yes, the woman who scheduled me insisted, in case the doctor had an emergency on the day of my appointment. What if they phone here and David answers? I can't take the chance. Later, when David's in the shower or outdoors, I'll have to call.

I glance across the table at my husband, a good man, an honest man. He deserves more than he's getting from this marriage. I wonder why he stays.

David and I were drawn together by mutual loneliness camouflaged as sexual attraction. I never hid from him the fact that I was living at the sanatorium, voluntarily. I had a private cottage by then and could come and go as I pleased. Staying on the grounds was an anchor for me, someplace I could pretend was home. And I still met twice a week with Dr. Bannar.

David seemed unfazed by this, even when he came to visit me there. Later I learned that his mother had spent time in psychiatrists' offices; maybe he thought all women did. He was interested in my past, but not morbidly so. He had some shadows of his own, he said. I never asked, but after we'd dated for a while, he told me.

He'd had a brother, only a year older. Michael was athletic and tall; David slight from bouts of childhood asthma. David had worshiped Michael and followed him everywhere. The day Michael drowned in the ocean, sucked away by the undertow, David was playing twenty feet away in the shallow waves.

They were ten and eleven. "If I'd been stronger, like Michael was, I might have saved him," David told me, lying on his back in bed in his apartment, after we'd made love. It was a single bed and his arm was hooked underneath me to keep me from rolling off.

"Probably not," I said, picturing his thin, boy's body knee deep in the water, in the horror. "It's hard to save anybody in the ocean. Especially if they're bigger than you are."

"I was scrawny then," he said, "but I never cared until Michael died."

I ran my hand over his muscled chest and understood why he lifted weights and ran every morning in the dark, what he was running from. I rolled on top of him and we made love again.

Our lovemaking was always urgent, but gentle, too. Neither of us could get enough. He would trace the scars on my neck with light kisses. Dr. Bannar told me sex could be a healing experience. David and I joked about that. "How about a little physical therapy this afternoon?"

When he asked me to marry him the spring he got his degree, I still had three semesters to go. But I agreed, knowing he was worthy of love, knowing I didn't quite love him because I was afraid to. Hoping I might grow into it.

On this snowy morning, as David gets up to refill our coffee cups, I ask myself if that has happened. We've been married almost five years.

The news over, the radio has switched to music and David turns it down. He picks up his empty plate and gestures for mine. I shake my head; three-quarters of my bagel still sits on my plate. He takes his coffee and leaves the room.

I feel great affection for David. I respect him and would miss him terribly if he were gone. Is that what loving a man is supposed to feel like? I've loved only women—Lenora and Cynthia, and maybe my mother when I was small. Love mixed up with pain.

I think of Lenora—and remember, like an electric shock, the visit yesterday from Harley Jaines. I've been so fixated on my appointment in Calgary that I'd blocked him out.

"I believe you have the power to set her free. You tried to tell the truth once…I'm asking you to try again." Heat rolls through my stomach like lava. I don't even know if this stranger is who he claims to be.

But that's rationalizing. Those eyes, that chin…yes, he is the man in the picture, Cincy's father. He's back from the dead and he obviously cares about Lenora. It can't be for money, because she has nothing. If she is paroled—or pardoned—would the two of them live together, happily ever after?

The idea seems so childish I can't even hold it in my mind. I decide to ignore the resurrected Harley Jaines. Maybe he'll disappear like a wisp of my imagination. So many things will go away if you ignore them long enough. Like that line from a poem, "The face of the mother with children/ignores and ignores…."

But unlike old memories, a pregnancy can't be ignored. This I must deal with immediately. Dr. Bannar would be proud of my ability to make a firm decision and take action, whether she agreed with the action or not. "Take responsibility for your life," she kept saying. "Take control."

Would she agree with abortion? I wouldn't know even if I could ask her. She always turned the hard questions back to me.

After breakfast, David stands in the closed-in back porch and dresses in thermal coveralls, ski mask and snowshoes. "Come with me," he urges.

"Maybe later."

I am glad his ski mask hides his disappointment. I tell myself I will go out after I make the phone call. As soon as David steps out into the snow, I go upstairs to the telephone in our bedroom.

As so often happens, all my worrying has been over nothing. The doctor's assistant is understanding when I tell her the pass is closed and I have to cancel. Why wouldn't she be? The blizzard isn't my doing, after all; it's an act of God. She cheerfully reschedules me for two weeks later. I hang up the phone with a buzzing in my ears as loud as the dial tone. My heartbeat jolts my chest.

Downstairs, I pull on my own thermal coveralls, boots and hood. I lash snowshoes onto my boots and step awkwardly out the back door into the white wilderness.

The cold makes me gasp. Tears form in my eyes and immediately turn into frost on my eyelashes. I scan the yard for David, but he's out of sight.

The mountainside is eerie as a moonscape and incredibly beautiful. I start off toward the hiking trail David maintains, which winds through our acreage and up the steep slope behind our house to a meadow that overlooks the valley for miles. I hope this is the direction he's gone; why didn't I ask?

On the trail, the trees become trees again instead of white

mounds. Their trunks are packed with snow on the north side and branches droop like the oily wings of cormorants I once saw along a northern coast after an oil spill. I slog along the trail, listening to the whirring silence of snow sifting through fir and pine, and my own labored breath.

After a few minutes, I stop. Trees surround me, and I can no longer see David's tracks or where the trail has gone. I search for landmarks, but any familiar deadfall or boulder is buried in snow. Everything is changed, as if I've never been here before.

Perhaps I haven't. I turn a circle but can't see the house. I don't even know which direction it is. This slope catches the wind, and my tracks, too, are fast disappearing. I begin retracing them but come to a halt when the space ahead of me seems to fall away steeply. I don't remember this drop-off....

I look straight up through the trees. *The woods are lovely, dark and deep / But I have promises to keep / And miles to go before I sleep / And miles to go before I sleep.*

"David!"

My scream sounds muffled in the snowy silence. I draw a deep breath and try again.

"David, I'm lost! *David!*"

CHAPTER 5

I stand rooted to the snowy slope like the fir trees around me, screaming David's name. My snowshoes sink inch by inch into foot-deep powder.

I listen hard into the rushing silence but hear only the sigh of the wind through the trees. My eyes strain to see past the flurry of whiteness until even the distinction of vertical pine trunks disappears, and I am snowblind.

Vertigo gathers momentum like an avalanche in my brain. I take deep breaths, fighting it, but lose the battle. The sky spins. I summon all my strength behind my hoarse voice.

"David! Can you hear me?"

Then I am falling.

Not through snow, but into a wall of leaping flames. The hillside, the sky, the world is engulfed in fire. Bright wings beat wildly inside my head, fighting to escape. I am running through flames...glass walls explode...my foot connects with something soft, something human that shouldn't be there. And I am falling through fire....

When my eyes jerk open, I'm lying in the snow. An unbearable nausea, like seasickness, washes over me. Cold burns my face.

I hear a muffled sound. David's voice?

My elbows tremble when I push myself up and struggle to my feet, clinging to a tree while the world swims around me. I hold my breath and listen.

"Roberta! Keep yelling so I can find you!"

Heat floods through my stiff limbs. His voice sounds far away, but I fix on its location and the vertigo disappears.

Keep yelling, he said. I can do that.

"I'm here! Over here!"

Breathless but weirdly elated, I suck in air and call out again. I struggle to move but am stuck in the snow.

A dark shape materializes from the whirl of falling flakes— Sasquatch in a red ski cap. An overgrown redheaded blackbird. I start to laugh.

By the time David wraps me in his insulated arms, I'm giggling wildly. I feel his warm breath against my cheek, but he isn't laughing. He holds me tightly until I quiet down. Then he turns me away from the drop-off and guides me through the trees with a gloved hand.

His breath comes through the red mask in steamy puffs. "Why didn't you tell me you were coming out? I'd have waited for you."

I don't answer. I don't remember the answer. It doesn't matter anyway. What matters is that he knows how to find the trail. My knees tremble lifting the clumsy snowshoes.

"Maybe we ought to mark the path with yellow flags or something," I suggest, trying to sound normal. But my voice shakes so that when I hear it, I start to laugh again, but only a little.

"Good idea. If I'd realized how low the visibility is, I wouldn't have come out until later. I nearly got lost myself."

This isn't true, of course. He's trying to make me feel better about my helplessness. David grew up in these woods; he came here with his parents every summer of his first eleven years. In the winter they used to cross-country ski here. After his parents divorced, he even came back once with his dad, before they gave up trying to talk to each other.

When I see the outline of the house ahead of us, my heart makes a painful leap that catches in my chest. If it were possible in snowshoes, I would run.

My confidence returns as we get closer to home, though I don't let go of David's arm. At the back porch I turn to look out across the white wonderland. The snowfall has lessened for the moment, the sky lifted. Mountain peaks shrouded in clouds angle downward in frosted slopes that sink away toward the valley.

Severely beautiful. We stand a moment in silence.

"How about some hot chocolate?" I say, as cold seeps beneath my layers of clothes.

"Sounds good. After I feed the birds, I'll come in."

Not many species of birds winter here, but David feeds the hardy ones every day. From our sunporch windows I can watch them gobble seeds and suet, insulating their tiny bird bones from the cold. Sometimes I spend entire mornings watching them scratch and peck atop our picnic table and beneath it. I wonder where they sleep in the subzero Canadian nights, and how they manage not to get lost.

That evening the TV weatherman says the blizzard is over and the pass has been cleared. I digest this news with mixed feelings.

The next morning David gets ready for work. "Why don't you get dressed and go with me?" he says. "You could poke around the museum this morning." He knows I love spending time there alone, especially in the Rungius gallery. The artist's wildlife and landscape paintings are breathtaking; I never tire of seeing them.

"At lunch I could drop you off at the shopping mall," David says. "Or the library."

"I'll be fine here. Really. I don't feel like going to town today."

He gives me a quick goodbye kiss before he goes out the door. I hear his Jeep start up and plow down the unshoveled driveway.

When I've cleaned up the breakfast dishes, I settle on the sunporch with my needlework. The butterfly on the pillowtop blooms yellow and black, its stripes vibrant in the warm cone of lamplight. The colors are satin beneath my fingertips. Secure in this familiar way, I let myself think about my postponed doctor's appointment, and about what happened yesterday morning in the snow.

The dreams of Rockhaven come less frequently now, just as Dr. Bannar predicted. Except for the nights when I don't take the sleeping pills she prescribed. Sometimes those sleepless nights are a refuge, a time zone separate and unconnected to my repetitious, panic-filled days. In the quiet dark, I take out the past like an old locket and turn it over and over in my hands. I try to believe that when I've done this a specific but indeterminate number of times, I will be able to put it away forever.

It isn't working. How long can I live this way before I step over the edge again?

At midmorning David phones, ostensibly to ask if I want anything from the store. I know he's checking on me; he's such a worrier. I list bagels and milk and whatever fresh vegetables at the market look edible today.

By lunchtime I have finished embroidering the orange-and-blue spots on the butterfly's hindwings. I am rethreading with black, looking forward to outlining the teardrop-shaped swallowtails, when the telephone rings again. Impatient, I pick up the receiver intending to tell David I'm not a child and he doesn't need to keep calling.

My stomach lurches at the sound of the bass voice that reverberates across the line. It needs no identification, but he gives one anyway.

"It's Harley Jaines."

The embroidery needle pierces my fist and a red droplet rises instantly on the knuckle.

"I've just come from the prison," he says. "Lenora wants to see you."

I watch the red drop swell on my hand. "I'd like to see her, but I don't think I can." I sound helpless as a child and hate it.

"I could drive you. I'll come this afternoon. Or tomorrow, if that's better."

"*No!* No. I can drive myself." But it's a long way to Spokane, more than four hundred miles. "Maybe next week, if it doesn't snow again."

In the long pause that follows, I bring my knuckle to my lips and suck away the blood.

"You've got to help her, Bobbie. You have to come to the hearing." His rumbling voice is gentle now; I am only imagining the menace behind his words.

"Maybe it would help you, too," he says.

The house ticks its irregular heartbeat in the silence. I think of Lenora's pale face in the sterile prison, then see her tanned and animated among the tangled vines of my childhood. I force deep breaths to stop the spinning in my head. "I'll talk to Lenora about it."

"When?"

"*I don't know!*"

He waits a beat. "If you don't come down by Monday, I'll come to get you."

"Don't threaten me! And don't come back here."

I jab the button on the portable phone so hard it flies from my hands and clatters to the floor. My hands are shaking.

This won't do—too much silence. I go to the living room and switch on the stereo. An old Elton John song floats through the house, a song Lenora used to love. I can hear it playing from her dusty radio on the sunporch, nestled among the leaves and loam on the potting table.

And suddenly I'm desperately homesick to see Lenora. I want to ask her if Harley Jaines has told me the truth. I'm slipping back toward that dark place where I've been before. Lenora is my anchor, but I abandoned her. I let her stay in prison all these years.

Could I really have changed that? Why didn't I try?

I know I must drive to Spokane.

David will want to go with me. That's okay. I could let him drive while I zone out, maybe sleep. Perhaps Lenora won't look so pale and lonely this time. I could talk to her about finding myself pregnant, how wretched it is to know what I must do....

No. I mustn't use her that way. I wipe my face on my sleeve and go back to the porch, wrap up in the afghan and stare out at the snow.

Lenora will ask questions that I can't answer. Emotions could swamp me. I know the dangers, but the thought of seeing her is soothing and a longing grows in my chest.

So I rationalize: If I go, Harley Jaines won't come here again. If I talk to her, Lenora will understand that I can't testify at her hearing. That I cannot save her because it's all I can do to save myself.

CHAPTER 6

In my earliest memory, I am lying in a bed with bars on the sides, a crib, and watching tiny speckles of light dance on the ceiling. I'm supposed to be sleeping. Instead, I listen to the music that seeps through the wall from the next room. I hear my mother's voice, and my father's and another man's. I don't know who he is but my mother does. I can tell by her voice, though I don't understand the words.

The music feels happy. I hear my mother laugh and then the front door closes and her voice is gone. Only the low, rumbly sounds of Daddy and the stranger drift through the wall as I doze off.

Later something wakes me—a dream. A noise, maybe. I'm frightened but not enough to cry. The light has receded into a thin stripe around the door. The music is still playing in the next room but I don't hear any voices. I throw one leg over the crib railing and hoist myself up—then I'm tumbling to the floor. I land on my big stuffed bear and roll off unhurt. I pick him up and get the door open and go out into the hall.

Daddy and the other man are sitting on the sofa in the living room with their backs toward me. Their heads are shadows in the lamplight.

"Daddy," I say, and both faces turn toward me, surprised. More than surprised. Frightened?

Then they both smile and my father comes around the sofa, fast, and sweeps me up.

"Well, look at you! How did you get out of bed all by yourself?" He laughs and the other man, whose face I cannot remember except for a frame of reddish curly hair, laughs, too.

Carrying me back to bed, my father kisses the top of my head. "What a big girl you're getting to be," he says. "Daddy's smart, big girl." His voice sounds sad.

I was fifteen when my mother finally told me the truth about my father. She didn't mean to. She meant to keep it secret forever. If she'd succeeded, it might have saved us all.

On Friday evening after dinner, I finally tell David about Harley Jaines. We argue about whether I should go to Spokane.

"You don't know who this guy is. He could be some kook," David insists. "We should have him checked out. I'll call the prison, find out if Lenora's had a regular visitor, if there's really a hearing coming up."

"David, I *know* who he is."

"Maybe, maybe not. Don't let him scare you into going down there if you're not ready to see her. I don't want you—" he pauses, choosing his words "—to make yourself sick again."

Crazy again.

Pinpoints of light float through my vision and blackness gathers around the edges. I curse my inability to handle a normal household argument, or any stress at all. I take a deep breath and blow it out the way a sprinter does, the way Dr. Bannar showed me. Breathe and blow. Keep the oxygen flowing.

David paces between the kitchen table and the sink, numbering the reasons I should not make the trip, while I sit huddled on my chair staring at the half-eaten food congealing on my plate, hugging my knees. Suddenly I wonder whether it is I who have shut myself in this house like a recluse, or whether he's keeping me here. Like a specimen in a jar. *Homo sapiens insanitus.*

I interrupt him. The confidence in my voice surprises us both.

"David. Regardless of Harley Jaines, I need to see Lenora. I *want* to see her. I don't think I'll ever be normal again—" *was I ever normal?* "—until I've done this."

He looks at me as if I've already lost it. Worry and fear show in his eyes.

I spread my hands and state the obvious. "Hiding hasn't worked."

He shakes his head, defeated, then he comes to stand behind my chair. Without speaking, he places his hands on my shoulders and lays his cheek on the top of my head. I know he means it as a gesture of love, and it makes me feel like an unresponsive mother.

"I'll drive you down on Sunday," he says. "I'll go in tomorrow and finish setting up the new exhibit so we can stay overnight in Spokane and drive back Monday."

My muscles stiffen but he doesn't seem to notice.

"It'll be all right," he says. "I'll take care of you."

I picture the two of us in the car those long hours, tension hovering over us like a back-seat driver.

On Saturday afternoon, when David goes to the museum, I pack my small suitcase and load it into the Honda. I put out extra food for the birds, and leave a note on the kitchen table.

David—I'm sorry, but I need to do this alone. Please don't worry. I'll call tonight. Love, Roberta.

When he reads it, he'll be horrified.

I lock the house and stand for a moment on the shoveled driveway, my breath coming out in white puffs of worry. *Breathe and blow.*

What will I need that I didn't pack? I haven't taken even a weekend trip for so long I feel disoriented about sleeping somewhere else. I worry about toothpaste and contact lens solution. This is simpler than worrying about what will happen when I reach my destination, or the recurring images of my car drawn magnetically toward a snowy precipice like a jumper to the edge of a bridge.

I climb in the car and start the engine. Should have warmed it up. I pull on gloves and fasten my seat belt, breathe and blow. At the bottom of the hill beside our mailbox, I turn left toward the main road.

The snow mounds high along the roadsides, but the sky is a bright, blinding blue. I fumble for my sunglasses. Ten hours to Spokane, maybe more, but I've made a plan: drive until dusk, get a cheap, safe room somewhere and sleep like a glacier. I've brought medication to make sure of it. Then I'll finish the trip Sunday morning, find a room in Spokane and locate the prison. It's been so many years since I visited Lenora there, I can't remember where it is.

I should have called ahead. I think regular visiting hours at the prison are on Sunday afternoon—at least, that's how it used to be. I may not get there in time for that, and I seem to remember every visitor's name had to be on an approved list. It's possible they won't let me in.

Hope rises at this thought; I wouldn't have to face her, and it wouldn't be my fault. But if I don't see her tomorrow, I'll have to try again. Because what I told David was true. Though I'd never admitted it before even to myself, I must see Lenora again.

I keep driving, my fists stiff as stone on the wheel.

At the main road, instead of turning east toward Calgary to catch the superhighway south to the U.S. border, I turn right, toward the resort areas of Canmore and Banff, the scenic route. The trip will take a bit longer this way, which I recognize as avoidance behavior. But the route is beautiful, and I know the roads will be cleared of snow, for the ski traffic. *Tourists uber alles.*

David and I drove this road together when we moved to his inherited house, but I haven't traveled it since. The scenery is even more spectacular than I remembered. Perhaps that's because I'm seeing it alone, in captured glimpses like photographs, while I concentrate on the two-lane road. After an hour my hands cramp from gripping the wheel so hard. I slump back in the seat and will myself to relax, shaking out one hand and then the other.

Another two hours slip easily beneath my wheels; I'm beginning to enjoy the drive. Being on my own like this is scary, but heady, too.

David made waffles and eggs for our late Saturday breakfast, but by five o'clock I'm hungry again and desperately need to pee. Up ahead I see a roadside hotel where tables and chairs sit outdoors on a wooden deck with a view of snowy peaks. Today the tables are covered with snow and the deck deserted, but I like the looks of the place and pull into the parking lot.

The small dining room is cozy, with rose-colored tablecloths and a smoke-stained fireplace where yellow flames leap and crackle. I use the rest room first, then choose a table where it's warm but not too close to the fire, and order a sandwich.

Only a few other diners come and go. I listen to their conversations while pretending to concentrate on my food. An old woman tells her younger companion whose face I cannot see, "You're still looking for what you can get, honey. It isn't what you *get,* it's what you *give.*"

The sandwich is plain with store-bought potato chips on the side, but the bread is good and the chicken tastes fresh. I consider staying here for the night, but the food has restored my energy and I want more miles behind me. By five-forty-five I'm back on the road, switching on my headlights in the early darkness of mountain shadows.

The route winds south through Kootenay National Park and finally joins a thin, Canadian version of the Columbia River just below its source in the Columbia Reach. I catch glimpses of it in the headlights.

I'm following the river that leads back to my childhood, the same waters where I once tried to drown. That history seems like a hundred years ago. And it seems like yesterday.

By the time I reach the outskirts of Cranbrook, my chest feels heavy and my contacts grate like sand in my eyes. I stop at the first motel that looks well lit. The room is spare and clean, un-complicated, and suits me perfectly. I take my sleeping medicine first thing, a nice big dose, then a hot shower. I rush through the other bedtime rituals and fall into bed, asleep almost as soon as my head hits the pillow.

At daybreak, in the peculiar blue light that filters through the motel curtains, I awake and think of David.

I forgot to call. *Damn.*

I roll over and switch on the bedside lamp, find my glasses and read the instructions for dialing long distance. David answers on the third ring, his voice husky from sleep though he sounds alert. "Roberta?" is the first thing he says.

"Yes, it's me. Sorry I forgot to call last night. I was so tired...."

"Where are you?"

I can tell he's both angry and worried. "Umm." I try to remember the name on the map. "Cranbrook, I think. Yes, that's it."

"Are you okay?"

"I'm fine. I enjoyed the drive, actually. The mountains—"

"Stay right there. I'll come to you. I can be there before noon."

"No, sweetheart. Don't do that. I'm fine, really. I'm going to get some breakfast and get on the road so I'll be in Spokane early."

"Roberta—"

"I'll try to see Lenora today, and get a room in Spokane for the night. I'll call again this evening. Be sure the answering machine is turned on if you go out." I pause for courage. "How is the exhibit coming along?"

I hear his sigh and the rustle of bedding and picture him sinking back onto his pillow. "What if you can't see her today?"

"I don't know. Maybe they'll let me come back on Monday. Meanwhile I'll find a mall and window shop."

"You hate shopping."

"Not through windows."

"What if you run into that Harley character?"

"What if I do? He's not going to *hurt* me, David," I say, feeling the irrational flutter in my stomach that betrays my confidence. "After all, I'm doing what he asked. So far, at least."

"You're scaring me, Roberta."

"I know and I'm sorry. But right now, it can't be helped."

"I love you," he says.

Why is it easier for him to say this over the phone than when I'm right in front of him? This small weakness endears him to me; my own flaws hang unfurled like tattered flags.

"I love you, too." And when I say it from this distance, I realize it's true.

Back on the road, I turn on the radio for company, find only static and switch it off. The snow along the roadsides thins and grays with decreasing latitude as I near the checkpoint at the U.S. border. It reminds me of Christmas morning when I was eleven, the Christmas of the shell necklace.

Shady River, Oregon, 1974

On my almost-new bike, I gasped and teetered up the slope to Rockhaven in the winter morning stillness. Whatever remorse I might have felt for abandoning my mother to her bottle on Christmas Day dried up with my tears in the freezing air. I left the bike in the driveway and rang the bell.

They greeted me at the door as cheerfully as if I'd remembered to call before I came.

"Merry Christmas, Sarsaparilla!" Cincy chirped.

"Merry Christmas," Lenora said. "Come into this house!" Her smile made me feel like a real person instead of just a kid.

I stood red-nosed on the flat space of concrete that served as their porch, my lips thick and numb with the cold. "Come look at my new bike!"

"You got a *bike?*" Cincy shrieked. "Outta sight!"

She bounded out of the house, wearing flannel pajamas and rabbit-eared house shoes.

Lenora came, too, carrying her coffee mug and lifting her terrycloth robe off the ground. Her hair hung loose down her back and glistened like mink in the morning sunshine. I pictured my mom's short, kinky hair and felt guilty for making the comparison.

Pulling my red Stingray erect, I held it for my friends' inspection. They circled and exclaimed until my face hurt from grinning.

"Come in and eat breakfast with us," Cincy said, dancing in the cold. "We can go riding after it warms up out here."

I lay the bike gently on its side and we all three sprinted for the warmth of the house.

Christmas carols played from a radio somewhere in the living room, and the house smelled like cinnamon and candles. The whole sunporch was their Christmas tree, except the one end Lenora kept sealed off for controlled research. I'd recently learned she was a real scientist, a lepidopterist.

Strings of tiny colored lights looped around the tallest plants and wound across the ivy-covered ceiling. Glass ornaments and silver icicles draped the other greenery, shimmering with every breath of movement. A few nights before, Cincy and I had sat on the porch with all the other lights off, whispering about the mysteries of Christmas and our approaching teenage years. In the dark, the place looked enchanted.

This morning, though, it was sunny and bright. Cincy and Lenora were having breakfast there. Lenora had set up a card table in a narrow space among the plants and covered it with a red cloth. She crowded in another chair for me and insisted on sharing her omelet.

Cincy went to get me a glass of orange juice and returned with two small packages tied in curly bows. She laid them in front of me one at a time.

"This one's from me, and this one's from Mom."

My smile fell. "But I didn't get you anything." I searched Cincy's face, appealing.

She made a brushing motion with one hand. "You weren't *supposed* to, Gwendolyn. These are no big deal, believe me."

She flipped her long hair behind her shoulder with a toss of her head, a motion that had become characteristic lately. "Go on. Open them."

I tore into hers first, finding a pair of knitted gloves. They were white, with red-and-blue reindeer marching around the backs and palms between borders of holly. "Ooh, they're pretty," I said. I pulled them on and flexed my fingers.

"I told you it was no big deal," Cincy said. "Grandma got me an extra pair and I knew you'd lost yours."

"Thanks," I said, adopting her lightheartedness. "My hands were frozen to the handlebars on the way up here." But I wished desperately that I had presents for them.

As soon as I picked up Lenora's gift, I could tell it was a book. I tore off the paper. "Wow."

I ran a gloved hand over the picture of a tiger swallowtail on the cover and read aloud, "*The Golden Nature Guide to Butterflies and Moths,* 423 illustrations in color." I glanced up at Lenora, feeling she'd entrusted me with something special. "Thanks. I love it."

Lenora winked at Cincy. "See, I told you."

"I know," Cincy said, faking disgust. "Science. Gross." She flipped her hair. "Come look at my Christmas loot!"

I tucked the book in my arm but hesitated. "Want us to help with the dishes first?" I asked Lenora.

She smiled. "Thanks, Bobbie, but since it's Christmas, I'll let you off the hook." We streaked to Cincy's room.

Later in the day the temperature rose into the forties and we rode our bikes across the bridge and into town.

"I ought to stop by and check on Mom," I told her.

We parked in the driveway and entered through the kitchen. Cincy needed to use the bathroom, so I steered her down the hall and went into the living room alone.

The room smelled sour. Mom was asleep on the sofa, still in her sweat suit, the TV playing. She hadn't even roused when we came in. Asleep, her face looked much older than thirty-five.

"She's okay," I told Cincy when she came out. "Anyway, she's still breathing." I had begun to develop a caustic edge about my mother's drinking when I talked to Cincy. I never mentioned it to anyone else.

On the way back to her house, we traded and rode each other's bikes.

Late that afternoon Cincy and I were watching *It's a Wonderful Life* on TV when I heard the phone in the kitchen ring and Lenora answer.

She called into the living room. "Bobbie, your mom wants you to start home now, before it gets dark."

"Okay."

"I'll sack up some Snickerdoodles for you to take to your mom," Cincy said.

I went to Cincy's room and put on my coat and new gloves. Luckily, the butterfly book fit into the oversize pocket of my car coat. My new bike didn't have a basket yet.

As I came back through the dining room, I heard Cincy's subdued voice in the kitchen. "Isn't there something you can do to help her? Maybe she just needs a friend."

I froze, my throat squeezing shut.

What was she talking about? *She* was my friend! And I didn't need any help.

"I don't think so," Lenora answered. "Every woman has her own demons to fight. I don't think Ruth *wants* to stop drinking yet."

Heat flashed to my cheeks. *They had no right to talk about my mother.*

Despite my indignation, a realization spread over me, slow and thick as syrup. Alone in the dusky dining room with my hands clenched into fists at my sides, I understood for the first time that my mother was an alcoholic. Neither Cincy nor Lenora had said the word. It simply burbled up from within me like a belch, embarrassing and unwanted.

My mother is an alcoholic. And I knew beyond a doubt that this was how other people saw her.

If this was how people saw Ruth, how did they see me? The child of the alcoholic, an object of pity? Was that how Lenora and Cincy saw me? Did they include me in their family out of pity instead of love?

The edges of my world crumbled beneath my feet; my head reeled.

I waited two beats until I could control my voice, then yelled toward the kitchen. "I'm going now! Thanks for the presents!" And fled out the front door.

Cincy caught up with me as I climbed on my bike. "Wait! Here's your cookies."

"Thanks." I tucked them in my other pocket, avoiding her eyes, and pushed off down the driveway.

The tires wobbled until I caught my balance, then began to pedal recklessly, gaining speed. I could hear the blood zinging through my veins, *alcoholic, alcoholic,* while I careened down the hill on the red bike my mother gave me, far too fast for my beginner skills.

The sun hung on the horizon in a lonely strip of sky between the river and a bank of gray clouds. By the time I reached the bottom of the hill where the drive turned left, my nose was running and I was flying.

My tires hit a patch of loose gravel and skidded sideways. The bike waffled and the steep edge of the road loomed close. Beyond, a rocky slope descended into a gulch that led toward the river.

I gritted my teeth, my heart pounding. Part of me wanted to give in, go sailing into the chasm. But some other, stubborn girl rose up on the pedals, gripped the handlebars, and fought for balance.

I would *not* go down! Damn it, I *would not!*

In the still, cold air, I controlled the skid inches from the precipice and sailed onward toward the bridge. Cincy's voice echoed down to me like a benediction.

"Ride 'em, Sarsaparilla!"

Canadian/U.S. border, 1990

As I wait at the checkpoint before crossing into Idaho, the benediction echoes in my mind. What happened to that determined little girl I used to be? Would the baby I'm carrying resemble her, or the flimsy sister I've become in the eons since then?

The thought scares me. It's the first time I've imagined this brief embryo as an actual person.

In the insulated time warp of the warm car, I remember a resilient little girl playing out the mystery of metamorphosis with the moon on her hands. And I allow myself to picture my accidentally fertilized ovum as a real baby, then a child, and eventually a young woman totally separate from me. I imagine curly hair like my own and sturdy legs, poor girl. But when I try to fix an image of her face, the features become the thin, aging visage of Lenora the last time I saw her, in prison.

It's not what you get, the old woman at the restaurant said, *but what you give.* I should have asked her, is it what you give that makes you happy, or that kills you?

CHAPTER 7

Shady River, 1978

In our teens, Cincy and I invented a game that began, "If your father were here..." The scenarios started realistically, but quickly progressed into wild fictions full of money and adventure.

"If your father were here," I told her, "he wouldn't let you date Stan Stenson even if he asked, because of that motorcycle."

"Well, if *your* father were here," she countered, "he wouldn't let you stay after school *supposedly* working on your science project with Petey Small. He'd ride up to the school on his white horse and throw you across the saddle and carry you away...."

Each new layer outdid the last, until finally our fathers metamorphosed into fantasy lovers. *"But he isn't your father at all, see, he's this warrior from the next village who's loved you from afar...."* And we were swept away into nonsense and laughter.

It was a surefire method for cheering ourselves up.

Cincy's favorite fantasy was one about a fellow I'd named Lionel, who was involved in international espionage but returned to her, his one true love, for fixes of wild lovemaking before disappearing again into the mist along the river. Cincy made me tell this one over and over, adding her own creative twists. Whenever we saw a handsome stranger, she'd dig her elbow into my ribs and choke out, "It's Lionel, come to take me away!"

"Take me, too!" I'd whisper.

But nobody ever did. Instead we went to school, and to her house afterward. Cincy grouched about her homework; I whined about the contact lenses I couldn't afford. I'd convinced myself that my life would blossom if only I could get rid of my glasses.

"If your father were here," Cincy scolded, "he'd tell you that you're beautiful just as you are." Then she shrugged, grinning. "But he'd buy you the contacts anyway."

Sometimes, when I was alone, fragments of my missing father rose in my consciousness like a chronic toothache. The memory hurt only when I returned to it, touching my tongue to the aching spot to probe the pain. By the time I reached puberty, I was accomplished at this. Whenever I wanted to pity or punish myself, whenever I longed for the drama and sweet suffering that defines adolescence, I called up the mystery of my father's desertion.

Sometimes, to punish both of us, perhaps, I asked my mother about him.

How had they met? Did I look like him? What was their life like before I was born? She gave short, offhand answers with a nonchalance I knew she didn't feel.

I saw fine lines etch the pouches beneath my mother's eyes, and watched her jawline melt into middle age. In rare teenage moments when I felt giddy and invincible, the sudden contrast to my mother's life impaled me with guilt. I tried to imagine cleaning other people's hotel rooms day after day, coming home to a daughter and nothing else.

"Why don't you and Ying Su take off to Portland for the weekend?" I urged her. "Go shopping, go to the movies." Ying Su worked with her at the inn.

"Maybe sometime I'll do that," Mom said, but she never went. I even suggested she flirt with the hotel manager, invite *him* to Portland.

"Now you're being ridiculous," she said. "He's younger than I am."

"So what?"

She gave me one of those mother looks and changed the subject.

When my questions about my father got too pointed, Mom claimed ignorance. She didn't know where he lived now. She didn't know where he worked. No, he never sent money; she didn't want him to.

Once, though, she found an old snapshot of the three of us. "I'd forgotten about this," she said, her voice sounding far away. "Keep it, if you like."

The blurry images of a young couple and their shapeless, androgynous baby fascinated me. I resented that she'd kept the picture from me all these years.

In the photo, my father's hair looked dark, much darker than mine. He wore glasses like me and behind their rims I could see bushy eyebrows that explained why mine required continual tweezing. The faces in the photo were small and partly shaded. Even when Cincy and I examined it with a magnifying glass, lying in her bed on a summer night in our baggy T-shirts, I couldn't be sure of the color of my father's eyes or the shape of his nose.

"He's handsome," Cincy pronounced.

I couldn't see it. "You're just being polite."

She punched my arm. "Don't you dare accuse me of such a thing."

I laid the photo on the nightstand and switched off the light. Cincy's room, built partly into the mountain, had no windows, so when the light went off it was like a cave. If we left the door open, a faint rectangle of moonlight from the living room windows relieved the blackness, but that night the door was closed so our talking wouldn't keep Lenora awake.

It was well after midnight. We'd gone swimming at the new municipal pool all afternoon, and I'd cleaned Mom's house in town before going. My muscles felt tired and my skin pleasantly sunburned.

"I'm going to be sore tomorrow," I said, stretching my legs out on the cool sheets.

"Whereabouts? I'll give you a rubdown."

She sat beside me in the darkness, massaging my shoulders and back while I groaned my appreciation, or giggled when she hit a ticklish spot. Then she rubbed my feet and calves.

"You should be a professional masseuse," I told her sleepily. "You could work at one of those ritzy spas giving massages to rich people and getting hundred-dollar tips."

"No way," she said, her voice deep and laughing in the humid darkness. "I wouldn't do this for anybody but you."

"Not even Stan Stenson?"

"*Well....*"

Our freshman year, Cincy blossomed into a long-legged beauty. She had the black satin hair and dark eyes of her Cherokee ancestry, with high cheekbones and Lenora's small mouth and slender nose.

Despite her looks, she wasn't the least conceited. She talked to everybody, even the nerds and thugs most kids shunned as if they had VD. Social distinctions didn't exist for Cincy. I considered it one of her best qualities, recognizing in myself a reticence toward people who were outwardly as uneasy in the world as I felt but kept hidden. I'd look at one of those kids and think *there, but for the grace of Cincy, go I.*

As it was, I merged with the great gray middle class of students, accepted because I was decently groomed and a friend of Cincy's, respected and *sus*pected because I was smart. Boys talked to me, but they didn't flirt. Girls talked to me, but they didn't confide.

Most of the time I was satisfied with that. I had Cincy, after all. My only other friend—besides Petey Small, my science buddy—was the athletic, red-haired Samantha. Like me, Sam existed mostly in her own world, where sports filled her brain space the way science did mine.

Samantha talked Cincy into running track. If our small school was weak on academics, it was huge when it came to sports. Sam said Cincy was a natural athlete. Her long legs pumping around the cinder oval that ringed the football field reminded me of waves on the ocean, rhythmic and tireless, though I'd seen the ocean only on TV. My own legs were far too short for speed. At five-two, I refused desserts, fighting the natural resemblance to a pear that defined my mother's figure.

Cincy ran, but she didn't care about running. Coach Hastings said she could have won any of the long-distance events if only she would concentrate. He put her in sprints, which he said were better matched to her short attention span, and when she won without half trying, he just shook his head. "She's amazing," he said to me once. "I love to watch her run."

She didn't care about her studies, either. In fact, aside from hanging out with me, only one thing interested Cincy. While I was preoccupied with books and butterflies and the gray dread of going home at night, Cincy's curiosity turned to boys. How could it not? Whenever she walked down the hall at school, their adolescent lust followed her like a cloud of gnats.

Sometimes she seemed oblivious to their attention, and other times she'd flirt outrageously. Usually she just got that knowing smile—the one I'd first seen in the lunchroom during second grade—and gave me a wink.

I grinned back. "There's a mean streak in you, Cynthia Jaines. I like that."

One guy after another began to walk or bike up the hill to Rockhaven, and Cincy would go off with him to a football game or a movie at the Mount Hood Theater. The movie house was the only entertainment in town during cold weather. Cincy and I spent a lot of Sunday afternoons at the Mount Hood, with our feet sticking to the floor and the aroma of stale butter prickling our noses.

If a boy had asked me out, which none did, I knew Ruth would say fourteen was too young to date. But Cincy never asked Lenora's permission, she just floated away with a jaunty wave. The first time Cincy left on a car date with a guy who was sixteen, Lenora frowned in silence, and I foresaw trouble in paradise.

I'd always envied Cincy and Lenora's easy relationship. Lenora believed in letting Cincy make her own decisions. They were on the same team, she said, partners. Whereas Ruth and I were perpetual adversaries. My mom criticized everything I did, it seemed to me. But in truth, our arguments traced directly or indirectly to two sources: her drinking, or her resentment of my friendship with Lenora and Cincy.

I suppose the friction that developed between the Jaines women was inevitable. But I knew nothing then about adolescent psychology; what I saw was the crumbling of an ideal. And with so few ideals to believe in, the loss made my stomach hurt. Without being asked, I tried to mediate by voicing the worries I read on Lenora's silent face.

"Cincy, Danny Soames is too old for you," I told her as she stood in front of the warped, full-length mirror on her closet door drawing dark red on her lips. "And too fast."

Cincy cocked her head and undid one more button on the front of her blouse—a sort of barometer of how much she liked each boy she dated. Her hair shone like glass.

The red lines widened into a smile. "You think he'll take me into the woods and have his way with me?"

"If he did, what would you do about it?"

"Well, Grandma, I'd poke out his eyes and kick him in the balls, just like you taught me."

"Get real. He's on the football team. If he decides to rape you, you're dead meat."

"I think the expression is *hot, red meat*."

"Yuck! Cincy!"

She laughed. "Stop worrying, Rapunzel. I can handle Danny Soames."

"Oh, yeah. He'd *love* for you to *handle* him."

In the mirror, Cincy's eyebrows wiggled up and down.

"Aren't you going to brush your teeth?" I reminded.

"Naw. Kisses don't taste right when your mouth's too clean."

We laughed it off, but secretly I wondered if it were true. I had no way of knowing.

"If your father were here," I said, "he'd meet Danny on the front porch with a shotgun."

She dropped her lipstick into a tiny shoulder bag and snapped it shut. "Well, he isn't here. But I'll tell Danny that if he lays an unwanted hand on me, *you'll* hunt him down and see that he makes an honest woman of me."

"Making you honest is too big a job for anyone, let alone a jockhead."

Cincy smiled and shot me the bird.

I watched them drive away in Danny's dad's new Chevrolet, feeling that I'd failed as a parent.

That semester my science teacher, Mr. Jenkins, directed us to choose a research project. For me there was no question about a subject. I consulted Lenora, and she handed me an issue of *Nature* magazine with an article about Old World swallowtail butterflies.

One of them was *Pharmacophagus antenor,* found only on the island of Madagascar off the southeast coast of Africa. It was the only African swallowtail known to feed on pipevine, and its evolution was speculated to reveal links to the age when the earth's plates shifted and separated to create the continents.

In the photos, the antenor's black wings appeared delicate and narrow. The forewings were marked with white spherical spots that melded along the bottom of the hindwings into rounded crescent-shapes of pale yellow to red-orange. The antenor had a wingspan of five to six inches and a life cycle virtually undocumented by science.

"This is neat," I said, returning the magazine, "but I don't see how I could make a science project out of it."

Lenora sat on a tall stool on the sunporch, methodically examining the leaves of a willow branch for eggs. The porch was warm with rare November sunlight, and butterflies fluttered overhead. Most species couldn't fly unless the temperature was near eighty.

"Remember Zoroaster, the *Morpho rhetenor?*" she asked.

I recalled the iridescent blue beauty Cincy had introduced to me on my first visit.

"It was from French Guiana in South America," she said. "That red-and-black one up there," she pointed, "is from Asia."

I looked up, nodding, but I still didn't get it.

"How would you like to be the first American ever to raise a generation of *Pharmacophagus antenor* and document its complete life cycle?"

The light came on. *"You could get one of those?"*

Her eyes sparkled. "The university research facility obtains lepidoptera specimens from approved foreign sources under a special permit for scientific study. That's what the quarantine area is for," she said, nodding toward the one end of the porch sealed off by a glass door. "I have an acquaintance in Florida that I met at a conference who's offered to fund research to investigate the relationship of that species to other members of the swallowtail family."

I loved it when she talked like a scientist to me. Ever since I'd learned she did actual scientific research on her sunporch, I'd spent more and more time there. And made straight A's in science class. I knew her income depended on grant money from various sources.

"You could be my research assistant," she said. "I want to put the immatures—caterpillars and pupae—under the dissection microscope and compare them to some specimens we could get on loan from Sarasota or maybe Yale."

"Far out," I whispered. And it was—far out of my limited range of understanding about her work. But I understood quite clearly that she was offering to *include* me, to share with me the mysteries of the butterflies. My chest inflated to the point of exploding. "How long would it take to get them? I'm supposed to do the project this semester."

"It might take a while," she admitted. "Only eggs or pupae can be transported successfully, and we'll need to import the Madagascar variety of pipevine, too. I'll see if the university has a contact in Madagascar, and tell them it's a rush so that our research will be ahead of Britain's. That always pulls their chain. But the U.S. Department of Agriculture might give them trouble about importing the plants."

"Couldn't the caterpillars eat American pipevine?"

"Maybe, but not the first generation. Later on, if we get a second generation going, we could see if the larvae will adapt to the pipevine that grows farther south in the States. Or maybe try the ginger plant we have locally that's related to pipevine."

"So if the government vetoes the plants, the project is off?"

Her eyes took on a devilish light. "Not necessarily. There are other ways. In France you can buy lepidoptera eggs, pupae, even food plants—cash and carry. Smuggle them through Customs in your handbag, if you've got the nerve."

My eyes widened. "Have you ever done that?"

She pursed her lips like a kiss. "I'm not at liberty to say."

My grin stretched so wide Lenora laughed at me. I was practically hopping. "This is so cool! Can you call the university now?"

"Shouldn't you talk it over with your teacher first? Better find out if he's willing to be patient, in case your project doesn't get moving until the semester's nearly over. And there's always a risk that the specimens will die without reproducing."

I waved it off. "I can talk Mr. Jenkins into it. No problem. I'm his star pupil."

She smiled, approving my rash confidence. "If we can nurse a few through the pupal stage and get the adults to lay eggs on domestic pipevine or ginger, though, it's possible we could keep the generations going indefinitely."

Her voice held genuine excitement, and I let myself believe that part of it was because we'd be working together. I ran to bring her the phone, nearly tripping over its twenty-foot cord, so she could call her friends at UO.

On a Saturday morning, the two of us drove to a forested valley in the Cascades in search of wild ginger. Lenora wanted to begin cultivating it on the sunporch so we'd have a supply at hand. She thought we could buy pipevine at a nursery in Portland.

Cincy had declined to come with us, opting to sleep in after a late date on Friday night.

Morning frost glistened on the foliage along the quiet roadside. Lenora parked beside the road and we tramped off into the tangled wilderness, carrying our buckets and digging tools. Our breaths made cloudy puffs in the still air.

Before long she identified the plant, even with its leaves wilted by the cold. I spaded six starts into plastic containers and we wedged them onto the floor of the back seat in the old VW. I remember the earthy smell in the car as we sped back along the river road, jabbering like mountain jays.

On Monday, I conferenced with my science teacher. Mr. Jenkins was soft-spoken and intelligent, and he knew of Lenora's work. He accepted my proposal on the conditions that I could manage to obtain at least one specimen this semester, and that I would keep a daily journal of observations and outside readings on lepidoptera. He suggested that I enroll in his advanced biology class the next year and follow the project through for classroom credit.

I felt singled out for greatness. Had Mr. Jenkins not been such a frail-looking fellow, barely taller than I, with wire-rimmed glasses, thin hair and a pregnant wife, I'd probably have developed a huge crush on him.

Instead, I adored Lenora.

On an afternoon that smelled of spring during second semester, I found Cincy waiting for me in the hallway after school.

"Come with me to watch the guys' baseball game against White," she said, a note of pleading in her voice. We hadn't been spending much time together lately.

She waited until I worked the combination on the locker we shared, then tossed her books into the wasteland of snack wrappers and crumpled notebook paper at the bottom. Her books disappeared like a pebble in a pond.

"I heard strange sounds from that mess yesterday," I said, pointing. "Something grotesque is mutating down there." I stacked my English book on an upper shelf and retrieved history and geometry.

"Come on. Come with me."

"I have no interest in jocks," I said loftily. Which was almost true—except that Petey Small played shortstop for the Shady River Cougars. "Besides, I have to feed the animals."

Lenora had left that morning before daybreak to join a conclave of entomologists at the university in Eugene. She'd been fussy as a new mother the previous evening when we'd gone over the list of chores I'd promised to attend to in the greenlab. As if I hadn't done them all a zillion times before.

I prayed she could find out something about our Madagascar specimen while she was there. Weeks had gone by since we'd placed the request, then months. Other students had turned in completed projects on volcanic rock and cross-pollination. Mr. Jenkins's wife had delivered twins. And I still had nothing but reports on my outside readings to write in my science journal. Mr. Jenkins had suggested I shift my project to an accessible species, but I declined.

Cincy and I walked outdoors into the school courtyard, crossing through a pool of yellow sunlight. It was April, a warm afternoon that smelled of spring after several gray days in a row. Masculine voices and the sound of leather smacking leather drifted up from the baseball diamond south of the building.

For a moment my chest swelled; the school year was almost over and I still couldn't believe I was in high school at last. A brief fantasy from some goofy beach movie floated through my brain—of weekend dates in summer, troupes of babbling teenagers hanging out at the drive-in, making out in somebody's white convertible.

Who wrote that stuff? Did anybody, ever, really live like that? Still, the image and the sunny afternoon filled me with a familiar restlessness.

"Come on," Cincy urged. "It isn't as if those worms can't find the food they're sitting on."

She knew they were caterpillars, not *worms;* she did this to annoy me.

"Mom won't be back until dark at the earliest," she said. "We'll be home long before that."

There was more to it than checking on their food. One of the cocoons might be hatching. A field mouse might have found its way onto the porch, a fairly regular occurrence that had resulted in the loss of several chrysalides last fall. However, I had gone up to Rockhaven on my lunch break, and everything was fine. It wasn't likely that the critters needed attention only a few hours later.

I glanced toward the practice field and scanned the uniformed shapes in purple jerseys for a tall, skinny number seven. He was taking practice swings with three bats, loosening up.

"Okay," I said. "For a little while."

Petey got one hit and made a couple of good throws to first base. I hoped he could hear my voice among the cheers. Cincy and I were home by five.

But it was too late. Lenora's VW sat in the driveway before the open door of the peeling garage.

"Damn," I said aloud. Even then, I wasn't seriously worried. I walked into Lenora's wrath unprepared.

I found her on the sunporch, bent over one of the gallon jars we used for hatching new specimens. Common butterflies like monarchs and red admirals spent their entire life cycles at large among the vines, eating, mating and pupating without supervision. Rare or difficult species that were under study, however, were isolated during pupation for their protection. I had placed the tulle netting over this particular gallon jar and secured it with a rubber band myself.

Lenora turned toward me with her fists on her hips. Her face was flushed. "I thought you were going to take care of things!"

Stricken, I glanced from her eyes to a misshapen creature dangling from a stick inside the jar.

It was a *Protesilaus aguiari,* a long-tailed white swallowtail of the Amazon region with pale, zebralike stripes. Rather, it was supposed to be. What hung now on a naked twig was a black, prehistoric body attached to a crumpled mass like dried tobacco leaves on its back.

"I checked on it at lunch and didn't see any signs of hatching," I said lamely.

Her voice was ice hard. "How does it look now?"

I'd never heard her use this tone, not even to Cincy. A lump swelled in my throat.

"If you'd been here even an hour ago, you'd have seen that the pupa case wasn't detaching properly. You could have pulled it free and saved the specimen, not to mention six months of work."

Lenora's hand moved swiftly into the jar and removed the deformed butterfly. She dropped it to the floor and crushed it under her foot.

My breath sucked in, locking in my rib cage. I turned away to avoid seeing what was left of the ill-fated swallowtail.

The butterfly couldn't have lived that way, I knew. There was no room in the insect world for deformity. Still, her swift mercy killing brought my hastily eaten lunch to the back of my throat. Never again would I neglect my responsibilities.

I fled to Cincy's room. She saw my tears and demanded an explanation. When I told her what happened, she commiserated as best she could.

"It was just a bug, Rapunzel," she said gently, stroking my head. "You can't get so emotionally attached to your patients."

"It's not that," I said, my throat still tight. "It was the look in Lenora's eyes. She's really disappointed in me."

Cincy inspected my face, frowning. She spoke slowly, like someone talking a fool back to reality. "Bobbie, *why do you care?* She's not *your* mother."

Something in her expression warned me not to voice the response that rose immediately to my lips.

Yes, she is. And much, much more.

CHAPTER 8

Shady River, 1979

The day the carton arrived, I was carrying in my jeans pocket a warning slip from Mr. Jenkins. Without satisfactory progress on a project, I would receive an *I* in science for the semester. The paper scalded my skin as Cincy and I trudged up the hill to Rockhaven after school.

I didn't confide my shame to Cincy, though I could have. Her grades had become another thorn in her relationship with her mom, and Lenora didn't keep quiet on this topic the way she did about Cincy's dates. It made things worse when Lenora praised my grades, which were usually A's. Ruth, on the other hand, was consistently unimpressed by my scholarship. *"That's nice, honey. Get the laundry out of the dryer, will you?"* Cincy had taken to visiting Ruth sometimes, a strange behavior that unnerved my mother as much as it did me.

The minute we walked into Rockhaven, I saw two brown cartons on the dining room table. I knew immediately what they were.

"Lenora?"

She came in from the sunporch, smiling. "Just got back a few min-utes ago." Indeed, she sounded breathless. I didn't ask her "Back from where?"

Neither Lenora nor I ever mentioned the *Protesilaus aguiari* inci-dent after that one painful afternoon, and I never gave her cause to scold me again. I had redoubled my efforts in the greenlab to win back her confidence.

Both Cincy and Lenora hovered close as I carefully opened one end of the smallest cardboard box. Lenora said nothing, but I felt her excitement. Inside the box was a small cage made of metal grid, like a magnified screen. I worked the tips of my fingers into the wire and pulled it from the carton. Holding my breath, I opened one end of the cage and removed a mound of white, gauzy packing mate-rial. At its center lay an elliptical brownish-green shape about three inches long—a pupa.

I unwrapped the delicate packing and held the strange thing on my open palm. It looked like a rolled, dried leaf except at one end, where a long slender tube like a proboscis lay sculpted against its body.

Lenora leaned close to examine it. "It looks more like the pupa of a moth than a butterfly."

"It looks like a toad turd," Cincy said, but not critically.

The brown thing twitched, tickling my palm.

Cincy screeched. "*Eeeww!* The turd's alive!"

Even Lenora giggled. Quickly I cupped my palm to prevent the pupa from falling and laid the creature back inside its cage, goose bumps prickling my skin.

Lenora searched the white packing material, then inside the box. "Only one," she said, frowning. "And no eggs."

I began to glimpse the high-risk factors of scientific research. Until this moment, I never doubted that we could rear an entire gen-eration of rare lepidoptera. But that couldn't happen from one pupa.

The other carton contained the pipevine, still moist inside its plastic bag. "I'll get this plant potted and dosed with fertilizer," she said. "You fix a place for the pupa."

In a glass aquarium I'd borrowed from the school science lab, I prepared a bed of the domestic pipevine and ginger we were growing indoors on the sunporch. I imagined the brown pupal case splitting open, the butterfly emerging to dry its crumpled, wet wings. I prayed to whatever science gods there might be for its survival. And that Mr. Jenkins would see fit to remove my "incomplete" from his grade book.

What if the single pupa never hatched and I couldn't produce even one specimen to show for my project? If the adult butterfly had no mate, we couldn't raise caterpillars and observe an entire life cycle, let alone compare this swallowtail with its Old World and New World relatives. I clung to a hope the pupa would hatch, but disappointment gathered darkly in my stomach.

For a long time that afternoon, I watched the dormant antenor resting in its new home. Maybe it was female—Madame Antenor. The idea made me smile. Maybe she already harbored fertilized eggs inside her mysterious abdomen, and maybe she would lay them on the pipevine and they'd hatch and begin to eat—

And maybe I'd turn into a raving beauty with perfect eyesight overnight.

Three weeks later, Antenor-X, as I'd taken to calling my sexless specimen, had not emerged. It lay still as a rotting log on its bed of leaves in the glass enclosure. My journal was a study in monotony. The only thing that saved my science grade was the arrival—thanks to Lenora's continued badgering of her contacts at the university—of a tiny cluster of eggs purported to be those of the Madagascar swallowtail.

On the last day of school, my journal entry for Mr. Jenkins declared dramatically, "The Great American Lepidoptera Experiment:

To Be Continued." On the strength of my optimism—and a ninety-five-percent average aside from the research project—Mr. Jenkins gave me an A.

That was the summer everything changed. Or perhaps it happened slowly, like land masses drifting apart into separate continents. I began to detect a subtle distance growing between Cincy and me, and between me and my mother, that summer I turned fifteen. Cincy and Lenora couldn't seem to talk without arguing, so they rarely talked at all.

I got a job at Tucker's Variety Store, a landmark in downtown Shady River. In those days, the big chains hadn't set up shop in every little burg, and Tucker's made a decent profit selling zippers and thumbtacks, school supplies and lightbulbs, from an old wooden building on Main Street. Mr. and Mrs. Tucker hired high school kids to stock shelves and help customers find things, while the two of them took turns manning the single cash register.

The store was small by modern standards, but it had one of everything and a pleasant, dry-goods smell. Tuckers' prices were a few cents higher than in the big chain store twenty miles upriver, but people shopped at the hometown store because it was handy, and because of the complimentary pot of coffee Mrs. Tucker kept fresh all day long. Even people who didn't drink coffee seemed to like its friendly aroma and the idea that something was free.

"Personal service is the only marketing weapon the small businessman has left," Mr. Tucker quoted. "Smile and be nice to the folks!"

If personal service was one secret to his success, frugality was another. Other than the coffee, which more than paid for itself, Mr. Tucker counted every penny twice. He hired a dozen kids and worked us only a few hours a week, so he could pay less than minimum wage and avoid social security taxes. But he was good to us, and I was grateful for the job. My only other hope for income was baby-sitting my science teacher's twin boys, and the Jenkinses didn't go out often.

When Mr. Tucker learned I was saving for contact lenses, he suggested I open a savings account at Shady River Fidelity Bank. Every other Friday I crossed Main Street and deposited most of my meager paycheck, keeping out a few dollars for spending money. It was the first money I'd ever had of my own. That summer I was reading Ayn Rand's *Atlas Shrugged,* and I'd leave the bank feeling like Dagny Taggart. My dreams included success and romance, but never marriage and children.

Cincy had to take a summer class in algebra. Afterward she hung around the gym and watched the boys shoot hoops until I got off work. If we had money, we'd stop at Bixler's on the edge of town for French fries and a cola before biking across the river and up the hill.

Within a week after the school term ended, the imported swallowtail eggs had hatched. Suddenly my project moved as fast as it had gone slowly during school. Fifteen hungry, horny caterpillars roamed the aquarium, devouring pipevine leaves down to exposed stems. I placed a piece of window screen across the top to keep them inside.

Like the mother of teenagers, I was appalled by the appetites of my children. Thanks to Lenora's green thumb and Miracle-Gro, the imported pipevine had flourished, but I worried that they'd defoliate the plant and want more. I watched in awe as they split their skins and emerged larger and hungrier into the next instar, the stages between molts. They were beautifully patterned with black, white and rust stripes around their bodies, which were large at the head and tapered toward a smaller, blunt end.

Lenora, too, was mesmerized by the caterpillars' phenomenal growth. I assisted her with other studies in the greenlab, and with the endless tending and watering required by the jungle of plants, but she was careful not to encroach on my responsibility for the chamber of eating machines.

The original pupa never hatched. Lenora examined the still case using a tiny probe like a dentist's tool and a magnifying light, and pronounced Antenor-X dead. My grief was short-lived; the demanding exuberance of the caterpillar tribe precluded mourning. I had mouths to feed!

Most of the time, Ruth didn't seem to care that I was gone so much, or even notice. She came home from work tired, and the way I saw it, my absence relieved her of any duty to make conversation when what she really craved was quick intercourse with the green depths of Julio Gallo. And I was relieved of watching.

On rare days we were both home and awake, Ruth's cynical remarks about Rockhaven and my "preoccupation with bugs" grated on my nerves. I tried to ignore them. But as the weeks simmered into July, she shifted her barbs toward Lenora and Cincy.

I fired back. Fiercely. The emptier Mom's bottle, the more acidic her comments, and the freer I felt to lash out in response. I resented her resentment. Our shouting matches made my stomach cramp, and I resented that, too. I bought an extra toothbrush and stashed some clothes in Cincy's bedroom, and I began sleeping over at Rockhaven more nights than I went home.

At twilight on the Fourth of July, Lenora and I climbed onto the roof to watch the fireworks set off by the Shady River Chamber of Commerce on the high school football field. Cincy had a date with Payton Mills, son of the wealthiest family in town. She'd split up with the boy who'd been her science lab partner shortly after she set their experiment on fire and jeopardized both their grades. As for my own lab partner, I hadn't seen or heard from Petey since school was out.

From atop the cracked wooden shingles of Rockhaven, I pictured

Cincy and Payton below in the darkness, sitting in the bleachers with their necks craned skyward while the crowd oohed and aahed around them. I suspected she was having sex with Payton, but she hadn't told me, knowing I'd disapprove. The subject hung between us in throbbing blocks of silence. And that was silly, I decided, while Lenora and I watched colored explosions spangling the sky above the river. Cincy and I had always talked about everything. Tomorrow I would simply ask her about Payton, being careful to keep any judgment out of my tone.

The lights shimmered in the slow-moving water and a welcome breeze ascended to us across the treetops that sloped away below. Except for an occasional hum of approval, we watched in silence, while a huge silver moon arose in the east and threatened to upstage the show. In Lenora's company, I always felt content.

That night while I was sleeping, one antenor caterpillar strained and gyrated inside its too-tight skin until the girdle at last split and fell away, revealing the greenish-brown casing of its chrysalis. Lenora came into Cincy's room early the next morning to get me.

The warmth of her hand on my arm woke me instantly. My first thought was that something had happened to Ruth, but Lenora was smiling.

"Come out to the sunporch." In a whisper, her low voice sounded like the hum of bees.

Beside me, Cincy turned her back and pulled the sheet over her head. She'd come in late; I barely remembered her climbing into bed. Grabbing my glasses, I followed Lenora without stopping for shoes or clothes, my T-shirt nightie skimming the backs of my knees.

Together we peered at the pupa, attached by a silken sling to an angled twig in the aquarium. On a branch above, another sibling hunched and wriggled, preparing for its final molt. Lenora and I looked at each other and grinned.

In the kitchen we gave high-fives and celebrated with chocolate milkshakes for breakfast. When Cincy got up an hour later and we showed her, with great fanfare, the portentous event, she just shook her head. Lenora and I laughed.

I had to work at Tucker's that day and my work clothes were at home, so there was no time to ask my bedmate about her sex life until the next night. My timing wasn't great. Cincy had been moody all evening, barely speaking to Lenora or me, and when she did speak she was cranky. But I was determined.

After supper—waffles and salad, which Cincy barely nibbled—I found her sprawled facedown on her bed.

"Are you okay?" I asked.

"Sure. Just tired."

"Because I think we should talk."

"Jeez."

I plopped on the bed, tossing her slack body up and down. "Have you had sex with Payton yet?"

Cincy's muscles went rigid, and she waited several seconds before answering. "What if I did? What do you care?"

"Care! I want details!" I tried to make my voice flippant, the way we used to talk in the days before she was always with some boy and I was always with Lenora.

During the school term, I'd overheard rumors about the guys labeling Cincy "hot and ready." I hated gossip and I wouldn't hurt Cincy by repeating it. But I worried, and Cincy read me like a book.

She rolled over and propped up on her elbows. The anger on her face surprised me. "Yeah, I let the wimp screw me. And he isn't the first, either."

I tried not to be shocked, and failed. *"Why?"*

"What do you mean, why? Because *it feels good*."

She was scaring me, deliberately, and it pissed me off. "You don't even like Payton!"

"I can't stand him." She fell back on the bed and turned away from me. "I'm just poor white trash to him."

Heat rose to my face. "Did that jerk *say* that?"

"Not to me. But Patty Johnson told me he said it to her brother."

"Patty's a bitch."

"Yeah. But Payton still said it. I don't care. I *am* poor white trash, after all."

"Cincy, stop it! What a stupid thing to say!"

She rolled toward me again, and her tone was biting. "Well, we are poor, and I'm *mostly* white. And there's no question I'm trashy. Add it up."

I reacted without thinking—I slapped her face.

It sounded like the snap of elastic and left an echo in the silent room. Cincy froze.

I drew back my hand, horrified.

"Oh, Cincy," I whispered. "I'm sorry." I crushed the offending hand in my other fist.

She held her head stiffly, her face blank except for the red mark on her cheek. "Go ahead. Beat me, lie to me, call me names." Her voice was full of misery. "I'm a worthless piece of shit and I deserve it."

I jerked my fists over my ears so I couldn't hear her. "Stop it! Quit talking like that! What the hell's wrong with you?"

She met my eyes and hers were pleading. Tears spilled down her unblemished skin. "You think you know me, Rapunzel," she said softly, "but you don't have a clue."

"Then explain it to me! I'm no psychiatrist. What the hell's going on?" I was crying now, too, and yelling. "You're gorgeous, you're popular and your mom lets you do whatever you want. How do you manage to come up with this inferiority shit?"

Suddenly her face changed color. She jumped off the bed and ran for the bathroom.

I sat where I was and listened to her retching. When she stopped, I went to the bathroom door and knocked softly.

"I'm sorry, Cincy. Are you okay?"

"Go away," she said. "Leave me alone. *Please*."

I turned and walked toward the sunporch, baffled and depressed, guilty of more than just slapping her—but I didn't know what.

Something had changed. Permanently. I didn't know why, and Cincy couldn't tell me.

My stomach leaden, I went back to the world I understood, among the butterflies.

Chapter 9

Interstate 90, near Spokane, 1990

A semi pulling two trailers roars down the on-ramp beside the highway, scattering my memories. Panicked, I glance in the rearview mirror, preparing to pull over and give the truck room. But there's a red car coming up fast in the passing lane, and a white van close behind me. I'm blocked in.

The semi bulls its way into my lane and cuts me off. I hit the brakes hard. Behind me the van's tires screech; I jerk the wheel to the right and head for the ditch.

In two seconds it's over. The van zooms past in a blare of horn that pinches off to silence. I switch off the motor and sit panting, my front bumper nosed into a dingy snowbank, my hands shaking and white on the wheel. The other vehicles disappear over the horizon.

I lay my head back on the seat for a few moments, listening to the rush of blood in my ears, then fish a tissue from the console and blow my nose.

My car isn't damaged, nor am I, I tell myself sternly. But my pulse still pounds. I retrieve my coat and purse from the floorboard and start the engine, carefully back out of the ditch, and wait for a long, long opening in which to creep back onto the road.

I've got to pay more attention to driving.

A road sign reads "Spokane 10." In a few miles I hit the outskirts and traffic thickens. Sunshine warms the car and I drop my speed, struggle out of my blazer and toss it on top of my coat on the seat. With the passenger-side window half open, I'm amazed how much warmer it is here than at home.

Home. I've lived there four years, and this is the first time I've thought of David's house in Canada as home. Maybe it's a good sign. Then I think about David and remember his voice on the phone, his anger and frustration.

Ahead there's a clean, uncluttered service station and I pull in to gas up and use the rest room. I carry a diet soda to the register and ask the clerk for directions to the women's prison.

She gives me a strange look. "I have no idea. Just a minute." Turning toward the back, she yells, "Gus!"

When Gus appears, I tell him the street address and he unfolds a city map from the rack by the cash register. He points out a route with a thick finger embedded with grease around the cuticles. The grease could be from repairing cars or from fixing his hair this morning. I trace the route with a pen, put an *X* on the location of the prison, and buy the map and a Spokane newspaper along with the gasoline. Gus smiles, flashing a gold front tooth.

The Washington State Women's Correctional Facility sits on the opposite edge of the city in a sparsely populated area. Nobody wants to build houses or schools close to a prison, I suppose, even a women's prison. I drive west on I-90 and take the Grove Street exit south, then back east on Thorpe Road. Off to my left, jet airliners drift downward toward the Spokane airport north of the interstate.

In twenty minutes, I'm there. The prison sprawls in an open, flat area off a two-lane asphalt road. Somehow I'd forgotten about the tall chain-link fence topped by looping barbed wire that surrounds the grounds. I can't even remember approaching the prison seven years ago. All other impressions were scorched away by the image of Lenora in her prison garb, her face ashen and defeated. What will she look like now?

Video cameras overlook the wide parking lot as I pull on my coat and walk up a hill to the main gate. It's before noon, and the parking lot is still mostly empty.

I see no one inside the gates as I approach. It's a ghost town of dormitory-style buildings built of stone blocks, and smaller metal structures that look transitory. Outside the gate there's a gray phone mounted to an aluminum pole. I pick up the receiver.

"Yes?" a male voice says. Presumably it's coming from behind the darkened glass in a small stone structure that sits fifty feet inside, behind a series of fenced cages. I don't remember any of this from my first visit, though I'm sure it was here.

"I'm here to visit Lenora Jaines."

"Family visiting hours start at one."

"I've driven a long way. Sorry to be early."

I hear reluctance in his voice. "MSU or RHU?"

"I beg your pardon?"

"Is she in minimum security, medium or max?"

"I don't know…I would suppose minimum."

"Your name?"

"Roberta Lee Dutreau."

"Hold on." There's a ten-second pause during which a cloud passes over the sun and a chill breeze infiltrates my clothes. "How do you spell that last name?"

"D-u-t-r-e-a-u."

"Jaines is in medium, but she don't have anybody named Roberta on her list."

"Maybe it's Bobbie. She used to call me Bobbie."

He asks for my social security number and finally concedes that I'm on the "special visitors list"—probably the doing of Harley Jaines—but special visits must be scheduled ahead of time.

"Look," I say, trying for a reasonable voice, "I've driven all the way from Canada. I'm sorry I didn't call first—I didn't know the rules. But since I am on her list, could I please see her today?"

Again there's a pause. "I'll have to check with the boss and see if it's okay for the one o'clock. Can you come back then?"

"Okay. Yes." I hang up and stand beside the fenced yard a moment, looking across the bare ground at the austere buildings. I wonder what it would be like to live here, to be pat-searched every day and take communal showers once a week. Details come back to me that Lenora's lawyer told me years ago: prisoners are strip-searched and given a urinalysis after family visiting sessions on weekends. This will happen to Lenora because I've come to see her. I wonder whether prisoners are allowed to refuse visitors, or whether boredom is such an effective punishment that they'll submit to any degradation to see a different face.

Chilled, I walk back to my car to wait, start the motor and turn the heater on max.

Lenora won't refuse to see me. She'll be happy. But I'll also see the hurt in her eyes because it's been so long.

I've sent letters, two or three a year. Pleasant, bloodless letters about David's career and the wildlife I see out my windows—the unspoken, fragile monotony of my days. Sometimes she writes back. But she never talks about prison life. She tells me what she's been reading, and asks whether I've heard from Cincy.

She'll ask me that today, if I see her. I think of Cincy then, and try to remember how long it's been since the last time she called.

I wonder where she is, and what she'll feel when somebody tells her that her phantom father is alive and wants to see her.

War hero or not, Harley Jaines can't measure up to the fathers we dreamed in our girlish fantasies. Fathers are only human, after all. God knows, my own father fell short of the fantasy, too.

Shady River, 1979

A thoughtlike impulse stirs inside the pupa of the antenor swallowtail, an awareness of itself. Swaddled in September darkness, it exerts a powerful stretch, like a bear rousing from hibernation.

Something splits. Perhaps a moment of terror accompanies the sudden loosening of boundaries, before oxygen flushes threadlike veins with the rush of impending escape. Now the forelegs, still clamped to its chest, strain outward; the body wrenches.

The head and limp antennae pop free of the casing. Exhausted, the creature waits. Breathes. Feels strength and impulse returning.

It flexes and writhes. The thorax and front legs emerge from the split pupal case. The butterfly rests a few moments, then tugs its entire body free. Moving one leg stiffly after another, it climbs a twig, abandoning the empty husk of its former life.

The night is a gentle sanctuary. The antenor breathes humid air through spiracles along its sides while fluids engorge the veins in its crumpled wings. Slowly, unevenly, the membranes unfurl, a flower unfolding with time-lapse grace.

At last the shimmering black wings stretch taut and the veins harden into ribs. The miracle is complete.

Sluggish and vulnerable, the antenor opens and closes its wondrous new limbs, clinging to the twig for balance. Imprinted in its genes is the knowledge of flight and of procreation. Opening and closing, drying its wings, it awaits the warmth of the sun.

This is the way I imagined it, although I wasn't there to see.

When school started my sophomore year, I returned to spending nights at home. My mother and I observed a tacit truce: I never mentioned anything connected with Rockhaven, and neither did she. We ignored my secret life, like a married couple ignoring the shared knowledge of the husband's mistress.

I worked at Tucker's after school on Tuesdays and Thursdays, and on Saturday mornings. At Shady River High, my days revolved around honors biology with Mr. Jenkins. Surprisingly, I also enjoyed the art class Lenora had talked me into after seeing illustrations of the antenor caterpillars in my science journal.

Every afternoon, or after dark on the days I worked, I ascended the hill to Rockhaven to check on the mysterious, silent pupae. But that was only part of what drew me up that winding slope; I didn't feel grounded unless I'd made contact with the Jaines women each day. Using my own key, I came and went at will.

Cincy and I still shared a locker at school, but this year we had only one class together and the history teacher's seating chart separated us by three rows. If we met at lunch in the cafeteria, one guy or another always invited himself to join us. It wasn't my company they craved.

I missed our rap sessions that had nourished me through grade school and junior high. Mostly our conversations happened while I sprawled across Cincy's bed and watched her dress for a date. The more she and Lenora argued over her grades, the more Cincy went out. That fall she actually dated Steamy Stan Stenson, who rode a motorcycle and smelled of motor oil and danger. I couldn't believe Lenora let her go. I'd begun to sense that Lenora was afraid to give her an ultimatum. If she said *don't go,* and Cincy went anyway, then what?

As Cincy zoomed off on the back of Stan's bike, I wondered if she was having sex with him, too. After our last confrontation, I dared not ask for fear of spoiling the delicate peace we'd made afterward.

With Cincy gone, I went back to the greenlab to check on the five Malagasy chrysalides. I refreshed their habitat and made my journal entry, then set about the tasks of repotting, watering and pruning the new plants we'd quarantined until we made certain no pests were aboard. Working independently, I felt Lenora's quiet presence even when she wasn't there. When she was, I assisted in her research. She kept an eye on the Malagasies while I was at school or work.

On late afternoons, when the light cast patterned shadows through the canopy of leaves and I was alone in the lab with chores completed, I sat on a stool and sketched each denizen of the sunporch. I liked the process of drawing but was never quite satisfied with the results.

"*That's* typical of an artist," Lenora said, laughing. She surveyed my series of colored-pencil drawings. "These are absolutely wonderful. You ought to frame them."

So I decided to frame one for my mother's birthday, a peace offering of sorts. With skewed teenage logic, I hoped my interest in art might somehow neutralize Ruth's aversion to science.

At Tucker's I bought a natural wood frame and took it to art class, where Mrs. Burke helped me cut a dusty-mauve mat for my drawing of *Mourning Cloaks on Poplar.* She said it was my best composition.

The picture showed a trio of butterflies in a subtle triangle, one in flight, one perched on a branch with its wings closed to show its barklike camouflage. The third butterfly, the focal point, spread its indigo wings to the light. A butter-yellow band edged the sculpted wing tips, and inside that, where the indigo was darkest, a row of iridescent blue dots. I lamented about not getting the colors exact, but Miss Burke brushed aside my regrets.

"This is art, Bobbie, not photography," she said. "You've done a fine job."

I wrapped the framed picture in butcher paper and drew a red-checkered ribbon and bow on the outside in colored pencil. Pleased with the arty look of the package, I packed my other sketches in a cardboard portfolio to show Mom after she unwrapped her gift.

On an windless afternoon in late September, my mother's birthday, I biked home from Tucker's with the portfolio balanced across the handlebars. I told myself it was silly to be so excited and nervous about showing Mom my drawings.

Dusk collected in the untrimmed shrubbery and beneath the sagging carport by the time I arrived. The bluish light of the TV flickered through the living room window. I parked the bike beside Mom's car and went inside through the back door.

The kitchen was dark and held no smells of supper. My stomach growled and I promised it a sandwich—later.

"Mom?"

No answer. I laid the portfolio on the kitchen table and carried the wrapped picture into the living room.

Ruth lay on the sofa in front of a cops-and-robbers program, sound asleep. I leaned over to rouse her when my foot bumped the empty bottle on the floor. Its final contents dribbled a dark ring on the faded rug. The yeasty smell of bourbon stung my nose.

"Three six three, Ruth drank whis-key," I chanted. But as I looked down at the sunken eyes and slack mouth, flippancy deserted me. In the reflected light of the TV, her skin looked eerie and translucent. Except for the slight rasp of her breath, my mother looked dead.

One day I'll walk in and find her this way, I thought, *only she won't be breathing. I'll just walk in and find her drunk to death.*

Suddenly I was furious. The floor weaved beneath my feet; my shoulders trembled. Ruth's face shimmered before my eyes like fumes of bourbon.

"Damn it, Mom!"

I threw the picture on the floor and heard the glass shatter. My voice rose another notch. *"Happy birthday."*

Ruth's eyes opened. She smiled, hearing only the last phrase and missing the sarcasm. "Don't remind me," she said.

"Did you drink that whole bottle since you got home?" I demanded. I felt like fighting.

Her jaw tightened, but she wouldn't meet my eyes. "Nope. I started on it at lunch."

"Swell. Now you're drinking on the job. Tired of working at the inn, are you? Feel like getting fired?"

She struggled to sit up. "Don't you talk shitty to me, young lady."

I looked at my mother, listing at an unnatural angle on the battered sofa, her eyes glazed and defensive, her hair matted as a worn-out scouring pad. I wanted to strangle her.

The phone in the kitchen rang, but I ignored it. If Ruth heard, she didn't acknowledge it.

"I'm sick of this, Mom. Do you hear me? *It's got to stop!*"

Her head wobbled, but the glazed eyes didn't register any emotion I could read.

"If you get fired at the inn, you won't be able to get another job, because everybody in Shady River knows you're a drunk. An alcoholic." I'd never used the word to her before. "You've got to go to AA or somewhere and get some help. If you don't, I'm going to move out. A kid shouldn't have to come home and find her mother drunk."

I thrust my face close to her, talking loud to mask the tremble in my voice. "Do you understand me, Mom? *I'll move out.*"

I saw the mean glint of the whiskey come into her eyes, and instead of being afraid, I was glad. *Yell at me! Get up and hit me. Act like you care!*

Her mouth smirked. "And I suppose you'll move into that spook house with those lesbians? I'd rather have the whole town think I'm a drunk than what they're thinking about *you,* young lady."

Her best shot didn't faze me. "That's a lie and you know it. You're jealous of Lenora and Cincy because they're more of a family to me than you are."

But I only thought she'd taken her best shot.

"Family." She sneered. "I guess you think *family* means someone you can trust. Let me tell you, Miss Book Reader. Family will screw you over just as quick as a stranger. Quicker. All you get from family is bad genes. And betrayal."

A prickly feeling ran up my neck. This was a theme I'd never heard from her before. "Are you talking about my father?"

"Yes, your *father!* And my brother!" Her voice slurred, and her eyes moved toward some image I couldn't see. "Even my sister, who should have known better, taking up for them."

Suddenly weary, I threw myself into the lone chair, nearly tipping it over. "What the hell are you talking about? Do you even know?"

She didn't answer.

"You're using other people as an excuse for drinking," I said bitterly. "Nobody forces you to drink. I used to think it was my fault, but it isn't. You choose it yourself."

I leaned forward, challenging, refusing to be ignored. "I always thought you started to drink because Dad left us. But I had it backward, didn't I? He left *because* of your drinking, didn't he? You drove him away!"

Her head snapped erect and her eyes turned small and hard. "Your father," she said distinctly, "was a flaming queer. *A homo. A fag. A queen.*"

"You're lying!"

But I knew she wasn't. The dark pain of truth frightened her face.

A tingle like electric shock started inside my chest and streaked through my arms. I looked at my hands, expecting to see my fingernails melted.

"He didn't leave me for another woman," she said, disgust twisting her face. "He left me for a *man*. My own..." Her eyes jittered. I could see regret forming already for the secret she'd exposed.

Sirens wailed from the TV and red light flashed against her face. Ruth crumpled, her chin drooping onto her chest. "My own brother."

She wiped away tears and saliva with the back of her hand, no longer talking to me. Her head rolled back and forth. "Little Joey. My flesh and blood, my best friend! I lost them both."

"You don't *have* a brother...."

I was standing behind the sofa, holding Winnie the Pooh by one arm...my father's face turning toward me, frightened...the other man's face turning, his hair dark red and frizzy just like my mother's, the face filling in...freckles, familiar eyes.

I stood up, feeling alone in the room. "Jee-sus H. Christ." So many things becoming clear. So many new questions.

The phone rang again.

I retrieved the mourning cloak picture from the floor and carried it to the kitchen. Broken glass rattled inside the paper.

Lenora's voice in the receiver was animated. "Bobbie! I've been trying to call. The first antenor has started to hatch!"

I pictured the splitting chrysalis, the miracle I'd waited for all summer about to happen. I took a deep breath and blew it out. "I can't come up right now."

A pause. "Bobbie? What's wrong?"

I experienced a moment of weightlessness in which I couldn't remember who I was or why I was holding the telephone.

"I'll see you soon," I said nonsensically, and hung up.

I made a pot of strong coffee and watched the water as it gurgled into the glass carafe. When it was ready, I shook Ruth awake and shoved a steaming mug into her hands.

"Drink it," I said. "We're going to talk. There's no putting the cat back in the bag."

CHAPTER 10

I lift my arms while a uniformed attendant pat-searches my body.

"Remove your shoes, please."

Her hands slide over and under my feet, and I wonder what kinds of contraband people carry inside their socks. I have locked my purse in the car, according to instructions, bringing only my keys and my driver's license. These were traded for a clip-on plastic visitor's badge at a pass-through window inside the front gates.

The guard takes my coat and leads me to a room she calls "secure visiting," an eight-by-eight cubicle with a glass partition down the middle. She says Lenora has requested to see me here, not in the communal visiting room where other inmates will meet their families.

When she leaves me alone, a chill runs over me. Three phones wait in silence on each side of the partition, and three stools, close together and bolted down. The room feels much smaller than these places look on TV. My pulse escalates and thumps in my throat.

I sit on a stool and wait. Somewhere an anonymous guard is escorting Lenora through hallways that lead to this room.

Breathe and blow. I wipe my palms on the legs of my pants. The cubicle smells like floor wax and plastic and feels claustrophobic, despite a window at one end that looks out into a hallway. Two shadows pass the window and then a door opens—surprisingly, on my side of the partition. A woman in gray cotton pants and a loose shirt steps into the tiny enclosure.

If it weren't for those sea-green eyes, I'm not certain I would recognize Lenora. I stand up and we face each other for an awkward moment. Then she smiles.

"Bobbie. It's good to see you."

The dusky voice has not changed, but it's the only thing. Her hair has gone gray and it's cut short in no particular style. Her skin, always moon-colored and smooth in my memories, now looks like skimmed milk. Tiny lines gather at her lips and the corners of her eyes.

Lenora is forty-six now, two years younger than my mother would be if she were alive. But this is more than normal aging. She looks...brittle.

I swallow hard and smile, though my eyes are blind. "Hello, Lenora."

She holds out her hands, giving me the choice to take them or step forward into a hug. I hesitate, then move clumsily to embrace her. I can feel her bones beneath the coarse fabric of her prison fatigues as she hugs me tight. My face fits against her shoulder.

I close my eyes, remembering. The ache in my chest expands, hollow and painful. Her smell is foreign, I think, slightly metallic, not the scent of earth and chlorophyll that should be hers. Finally her arms loosen and she steps back to look at me. I'm aware of the guard, watchful outside the window, the way you watch a suspicious dog without meeting its eye. I wonder if the room is wired for sound.

"You look wonderful," Lenora says. Her eyes are dry.

We sit awkwardly on adjoining stools, our knees touching. It would be more comfortable to use the two outer seats, but putting that empty stool between us seems unacceptable.

I keep my voice low. "Are you all right?" I don't know how to ask *Are you sick?*

She smiles and shrugs. "I'm okay. How about you?"

"I'm fine." I smile, too, but it doesn't feel natural. "Still crazy after all these years."

"You were never crazy," she says emphatically. "Even as a child, you were saner than anybody I knew." Her voice cracks a little as if from disuse. "You just *felt* everything so deeply."

You don't know how bad it got, I think.

She was incarcerated already when I went over the edge. She doesn't know that I didn't speak for a period of four months. Or about the panic attack in a parking lot when I sat down on the concrete and wet my clothes. But I don't want to discuss the levels of psychosis. I take a deep breath and meet her eyes. They, too, have faded, a cloudier ocean, but her gaze is no less piercing. I feel as if she's reading me, learning things without having to ask.

I've rehearsed this moment for miles, for years, actually, but now that I'm here I can't remember what I'd planned to say. "I've been embroidering butterflies for you," I say stupidly. "Pillowtops, I mean."

"Really!" She seems pleased but confused.

"I draw the patterns myself. You can use them in your new place. When you get out."

Her eyes recede somewhere. "It's hard to imagine living anywhere else," she says. "With a real bed and furniture. And a private shower." She laughs but there's no humor in it.

My throat knots. "Has it been...horrible?"

Of course it's horrible, you idiot; it's prison.

But Lenora answers thoughtfully. "Not as bad as I'd expected, after the first couple of years. Back then, I was certain I'd die from it. I've decided the human mind, if not the body, can adjust to almost anything."

She studies my face. "Harley badgered you into coming, didn't he? I'll thank him." She says this good-naturedly, as if Harley were some quirky cousin the whole family tolerates, instead of the sudden, hulking presence who showed up at my door.

"Where did he come from anyway?" My phrasing is indelicate once again.

She shrugs. "It's a long story. After he was reported lost in Vietnam, the government asked him—pressured him, actually—to go undercover. He hunted the jungles for American POWs. Later they sent him into Cambodia, where things were even worse. He won't talk much about those years."

"He couldn't have let you know he was alive, at least?"

"He wasn't. They 'disappeared' him. He had to stay officially dead so the government could deny they'd sent men in there."

"But how did he get—"

She lifts a hand, stopping me. "I haven't seen you in so long. I really want to hear about *you*."

Again she smiles, and I brace myself for the question I'm afraid she'll ask. *Where is Cincy? Why doesn't she come?* Instead she says, "Tell me about you and David. No children yet?"

Though I recover quickly, Lenora has seen me flinch. "I don't intend to have children. Too much—" I wave a hand, searching for a word "—instability in my genes."

She frowns. "Stability is more a function of environment than of heredity."

"That's a strange attitude for a scientist," I say, trying for a light tone. "But either way, a child of mine would be at risk."

"Bobbie." Her voice is firm, the mentor's voice. "You'd be a *good* mother. Overprotective, probably, but that's okay."

"I would *not* be a good mother," I snap. "I've no patience, and no frame of reference. Can we please talk about something else?"

Apparently we can't. We're both silent and I look away but she does not.

"Are you pregnant? Is that why you've come?"

"No! I am not."

Her frown doubts me. Cincy used to tease me about my inability to lie. It's not a virtue; it's a curse. Fleeing this subject, I leap from one cliff to the next and blurt, "Harley Jaines wants me to testify at your parole hearing."

Lenora's eyebrows rise. She leans against the glass partition and sighs deeply. She never used to sigh. Sighing signals resignation, and Lenora was never resigned. Prison has taught her this.

"Men do love to take over, don't they?" Her voice takes on a hard edge. "There's no need for you to testify. My new attorney says we have a good chance. I've served the minimum time—" a smile twists one side of her mouth "—and Lord knows I'm a model prisoner. I plan to be full of remorse."

Her eyes soften again and she puts her hand over mine. "Don't worry about the hearing, Bobbie. It's a long trip for you, and you don't need to rehash all that…history. I mean it. I'm just glad you're here today."

I squeeze her hand and feel my throat constrict. She has given me what I came for. Permission to withdraw, to abdicate responsibility.

For some reason it's not enough. I have to swallow before I can speak. "He says your attorney's going to try for a pardon instead of just parole."

Lenora removes her hand from mine. Her face solidifies. "That's absurd. I've explained that to both of them. Over and over."

"But you didn't set the fire," I whisper. *"I know you didn't."*

For a moment I see the imprints of her prison existence in her face, imprints that run deeper than the physical. When she answers her voice is severe.

"Don't meddle in this. A parole would get me out of here. That's all that matters."

"Meddle! I was *there,* remember? I'm not sixteen anymore. You don't have to keep protecting me. Even then I knew what really happened."

"You *don't* know."

"*My mother tried to kill me. To kill us both.* I've accepted that, yet I let you stay here. I didn't try hard enough—"

"Stop it!" The pain on her face cuts me. She opens her hands as if to speak but shakes her head, instead.

"Lenora?"

"I'm no hero, Bobbie. I never was."

"Why are you still punishing yourself?" I ask.

"And why are *you?*" Her eyes are flat when they meet mine. "Go home to David. Forget about me. Forget about Rockhaven. Quit using the past as a crutch, Bobbie. *Decide* to be happy, and do it."

She stands abruptly and knocks on the window. In the moment before the door opens, I am silenced by the paleness of her skin and a sudden thought of losing her forever.

The guard opens the door. Just before Lenora steps through, she turns back to me. "Have you heard from Cincy?"

I take a deep breath. "Six months ago."

"Is she all right?"

I pause. "I only talked to her on the phone."

Lenora nods. Her face looks drawn and waxy in the fluorescent light, a crone's face. I see her lithe and beautiful, the reflection of bright wings alive in her eyes.

The door closes and she is gone.

* * *

At the gatehouse, I drop the plastic visitor's badge into the bin below the window and walk to the double gates where I stand numbly, waiting. I hear the guard call something through the glass as if from another world. At first I can't make sense of what he's saying, don't even try; it's too remote from the roar inside my head.

Finally, I hear, "Lady, you forgot your ID and keys!"

I return to retrieve my things. The first gate rattles open and I step inside the wire cage, wait until that gate closes behind me. The second gate slides open and I am free.

The sky has turned gray and tiny snowflakes whirl without direction. I pull my coat close and head for the car, feeling blank, disoriented.

I don't understand what just happened with Lenora. Out-of-sync sound bites play over and over in my head.

Don't meddle in this!

I'm no hero. I never was.

You'd be a good mother, Bobbie.

He didn't exist. They disappeared him.

My mother tried to kill me.

Go home to David. Decide to be happy.

Decide to be happy.

Harley Jaines is waiting beside my car in the parking lot. My heart lunges, its rhythm skittering. There's no way to avoid him. He is leaning against the fender, wearing a parka that makes him look even larger than I remembered. Snowflakes catch in his blue-black hair. He watches me approach.

I stop and face him, keys in hand. While I'm deciding what to say, he disarms me with kindness.

"Thanks for coming. I know it was hard for you."

"How do you *know?*" My anger rises unexpectedly. "You've been gone too many years. How do you know anything?" I haven't spent enough time in my adult life being angry, I decide. There's power in it.

He surprises me again. "You're right. I don't know about your life, any more than you know about mine. But thanks anyway. You mean a lot to Lenora, and I appreciate your making the drive down here."

He looks down at the square toes of his cowboy boots with no indication of moving off my car. I watch him.

"She doesn't want me to come to the parole hearing," I say. "Forbade it, in fact."

He nods. "And you always do what you're told?"

"It would appear so. I came here, didn't I?"

Suddenly my knees won't hold me up anymore and I lean against the car door, too shaky to fit the key into the lock.

He glances at me. "You okay?"

"Do you care?"

"I don't, really. I care only about Lenora now. But you did do me a favor."

"No, I didn't. I came here because I wanted to see her. I care a lot about Lenora, too. More than you could possibly know."

"Then why would you refuse to set her free?" he says quietly.

It's useless to keep repeating that I have no such power. Impossible to explain why I've kept silent so long, fearing something even darker than the guilt of Lenora's imprisonment. Instead, I say, "Why would you let her think you were dead all those years? And let her raise your daughter by herself?"

He looks off into the flurrying snow. "I didn't know we had a daughter."

"She wrote you—"

"I never got the letters. I didn't know until I traced Lenora down a year ago."

I have no answer for this. I'm exhausted and want only to leave this place. "Please get off my car."

He doesn't move. "Doesn't it strike you as odd that Lenora would go to prison for something your mother did? Just to keep you from knowing your mother was capable of trying to kill you?"

"Did Lenora tell you my mother set the fire?"

"No. I figured it out from talking to her first lawyer."

"No, it doesn't seem odd."

But it does; it always has. I look across the parking lot toward the buildings so he won't see my doubts. A thin layer of white clings to the barbed wire and cinder block.

"Lenora knew how fragile my sanity was. She tried to save me from losing it, but things didn't work out that way. Lenora loved me," I say, like a benediction.

"She loves Cynthia, too."

"Of course she does. What's that got to do with anything?"

"You believe she abandoned Cynthia to save you?"

Wings flutter inside my rib cage—panic rising. "I don't know what the hell happened! That's what I keep trying to tell you."

The temperature has dropped and the cold metal of the car against my back seeps through to my bones. "Get off my car. I'm tired and I want to get out of here."

Slowly, Harley Jaines stands away from the car. I unlock it and get in, relock the door.

He comes to the window and speaks through the glass, leaning close. "When you talk to Cynthia, tell her about me, will you? Tell her I want to see her."

I pull away fast and leave him standing in the snow.

My head feels like a helium balloon. *Breathe and blow. Breathe and blow.*

At the exit to the prison, I can't remember which way to turn. Pinpoints of colored light float before my eyes. Finally I recognize the road I came on and drive back toward a main road where a couple of motels crouch close to the interstate. Unsafe to drive, I pull in at the Starlite Motel. The motel office looks like a remodeled drive-in restaurant.

As I unlock my room, my heart rate is way too fast and my tongue feels like sandpaper. I turn on the lights, pull the drapes shut, draw a glass of water and drink like a parched animal.

Still in my coat, I pace the floor. Dr. Bannar's clinical voice inside my head tells me to isolate what I'm feeling. I breathe and blow.

Urgent. What I feel is urgency, besides the fear, an urgency to do something. Take action. But what?

Shoot Harley Jaines?

Go home to David?

Go back to Lenora and demand the whole truth?

Lenora won't tell me. And without that truth, I'm doomed to this tightrope existence forever, where one careless step can send me plummeting.

My shifting glance falls on my purse, sitting open on the bed. I stop pacing.

I dump the bag's contents onto the bedspread and paw through the debris, then search the lining. In a small zippered pocket, my fingers close on a folded slip of paper torn from a phone pad at home six months ago.

On the paper is the last phone number I had for Cynthia Jaines.

CHAPTER 11

On the motel phone, I read the instructions for long distance calls, then start pushing buttons. Five rings. My lips are dry again and I lick them with a thick tongue. At last a female voice answers, but it isn't Cincy.

I clear my throat. "This is Roberta Dutreau, an old friend of Cynthia Jaines. Is she there, by any chance?"

"Oh, she hasn't been *here* for, like, a *long* time," the girl says.

"It's very important that I reach her—a family emergency. Do you have another number I might try?"

"Let me see.... Hang on a minute, okay?"

"Yes. Thank you."

There's a rustling like drawers opening and papers shuffling before she comes back on the line.

"I think Freddy still talks to her sometimes. Here's his number." She reads off ten digits.

I don't recognize the area code. "Thank you. Listen, may I leave my number with you, just in case you should hear from her?"

"Sure, I'll write it down—but I haven't talked to Cincy in, like, months." Her voice turns confidential. "She was pretty messed up when she left here, you know?"

"Yes. Well." I spell out my name and give the motel phone number and hang up.

Then I dial the number she gave me. Freddy's machine answers. His voice on the recording sounds friendly and blatantly effeminate. Again I spell my name, leave the motel number and my home phone, doing my best to sound sane but worried.

"It's an emergency," I say, enunciating. "If you know how to contact Cynthia, will you please ask her to call me immediately?"

As soon as I hang up, the phone rings. I jump, snatch up the receiver. "Yes?"

It's the valley-girl voice. "I thought of another place you might ask about Cincy," she says. "Here's the number."

I thank her profusely, dial the number and get another machine. It's a bar that isn't open on Sundays. Again, I leave a message.

Then I lie back on the bed and start to cry.

I cry for Lenora, and the years in prison that have left her withered and old. And for Cincy, who's been lost to me for years and lost to herself perhaps even longer.

And finally, I weep for me. For the child I'll never have and for David, caught in the net of my dementia. For twenty minutes or so I indulge this fit of emotion, stupid with self-pity. Dr. Bannar would be proud. She kept telling me to let it out, that tears could be cleansing. Back then I couldn't cry.

When the siege finally passes, I feel hollow and lonesome yet somehow better than I was, the panic quelled. I sit up and blow my nose. I clear my throat several times before dialing my home phone number.

David's calm baritone comes on the line but it is only the recording. I close my eyes, letting his voice fill my head and my body, and a longing rises that I haven't felt in a long time. *I do love you, David. I need you, and I think you need me.*

It isn't what you get, it's what you give, the old woman in the restaurant said. What have I ever given to David? I take his love, his strength and his patience, and give nothing in return. *I'll make it up to you,* I promise.

The machine beeps. In the hushed static that follows I can't find my voice. Finally I manage to identify myself and read off the motel phone number. My voice sounds nasal from crying and I clear my throat again. "I saw Lenora this afternoon. I'm okay, just tired. I'll try to call you again this evening." I pause. "I love you, David."

I walk next door to a chain restaurant and order an omelet and decaf coffee. I missed lunch and know I should eat, but it's hard to swallow the overcooked eggs. I dawdle until the coffee gets cold, then go back to my room and phone David again. When the recorder comes on, I hang up.

It's Sunday; he should be home. I picture him screening my calls, scuffing around the house in his over-run house shoes, frowning. My stomach twists. But that isn't like David. He's overprotective, but not vindictive.

I try the museum, the private number for the curatorial staff, but no one answers. A tremor begins in my stomach and moves to my brain. What if I lose him? Who could blame him for giving up on marriage to a cold and unstable wife? He has no family left to disapprove, and his friends will support him. They'd invite him to dinner, try to fix him up....

This is crazy. I'm making myself paranoid.

I undress and step into the shower, standing under the steaming water a long time, lathering my hair in a thick excess of motel shampoo. Toweled dry, I sit propped up on the bed and watch TV, swaddled like a mummy in an extra blanket. At ten o'clock I take my sleeping medicine and dial my home number again.

It's 11:00 p.m. in Calgary and David doesn't answer.

Still wrapped in the blanket, I crawl under the covers and wait for sleep.

The room is black as a cave when the phone rings at 2:00 a.m. Though sleeping heavily, I come awake fast and grab the receiver.

"David?"

There's a pause at the other end. "No, Bobbie. It's Cincy."

"Cincy." Caught in a backwash, for a few moments I cannot speak.

"I got a message that you need to talk to me," she says.

Her familiar voice sends a wave of warmth down my limbs, but it sounds strange, too, edged with something I can't discern. "Where are you?" she says.

"In Spokane, in a motel. I visited Lenora."

"What's wrong?"

"I...it's not really an emergency. I..."

"You haven't called me in a decade, Bobbie. I guess it *is* an emergency."

"I need to see you."

She pauses. "Why? Is Mom all right?"

"She looks terrible. But how else could she look? I...there are things I need to talk to you about. I can't do this on the phone."

Silence.

"Cincy?"

"I'm in California. Redding, in the north. If my car holds out, I can be in Spokane by tomorrow." No hesitation. If I need her, she'll come. My eyes burn. Where was I when Cincy needed *me*?

It isn't what you get, it's what you give....

Lying on my back in the motel bed, I close my eyes and lay one arm across my forehead. And wonder if I will feel this tired for the rest of my life.

"I'll meet you in between," I tell her. "How about at Rockhaven?"

She pauses. "Are you sure?"

"Yes." We set a time in late afternoon. I hang up and lie awake, waiting for morning.

Shady River, 1979

Most of my family history I learned from my mother the night of her birthday in September 1979, as I plied her with coffee and took advantage of her drunkenness. I once heard a policeman say that coffee won't sober anybody up, just make him a wide-awake drunk. It worked that way on Ruth. The parts of the story she didn't tell me I discovered on my own later, climbing back through the gnarled branches of our family tree.

My father was from the South. The Lees claimed some circuitous kinship to the famous Confederate general, and most of the sons in the clan were named after him. My father was dubbed Robert Elden, Elden being my grandmother's maiden name.

Great-great-grandfather Lee was a tobacco lord and lived on a plantation right out of *Gone With the Wind,* but over several generations the family money evaporated with mismanagement and indolence. Robert Elden wasn't indolent, though; he was determined to get an education from a good university and reclaim the prosperity of former Lees.

Mom married Robert Elden Lee when she was sixteen. He was eighteen and newly graduated from a small Alabama high school. I can only guess what drew them together, two loners in a peer society as fixed as bees'. Neither had dated anyone else, she told me. Mom must have worshiped his Old South manners and gentle good looks, so far removed from anything she'd ever known.

Born in Missouri, Ruth Marcott was the oldest child of an itinerant family that moved to Alabama when she was eight. They lived in a shack that had once been a chicken house. Her father, a barely literate day laborer, spent much of his sporadic earnings on cheap whiskey, and her mother's health was bad. From the age of twelve, Ruth worked odd jobs after school and during summer for twenty-five cents an hour, then came home to feed and supervise her brother and sister. Ruth was fourteen when her mother keeled over in the chicken pen and died.

Mom's brother, Joey, was twelve then, and Olivia nine. Joey was the smart one. He did well in school and everybody liked him. Ruth adored him. But after two years of being a teenage mother and breadwinner for the family, Ruth made her escape. She married my father and left home, never finishing high school. Joey stuck it out, earned a wrestling scholarship for college, and Olivia was left to cope with her drunken father alone.

Robert Elden Lee wasn't athletic enough to be valuable to college recruiters, and good grades from a country school in Alabama didn't count for much, either. His parents couldn't afford the school he chose, but his dreams were Ruth's dreams, so she went to work in a tire plant in Birmingham to put him through architecture school. Making tires, Ruth found, was hot, stinking, unglamorous work. Hours on the assembly line imprinted an oily black line that never quite disappeared around the white moons of her fingernails; her sweat smelled like rubber. But the job paid union wages and Robert did indeed graduate. He took an entry-level job as a draftsman and Ruthie, as he called her, quit work and got pregnant. The future they'd planned seemed poised to come true.

Then Robert began to change. His job didn't pay much and advancements were slow. He grew quiet and moody. Only when he played with me, his infant daughter, did Ruth see the old Robert, for whom she'd given so much.

By all accounts, I was a plump and placid baby. My father would carry me outdoors to watch songbirds flit through the magnolias and moss-draped oaks. Talking in a low voice, he'd hold me up inside the fluttering leaves, where I'd gurgle with delight. I believe that on some level I retain that memory; throughout my childhood, I sometimes dreamed of living among the leaves as a bird.

Before I was a year old, Ruth took a job as a waitress to ease the financial strain. But Robert receded even further from her, evading intimacy, then any physical contact. In silent, mounting panic, Ruthie came to the only conclusion she could. He must have found another woman. But she was afraid to confront him and force a choice. She knew, or thought she knew, what his choice would be.

On a day in August when I was three, a blue-black headache sent Ruth home from work unexpectedly. She found Robert with her brother, Joey, in the bedroom, their eyes glazed with naked desire.

If I had been in the house, perhaps Ruth would have controlled her rage for my sake. But I was visiting my grandmother Lee. Repulsed and devastated, her head shrieking, my mother seized an iron doorstop and hurled it at Robert, shattering the window instead. I can picture a flurry of white legs scattering from the bed. Ruth ran to the kitchen and grabbed a handful of weapons from a drawer. She wanted to kill them both.

The steak knife she threw clattered against the wall and fell to the floor, but the butcher knife lodged into the closet door frame beside Joey's cowering head. He grabbed his jeans and leaped through the broken window. Ruth threw a spatula after him and aimed an eggbeater at Robert's head before she crumpled in a corner, weeping. My father packed his things and left.

That night, Ruth bundled our clothes into the family car and retrieved me from Grandmother Lee's without a word to her about what had happened. We headed west on the first major highway.

When she told me the story, that September night while my antenor swallowtails emerged from their liquid sleep, I got a vague memory of headlights, the green smell of Southern summer night air through the car window, and the whiteness of a bandage on my mother's arm propped up on the steering wheel.

Ruth didn't tell me the part about setting afire the tiny house where the three of us had lived. This I learned from Aunt Olivia, later on. With me asleep in the car on a pile of clothing, Ruth returned one last time to the bedroom she had shared with my father. In the act of torching the bed, she somehow burned her arm, leaving the scar she carried for the rest of her life.

But even fire could not purge from Ruthie's mind the scene of my father's betrayal. She hopped from job to job across Missouri, Oklahoma and New Mexico, using assumed names to avoid being traced. At first she wrote to her sister each Christmas to let her know we were alive. She swore Olivia to secrecy. My aunt tried to persuade her to come home, and finally, when Olivia passed along a similar message from my father, Ruth concluded they were in league against her. Humiliated beyond repair, she cut off all contact.

The September I was fifteen, on my mother's thirty-seventh birthday, I sat in the faded rocker in our rented living room and listened to her confessions. Detached as a priest, I was quietly brutal in my inquisition. Near midnight we were both exhausted, and I let her escape into sleep.

I kept rocking, my head lolling back on the cushion of the musty-smelling chair. A stocky black spider scuttled up the wall toward the ceiling, his simple quest for food and sex more real to me than the story I'd just heard.

My mother's life might have played on the afternoon soaps. It was impossible to absorb so many bizarre details at once, so my mind chose one and fixed on it: My father hadn't abandoned us as I'd always thought. Ruth had hidden me from him.

Suddenly the tiny house felt airless, overcrowded by my drunken mother and the strangers of her tangled past. I couldn't breathe; I had to get out of there.

I changed into jeans and biked through the autumn night to Rockhaven.

It was well past 1:00 a.m. when I ascended the hill, but a small light burned on the sunporch. I knew Lenora was awake, attending the hatch of the Malagasy swallowtails. From the driveway I whistled the three-noted call that was our signal, then let myself in with my key. Cincy's room was dark, the door closed.

I stepped into the greenlab quietly. Lenora had posted herself on a wooden chair beside the caterpillars' terrarium. Her hand rested on a coffee mug, hidden on a crowded plant stand except for a thin curl of steam. Her long hair was looped into a knot on the crown of her head and was held in place with a pencil.

She looked up when I came in, her forehead pinched into a frown. When I hadn't come running at the news that the first chrysalis was hatching, she must have known something drastic had happened.

"Are you okay, Bobbie?" She examined my face closely, as if for bruises.

I took a deep breath and huffed it out before answering. "I've been better." The tremble in my voice surprised me.

I knelt beside her chair to peer inside the terrarium. Its glass walls shimmered through the moisture in my eyes. In the dim light, I focused on a silky, dark shape that clung to a twig, drying its wings in the warmth from Lenora's lamp. Perhaps five inches across, it was midnight-black with loose white splotches like dots from an artist's paintbrush. On the hindwings, reddish-orange crescents made plump moons on the black background. Its teardrop-shaped swallowtails were perfectly formed.

"It's beautiful," I whispered.

For one suspended moment, I forgot everything but the magic and incredible risk of the creature's transformation. Inside the protective shell of the chrysalis, all identifiable parts of the caterpillar had dissolved into a fragile genetic soup. The slightest trauma at that point could thwart the miracle of reorganization into this complex, winged beauty.

I felt my own insides melting and wondered whether they'd reassemble as a functioning person, or remain a gelatinous, emotional goop forever.

"Can I help?" Lenora asked.

I kept my eyes on the fanning wings. "I'm not going back to her house. Could I stay with you for a while?"

Lenora opened her arms and I buried my face against her and sobbed. She held me while I poured out the whole scene with Ruth, even the lurid revelation about my father. But I didn't repeat Ruth's accusation that Rockhaven was a house of lesbians.

Lenora listened, stroking my hair. A wave of longing swamped me.

Like father, like daughter. Could Ruth be right? My stomach rolled.

"I love you, Lenora. Why couldn't you have been my mother?"

Her voice was soft, unhesitating. "I love you, too, sweetheart. You're welcome here as long as you want to stay."

A gust of wind tossed the trees outside the sunporch and its timbers creaked and shifted. Still she held me, rocking gently. I closed my eyes and felt my body pulling apart. "I know you can't think about it now," she said, "but later, when the hurt's not so fresh, try to imagine what your mother's been through. Think about what you'd have done, in her position."

Cincy's sardonic voice from the doorway startled both of us. "Well, *this* is pretty."

I jerked away from Lenora.

Moonlight made an ivory silhouette of Cincy's T-shirt and long bare legs.

"Bobbie's had a rough night," Lenora said. "She's going to stay with us awhile."

Leaf shadows hid Cincy's face. I held my breath, trying to guess what she might be thinking.

Finally Cincy yawned. "Three six three?"

Mom drank whis-key. "Bingo." I exhaled relief.

"Sorry to hear it," she said, and yawned again. Her sleepy eyes wandered to the terrarium. "So how's the hatch coming?"

"Great," I said, eager to change the subject. "Come look."

"Hmm." She stayed put, then affected a Southern accent that unnerved me, considering what I'd just learned about my forebears. "I don't know nothin' 'bout birthin' butterflies, Miss Scarlett. See you in the morning."

Cincy turned toward the darkened house, then back again. The accent was gone. "You going to sleep in my bed or in Mom's?"

My breath caught. "I'll just bunk on the couch, if I sleep at all. I want to watch the other swallowtails hatch."

"Whatever." Cincy disappeared, leaving behind the vague scent of her perfume and something dark and unspoken.

I knew then that I could not stay at Rockhaven.

Something was happening between Cincy and Lenora, between Cincy and me, between Lenora and me. I was certain my presence would deepen the wedge, and I couldn't risk being forced to choose between them.

But if I didn't stay here, where would I go?

The distant sound of a train passing along the river vibrated the windows of the sunporch. Its lonesome whistle echoed in my breastbone.

I could not return to my mother's house. Only one other possibility remained. I would try to find my father.

CHAPTER 12

That night, Rockhaven's living room felt stuffy and abnormally warm for October. Tossing on my sofa bed, the sheet wadded and damp beneath me, I stripped off my T-shirt and flung it away. I lay awake in the ticking darkness, the smell of vegetation pungent to my nose. At half light, I padded to the sunporch wearing only my glasses and stepped into the green world of the butterflies.

Moist air wrapped my skin. I breathed deeply and felt the familiar oxygen rush.

How I would miss this place. And the butterflies.

On the lip of the open terrarium, a newly hatched antenor swallowtail sat poised for flight. Its beauty caught in my chest. A third one clung to its branch inside the glass box, pumping fluid into wet, crumpled wings. The fourth chrysalis still hung motionless on its silken thread.

I scanned the branches and matted canopy for the firstborn swallowtail. A dark flutter caught my eye. Antenor One fanned its dark wings on a rhododendron, seeking early sunlight. I raised my hand involuntarily, as if it might recognize me and come to perch on my finger.

Though I would abandon them, my magical children would survive. I knew Lenora would watch out for them.

I wished I could sketch the antenors, so I could carry a picture with me like the photo of a child. But there wasn't time. In the living room, I reclaimed my clothes and found Lenora's Polaroid camera on the buffet. She always kept it loaded. I shot a photo of Antenor One, a dot among the foliage, and a close-up of the newcomer on the terrarium.

When the photos dried, I tucked both pictures in my jacket pocket along with the butterfly book Lenora had given me. Returning the camera, I picked up a small photo of Cincy and me that sat atop the buffet in a faux-silver frame. We mugged for the camera, our hair windblown, arms dangling over each other's shoulders. I could feel Lenora's face behind the camera like a third presence in the photo. It was taken two years ago—before Mom and I fought constantly, before Cincy discovered sex and the power it gave her.

I turned the frame over and slipped the picture out, apologizing silently for the theft. I had to hurry. Lenora would be up soon, and I hadn't the guts to explain why I was leaving. I didn't even leave a note to say where I was going, for fear she or Cincy would come looking for me.

In the driveway, I pulled my bike erect and straddled it. The handlebars felt cool and damp to my palms, the morning surprisingly cold after the heat of the house. Early rays of sun washed the valley in a rosy mist as I coasted down the hill toward the river, my cheeks wet, my breath a thin fog in the chill air.

When my tires hit the bridge, I pumped hard, then coasted to a stop midway across to watch the river turn gunmetal blue beneath the rising sun. Wisps of fog levitated along its surface. Sitting astride my bike, I made my peace with the river gods. When I left the bridge on the other side, my eyes were dry.

With an hour to kill before I could be sure Mom had gone to work, I rode past Tucker's store, where I'd worked for more than a year. I felt a twinge of guilt for not giving Mr. Tucker any notice. But teenage employees were interchangeable; he'd replace me in a day.

Three blocks east, the high school lay sleeping. I missed the place already. Especially biology class with Mr. Jenkins. Would his twin boys grow up to be criminals, I wondered, or bankers? Or perhaps teachers, like their dad.

A few cars hunkered beside the track where early joggers bobbed along with determined steps. Nobody I knew; nobody who knew me. Petey Small was a runner, but his lanky form wasn't among them. My stomach felt funny thinking of Pete. Cincy had dated him recently and I'd tried hard not to let her see how much that hurt. I wondered if she'd done it with him, too. If so, I didn't want to know.

A single chime from the Presbyterian church bell tower signaled seven-thirty. I headed for the little house on Third Avenue.

Mom's car wasn't in the driveway. Disgusted as I was with her, it hurt to know that she hadn't called Lenora's to check on me, or to ask me to come home. I let myself in the back door and nearly tripped over Rathbone, who yowled and shot outdoors without even stopping to say hello. Stray cats were smart; they never really adopted anybody.

The house was dark and smelled faintly sour in the stillness. I cracked a window above the kitchen sink where a few dirty dishes had collected. Mom had opened her birthday present. My drawing of mourning cloaks lay on the kitchen table, jagged points of glass forming a sunburst around the edges.

In my bedroom, I took down from the top closet shelf the soft-sided bag I'd bought on impulse with money earned at Tucker's. It was tan and brown, inexpensive, more like a duffel bag than a suitcase. When I'd carried it home Mom had frowned. "What do you need that thing for?"

I didn't know, until today.

I crammed extra jeans, T-shirts, sweatshirts and underwear into the bag, along with toiletries and a box of Kotex. The box took up too much room, so I threw it away and stuffed the pads into a zippered side pocket. I stuck in the butterfly book with the antenor pictures inside and a paperback copy of *Jane Eyre* I'd started for English class. The book belonged to the school library, but what would they do, sue me? I felt a thrill of defiance; Cincy would approve. I'd probably mail it back, though, eventually.

When the bag was full, I looked around the room, examining each crack in the wall and stain on the rug with new eyes. The place seemed impossibly small and shabby, a summary of my life. Nothing in the room, or in this house, made me question my decision. I couldn't get out of there fast enough.

The bank lobby opened at 8:00 a.m. I withdrew my entire savings, five hundred forty-two dollars and thirteen cents I'd been saving for college. The teller, a sixtyish woman whose name I didn't know, watched me fold the change inside the bills and stuff them in my pocket. My bag sat beside me on the terrazzo bank floor.

The teller raised a penciled eyebrow. "Going on a trip?"

"Um. Sort of." I wondered if she would trace down my mother and call her the moment I was gone.

"Be careful carrying all that cash. That can be dangerous, you know."

I gave her a look of teenage disdain and said nothing. But the skin on my neck prickled as I stepped out on the street, the wad of cash like a grenade in my pocket. I hooked the bag over the handlebars of my red bike, bumped the tires over the curb and pedaled down a quiet street away from the river.

The Shady River train station sat stolid and quiet in the cool morning, its dark brick contrasting with square, unshuttered windows full of yellow light. I leaned my bike against the wall beside the front entrance.

Inside, at a hole-in-the-wall window, I purchased a coach ticket on the first passenger train going east. Destination: Boise, Idaho. Train fare was more expensive than I'd expected. I saved a few dollars by purchasing a ticket straight through to Salt Lake City.

On a scrap of paper torn from a littered bulletin board, I scribbled *This bike belongs to Cincy Jaines, 555-3779.* Outside, I wove the note through the tire spokes of my bike and stroked the back fender once before abandoning my old friend. Then I sat in a corner of the station lounge and studied a map the ticket lady gave me. I was the only customer in the station.

From Salt Lake I would travel across the central plains to Omaha, where I could catch a bus to Kansas City. The only clue I had to my father's whereabouts was Mom's sister Olivia. The last postmark I'd seen on a letter from her several years ago bore the unforgettable name of Licking, Missouri.

Farther down the line, I'd buy a Missouri road map and figure out where Licking was and how to get there. I wondered if Aunt Olivia looked like Mom and if I could find her without getting mugged or raped on a lonely road somewhere. And if I'd ever see my mother again.

What if my father turned out to be dead? My stomach shifted and rolled.

Maybe I was just hungry. I bought a package of cheese crackers and a grape soda from a vending machine and watched a few other transients straggle in. No one met anyone else's eyes.

The Amtrak puffed in only an hour late, which, it turned out, was remarkably good time. I loved its steamy, oily smell. For years I'd watched the trains pass through Shady River and wished to be onboard. Now I was. I took a window seat in a nearly empty car and stashed my bag in the seat beside me, hoping to avoid a seat mate. At last the train lurched, crawled forward and shuddered out of Shady River, pulling me out of my old life.

Dilapidated warehouses inched past the window, then tiny frame houses that were Shady River's version of slums. The houses looked only slightly worse than the one where I lived. *Used to live.* I glanced at the sun and tried to guess the time; I'd have to buy a cheap watch, I decided. Probably it was about eleven o'clock, the beginning of fourth hour at school. Cincy would be going to history, where the teacher would count me absent. I thought of faces and places I might never see again.

Suddenly I felt deadly tired. I folded my glasses into my shirt pocket and let the landscape blur into soft shapes and colors.

The train wheels settled into a hypnotic rhythm. *Racketa-racketa, racketa-racketa.* Leaning my head against the window, I sank into sleep and dreamed of making out with Petey Small on the river bridge while unseen cars thundered past, shaking the floor beneath us. I felt his body heat and the coolness drifting up from the river. When I looked up, Cincy sat on a bridge span above us, watching.

Chapter 13

Spokane, 1990

The sky is clear and cold at 9:00 a.m. I top off the gas tank at a Quick Mart and buy an oversize cup of coffee for the road. After two failed attempts, I find the correct entrance to Interstate 90 west and head out of the city, toward Shady River and the burned-out skeleton that once was Rockhaven.

The coffee scalds my tongue and tastes like metal, but the foam cup warms my fingers. Driving alone on a strange road is a challenge for me. I'd never driven a car before I met David; he taught me during college, in his secondhand, stick-shift Renault. Thinking of this, I smile, though there was nothing funny about it at the time. There was so much I didn't know that David had to teach me.

Today my pulse races along with the busy flow of traffic and it feels good to be here among the other drivers, my comrades in a busy, living world. Like them, I have a purpose, somewhere to go. It's a feeling I remember from my brief days as a teenage working girl in Shady River. David thinks I'm too fragile to take a job in Calgary, but maybe it's just what I need.

My thoughts drift ahead to Cincy. Though she has phoned me occasionally, I haven't seen her for more than five years, when I was still in college. I'd told her on the phone that I planned to marry David and a week later she showed up at my door, a gaunt ghost. I couldn't hide my shock when I first saw her.

"I want to meet him," she said.

"To see if you approve?"

She didn't smile. "And what if I don't?"

"You will," I told her. "He's wonderful."

She did seem to like David—how could she not? He was handsome and charming in such an innocent way, like a puppy.

Skimming down the highway, I rehearse how to tell Cincy about Harley Jaines: *The father you thought was dead is back, and he wants to see you.* Will she be excited, anxious to see him? Or will she reject him totally? It's hard to predict how Cincy will react.

Harley Jaines, though, is only the catalyst for this journey. I could have told her about him on the phone. There are other reasons I must see Cincy in person.

I glance at the Washington road map lying open on the seat beside me: fifty miles until Highway 395 branches south toward the confluence of the Snake and Columbia Rivers.

A freight train thunders across a viaduct, and suddenly I'm fifteen again, rattling across America to confront the twisted mystery of my own lost father.

Eastern Washington, 1979

I awoke on the train with the telltale heat and wetness in my jeans that every woman past puberty recognizes. Not unexpected, but inconvenient as hell. Especially when I realized I was not alone.

In the aisle beside my seat, a small boy with owl-like brown eyes stood staring at me. His dark hair sprigged up on the crown in an off-center fountain that jiggled with the motion of the train.

"Boo," I said.

"Boo to you," he said back, his face solemn.

I frowned meanly. "It's not polite to watch people sleep, you know."

"You were mumbling."

"Swell." I yawned and tried to stretch out my cramped legs. I had to get to the rest room, and quickly.

"You traveling alone?" I asked him, straight-faced.

He giggled. "Of course not. I'm only six."

And small for his age, I judged.

"My dad's back there," he said, bobbing his head toward the rear of the car.

"Tell you what. If you'll sit here and save my seat, I'll bring you back something from the snack car. What would you like? A beer?"

His grin was missing two front teeth. He reminded me of Petey Small when I'd first met him in second grade.

"I like licorice," the boy said.

"Yuck! Okay, you've got a deal."

I picked up my bag and he plopped down in the outside seat. I squeezed past him and made my way down the aisle.

The rest rooms were next to the baggage. I locked myself in a tiny cubicle hardly big enough to accommodate me and my bag at once. I attended to myself, washed up and splashed cool water on my face. The girl in the mirror was puffy-eyed and frizzy-headed. She looked like a runaway.

I followed the signs that read Cantina through three coach cars, with my bag hanging from one shoulder, bumping my butt as I navigated the aisles. Most of the passengers lay sprawled in sleep. The air in the closed cars smelled foul. I held my breath until I crossed through the cold little chambers where the cars linked together and the floor moved under my feet. It was like walking through a fun house.

The snack bar occupied a corner of the observation car, where wide, smeared windows rounded up and formed part of the roof. Formica-topped tables lined one wall, and cigarette smoke hung thick above a booth where two couples played cards. Outside the glass, the river still ran beside the train, wide and flat and peaceful, with wooded mountains clustered behind. In the hour or so I'd been asleep, we hadn't gone far from home. I wondered if anybody back in Shady River had figured out yet that I was gone.

At the linoleum-topped counter of the cantina, I made my purchases from an underemployed young fellow who had the smile of a con man. If he'd flirt with me the way I looked, I reasoned, he had to be seriously bored. I pocketed my change and made my way back to my seat, counting cars.

The kid was waiting for me. "They didn't have licorice whips," I said, tossing him a bag of jelly beans, "but there's some black ones in there."

His eyes got big, as if he hadn't expected me to keep my promise. I squeezed past him into my window seat and pulled *Jane Eyre* out of my bag before stashing it by my feet.

"Shouldn't you tell your dad where you are?"

The kid shrugged. "He said to get lost."

Nice. Looked like I'd have company for a while, but that was okay with me. There was something vulnerable and open in the kid's face, as if he didn't have it in him to tell a lie.

He fished out the black jelly beans with one finger stuck through a hole he made in the sack. "Where you going?"

I paused a minute, hunting for a simple answer. "To see my aunt Olivia. In Missouri."

"I'm goin' to my grandma's," he said, noncommittal.

"That ought to be fun."

"I guess. I'm gonna live with her. Mom's gone, and Dad says he can't take care of me and work, too."

"Bummer." Didn't anybody's father hang around?

"I've never met my grandma before," he said. "I wish she lived on a farm."

"Where does she live?"

He shrugged. "In town. I'll have to start school all over when I get there."

His brown eyes looked huge when he mentioned school, and freckles stood out on his nose like polka dots. Poor kid was scared to death.

"I really like school," I told him.

"You do?"

"You bet. I have friends there, and I like to read and learn things."

"I don't know how to read. We were just starting to learn some words at my school when I had to leave."

"Do you know your letters?"

"Sure."

"And how the letters sound?"

"Some of them."

I nodded knowingly. "You'll be reading like a whiz before the school year's over." I gave him a thumbs-up.

A thin black rim outlined his smile. He popped in another black jelly bean.

"What color do you like?" he said, holding up the bag.

"Orange."

He dug one out and handed it to me. Then we settled back and watched farmland and villages slide past the window.

The train had left the river now. I pulled out my Amtrak map and traced the line where we were cutting across the northeast corner of Oregon. If we kept stopping at every little burg, I'd be thirty-five before I got to Missouri.

"What's your name?" I asked the kid.

"Benny."

"Well, Benny," I said, and read from the map, "Hinkle—where we're stopping now—is a freight yard and railroad stop for two nearby towns, Hermiston and Stanfield. It is also home for a potato processing plant on the right—" we gawked out the window "—that makes potato chips and French fries."

We looked at each other and grinned. Benny licked his lips with a black tongue.

After Hinkle, I turned on the overhead light and read my book. The sun settled lower and cast a long, moving shadow beside the train.

My stomach growled. The kid must have been hungry, too, but still I'd seen nothing of his dad. I began to wonder whether Benny had been abandoned. What then? I looked over at him, working a maze in the tattered kids' magazine he'd found in the seat pocket. Maybe I'd take Benny with me. Like a puppy. I pictured myself showing up on Robert Elden Lee's doorstep with the little brother I never had. The image made me smile.

At the snack bar again, I bought a PB & J sandwich and a bag of chips to split with Benny. He eyed my cola longingly but drank the milk I gave him. Still no sign of good old dad.

The windows of the train grew dark and dots of light scattered across the countryside like fireflies. The lights inside the car dimmed, too. Benny stood on the seat and got two pillows and a blanket from the overhead bin.

Sometime during that black and rumbling night, a conductor whisked down the aisle with a flashlight, calling out "Boy-*zee* I-de-ho! Boise!" The train slowed and ground to a stop, the lights of a station flashing in the windows. Half asleep and cranky, I covered my head and dozed in and out, vaguely aware of a shuffle of passengers disembarking, newcomers hunting for seats. Finally the train shuddered and jerked and we were rolling again.

I awoke at daylight with a crick in my neck and severely scummy teeth.

Benny was gone.

On the seat beside me I found his jelly bean sack. He'd left the orange ones for me.

Aunt Olivia never married. If she had, I might not have found her. From a phone booth in the Springfield bus station at 2:00 a.m., I called information for Licking, Missouri, and gave the operator Mom's maiden name. And there she was, Olivia Marcott, 537-555-3990.

The bus didn't run to Licking. Rolla, sixty-three miles north of Licking, was as close as I could get. I debated whether I should call my aunt from there or hitchhike and show up at her door unannounced. If I called, she might tell me not to come.

Then again, why would she do that? It was Mom who had broken off communication, not my aunt. Assuming gay Uncle Joey had no children, I was Olivia's only niece. Surely she'd be curious enough to let me visit. I wrote her number on the corner of a phone book page and tore it off, trying not to damage the other numbers.

In a quiet corner where no one could see, I counted the money I had left after buying my bus ticket to Rolla. The bus was cheap, compared to the train. I'd had no idea train fares would be so expensive. Five hundred dollars had sounded like enough money to go around the world. Now I had less than a hundred left, and I didn't know where my father was or how much money it might take to get there. I sure hoped Aunt Olivia could tell me.

The bus didn't leave until 8:00 a.m., so I curled up on a wooden bench with my head on my bag, which now looked well seasoned at traveling. It was my fourth night sleeping in a public place. I hadn't had a shower since I left Shady River, and I was hungry. Where was the romance of the road I'd read about in books?

Spastic fluorescent light jittered against my closed eyelids, and tears seeped out between my lashes. I promised myself a cheap motel room in Rolla, even if it broke me. I would stand in the shower until the hot water ran out, and sleep in a real bed as long as I wanted. After all, if I showed up at my aunt's house looking and smelling like this, who could blame her if she slammed the door in my face.

"Good heavens! I can't believe you've come!" Aunt Olivia's voice on the phone sounded a little like Ruth's—through a megaphone. "You stay right there till I come get you," she warned. "Don't you even *think* of hitchhiking. It's too dangerous!"

The backwash from trucks zooming by on the highway rocked the phone booth. I'd had to come outdoors to call because a sign in my motel room read No Long Distance Phone Calls. It wasn't the friendliest establishment. When I checked in, the desk clerk had looked me up and down and made me pay cash up front.

"I'm sorry to put you to so much trouble," I said to my aunt.

"Trouble! Good heavens. I thought I'd never see you again! And I'm sure you don't remember me." She hesitated, hopeful. "Do you?"

"I'm afraid not. Sorry."

"Of course, you couldn't. You were only three. And you're what now, fourteen?"

"Fifteen. And a half."

"Good heavens! And you're alone? Ruth didn't come?"

"No." I felt exhausted in the face of my aunt's enthusiasm, despite ten hours' sleep in a bed that smelled like a cellar. "I can explain it better when I see you."

"Of course you can. I'll just throw on some clothes. Be there in an hour and a half. Lucky I'm off work today!"

Hanging up, I felt oddly disappointed to realize that Aunt Olivia had a job. The image of her I'd conjured in my head looked like a grandmother, but actually she was a few years younger than my mother. I guess I'd been *hoping* for a grandmother.

I shouldered my bag and zipped my jacket against a stiff wind that swept sand and French fry wrappers across the parking lot. I'd already checked out of my room, so I could either sit out in front of the motel for an hour and a half or spend a few of my dwindling bucks to pacify my nagging stomach. Not counting chips and colas, my last real food had been a hamburger in Kansas City, a day and a half ago. My jeans hung loose on my hipbones.

I ducked my head into the chilly wind and headed for a row of restaurants that bordered the interstate.

A poster in Denny's window advertised all the breakfast I could eat for $1.99, even at noon. I ordered eggs and bacon and Texas toast, and finished off with pancakes drowned in syrup. Sated, I put down two quarters for the waitress, who looked like she'd been on the road alone herself.

Aunt Olivia had described her car as an old white tank, and she wasn't kidding. Sitting on the motel curb, I spotted it a quarter mile away at the exit ramp, with six cars backed up behind. It was a big, fish-finned Chevy from some prior decade, loaded with polished chrome that sparkled in the sun.

As the car drew closer, I made out huge shoulders and a halo of frizzy hair behind the wheel. She parked beside the motel and extracted herself from the car—all five-ten, two-hundred-fifty pounds of her, minimum.

How could my mother have turned out so short if she had giant-genes in her DNA? Malnutrition?

Olivia wore a dark cotton muumuu with tiny pink flowers in diamond patterns and white jogging shoes with pink socks. Her hair was sunset red. She stopped in front of me, a monolith. I stood up to face her and tried to smile.

"Roberta," she said. The wind inflated her dress like a sail and I caught a whiff of her powdery scent as she scrutinized my face. "I can see Ruth, but you look even more like your daddy."

I feared a suffocating hug, but instead she held out both hands. Mine felt small and cold in her clasp. Her pale eyes watered behind plastic-rimmed glasses.

"I'm your aunt Olivia," she announced redundantly. "Good heavens."

"My friends call me Bobbie."

"Well, climb aboard the boat, Bobbie." She smiled broadly and gestured toward her car. "We have a lot of catching up to do."

We zipped down the interstate at forty-five miles an hour. The Chevy's dashboard looked polished and there wasn't a speck of dust on it. I suspected that beneath the homemade chintz seat-covers, the original seats were perfect, too.

"Cool car," I said.

"A '57. They don't make 'em like this anymore."

She had the bench seat pushed all the way back. I could stretch my legs full length without touching the slanted part of the floor-board.

Aunt Olivia ignored a stream of semis that clotted behind us until they could roar past one at a time. She leaned forward in the seat, gripping the wheel between two beefy forearms, and glanced sideways at me.

"Honey, you look like you've been rode hard and put up wet. Ran away from home, didn't you?"

The directness of her question surprised me. But if that was the ground rule, I could handle it. "I'm going to find my father."

"Well." She nodded. "That day was bound to come. Know where he is?"

"No. I was hoping you could tell me."

She nodded again, but she didn't say whether or not she knew the location of Robert Elden Lee. "How's your mama? I haven't heard from her in years."

I opened my mouth to say *she's fine,* then remembered the ground rule. "She's an alcoholic and she's depressed all the time."

I looked out the window, embarrassed. Beside the highway, rolling hills covered with trees reminded me of the Columbia Valley, except there were more oaks and the pines were shorter. "She works at a hotel in Shady River, Oregon. I'll give you her address, if you want."

"Does she know where you are?"

"No. And I hope you won't tell her."

"Why's that? You think she'd send the police after you?"

I thought about that for a minute. "No. Probably not." I didn't think Ruth cared enough to have me hauled back home.

Aunt Olivia's house wasn't any bigger than ours in Shady River, but it had red brick on the outside and on the inside it was spotless. Even the shelves that held hundreds of salt-and-pepper shakers showed no dust. I gazed through the glass doors at skunks and Aunt Jemimas and smiling fish and outhouses, all of them with little holes in their heads. No two pairs were alike.

"These are cool," I said.

She laughed roundly. "You think so? I'll leave 'em to you in my will."

Her furniture was old and cheap, but she covered it up with clean throws. A dark, old-fashioned area rug with a wine-colored border was worn down to the padding in a path from the TV to the kitchen.

"I just rent the house," she said, "but I've lived here since your grandfather died ten years ago, so it feels like it's mine."

"What did he die of?"

"Cirrhosis of the liver. Pickled in alcohol."

So Ruth was following her father's path.

Aunt Olivia plunked my bag down on the threadbare rug. "There's only one bedroom, so you can sleep with me or on the couch. How about something to eat?"

She called it supper instead of dinner and served it at five o'clock. I sat down to homemade vegetable beef soup with hot corn bread and butter. It smelled delicious.

"Vegetables," I said, smiling as I dipped my spoon into the soup. "I had vegetables in…1972."

Her laugh was as big as she was. "I eat a lot of vegetables," she said. "Hell, I eat a lot of everything!"

We had blackberry cobbler with ice cream for dessert.

The house had three rooms not counting the bath: a large kitchen where we ate, the living room and Olivia's bedroom, which had no door. This was a family accustomed to poverty, I decided, who never expected anything else. I wondered if Joey was that way, too.

That first night I discovered one possible reason my aunt wasn't married. She farted in her sleep. Maybe it was all that rich food. Lying on the age-scented sofa, I heard Aunt Olivia rip one in the night and I pulled the sheet up over my nose. Between gas attacks, she snored.

By the third night, though, I had learned to sleep right through it. I kept a blanket over my head and Kleenex tissues stuffed in my ears.

During the day, my aunt ran the cash register at a small grocery on the main road through Licking, which, I learned, was named for the natural salt licks in the area. At the crossroads, a sign noted "Seventeen Miles West of Success." I had a hunch it was farther than that.

When I got tired of sleeping and reading and watching TV during the day, I walked down to the store and sat with Aunt Olivia. There were hardly any customers and we spent the time talking.

She fattened me up with snacks and home cooking and stories of the family who were strangers to me. I didn't ask again for my father's whereabouts. I was stalling, and besides, I was in no hurry to move on. Then one evening she laid an address and phone number on the red Formica of the kitchen table.

"That's your daddy's," she said.

I looked up at her. Literally.

"He and Joey are still together," she said. "Bitchy as any old married couple. Your daddy's not an ogre, no matter what Ruth made him sound like. I don't approve of the way they live, but then it's none of my business. I'm just sorry for what it did to you. And Ruthie."

I stared at the piece of paper without picking it up, and swallowed hard. "Does he know I'm coming?"

"I haven't called him, but I'm going to. His health's always been frail and I don't want either one of us responsible for his heart attack." She laid an envelope on the table beside the slip of paper. "When you're ready to go, this'll pay your bus fare to Birmingham. There's no hurry. I've enjoyed having you and you're welcome to stay as long as you want."

She took off her glasses and wiped them and her wet eyes with the tail of her loose dress. "Good heavens," she said.

"I can't take your money." I'd accidentally seen her pay stub one day and I didn't know how she managed her groceries on it, let alone rent and utilities.

"Yes, you can." She pushed the envelope toward me again. "Don't insult me. Save what money you have for food. When you get there safe and sound, call and let me know—on your daddy's dime. He can afford it."

Aunt Olivia drove me to the bus station in Cabool, about the same distance south of Licking as Rolla was north. We were both quiet on the drive, thumping our feet to a fifties rock station on the radio.

At the depot, she walked out to the platform with me, where a big Greyhound steamed and rumbled. I mumbled my thanks and hugged her quickly, without meeting her eyes, before I climbed aboard. From the bus window, I saw her still standing there waving while the bus pulled away from the station and down the highway.

Good heavens.

The Greyhound speared east toward the Missouri border, then south toward Memphis. The miles rolled by, and I wondered what kind of man my father would turn out to be, bracing myself for the possibilities. I'd been too nervous to talk to him on the phone when Olivia called.

The bus route paralleled the Mississippi River, but not close enough that I could see the water. I was curious to see if the river was as muddy as everybody said, but when we finally crossed, it was dark outside and I couldn't tell.

My stomach felt like a jarful of wings. I was afraid to eat the lunch Aunt Olivia had sent for fear I'd upchuck on some unsuspecting fellow traveler.

I changed buses in Memphis. On the next leg, I tried to decide what I'd do if nobody was there when I arrived at the Birmingham depot. And in case my father did show up, I worried about what I'd say to him, and whether he'd like me at all.

CHAPTER 14

I-90, southwest of Spokane, 1990

Near Ritzville, Washington, I take the exit to state Highway 395. The road drops southwest through farmland and becomes four-lane again ten miles or so north of Pasco. There I turn west, following the signs toward Kennewick, and cross the Columbia River, the first time I'd been over the U.S. section in ten years. Even though I can't see over the bridge railings, I can feel the slow-moving water beneath my wheels, sliding homeward toward the sea.

At Kennewick, I exit the highway to find lunch. Outside the restaurant, I lay out all my change on the metal shelf of a pay phone and dial David's number at the museum, my forehead and palms suddenly damp. The Glenbow is closed on Mondays, but the curatorial staff usually works, especially when a new exhibit is set to open. It's past one o'clock his time; he should be back from lunch.

David's extension doesn't answer so I leave a brief message on his voice mail. He could be anywhere in the museum, working on the exhibit. At least he'll know I'm okay, somewhere in Washington, and on my way to meet Cincy. I wonder if he'll be angry that I'm not driving home today. I hang up feeling hollow.

The smell of the chicken salad sandwich the waitress brings sends jitters through my growling stomach. I eat it anyway, drink a cola and all my water. All that liquid will mean more rest stops on the drive ahead, but I'm too dried out to resist. At the gas station next door I fill up, consult my map and ask how to get on I-82.

Finding the entrance on the first try gives me a rush of confidence. I've never driven so far alone before, and never been away from David this long since we've been married. From this distance, I can see my insulated days holed up in the mountains aren't healthy—not much different from living on the grounds at Green Gables, where every movement was planned and monitored. I begin to realize the parallels between this journey and the one I took when I was fifteen to find my father. Only this time, I'm looking for me.

Birmingham, Alabama, 1979

The bus lumbered into the Birmingham station at 11:00 p.m. in a heavy drizzle. My father stood on the tarmac, water dripping onto his trench coat from the little metal tips of his umbrella.

From the bus window, I could see the reflection of his glasses in the misted light from a sentinel lamp. I watched him search the faces of each passenger as they disembarked. But I already knew his face. He didn't look that much different from the faded photo I carried in my wallet. Thinner and paler, maybe, but the dark hair and angular nose were the same.

When the bus was nearly empty, I picked up my bag and threaded my way down the aisle. I stepped down and walked straight toward him, my hair collecting rain.

He met my eyes and I saw recognition cross his face. He looked stricken. I couldn't tell if the look was panic or gee-how-you've-grown. Maybe both.

"Roberta?" His voice was midpitched, like a tenor. I had no memory of that voice.

"I go by Bobbie now."

Up close, I could see how the face in the photo had aged. He was taller than I'd imagined.

He stared, too, for a moment, then his face opened in a smile. "Wow. You're so—*grown*. And so *beautiful*."

I'd been on a bus for seventeen hours, hadn't really slept for two days, and my hair looked like a scouring pad. My father was a flatterer.

"Let's get out of the rain," he said, putting a tentative arm around my shoulder.

He held the umbrella over both of us while we walked toward the terminal, then opened the glass door for me. The air inside felt stuffy by comparison. I squinted in the bright lights. Before I could adjust, Robert E. Lee led me toward a bench where a guy in a black satin windbreaker stood up as we approached. The guy's hair was red and his face resembled my mother's.

Uncle Joey, the home wrecker. My father's homosexual lover.

I resented him immediately. Couldn't the bastard have stayed home and let me have one hour alone with my father? It didn't occur to me then that my father probably needed the moral support.

Joey and I sized each other up while Robert E. introduced us. Joey was half a head shorter than Robert and built like a concrete pylon. He hadn't wrestled in the lightweight division in college, that was for sure. My father called him Joe when he introduced us.

Joey's smile lifted only one side of his mouth. "Hi, kid. Welcome to Birmingham."

"Hi." It was all I had to say.

He looked at my father, dismissing me. "Ready to go?"

"Roberta," Robert said, then corrected himself, "Bobbie, do you have any luggage?"

I patted the satchel hanging from my shoulder. "This is it."

"Well. Shall we go, then? Let me carry that for you," he said, reaching for my bag.

I held tight. "It's okay. By now I'd feel naked without it." I followed Joey toward the exit, wishing irrationally that I hadn't said the word *naked*.

Joey held the door and Robert held the umbrella. Rain staccatoed on its nylon fabric like muffled machine guns. Walking between them, I pictured us as a trio of gangsters, with me going for a last ride. Sure enough, Joey opened the back seat door of a long, dark Lincoln. My stomach shivered. I was getting into a strange car with two men I didn't know. Anybody's mother would have told me not to do it, even mine.

I tossed my bag on the floorboard and crawled in. The back seat smelled like new leather and felt like satin. Robert got up front, with Joey driving.

"I'll bet you're hungry," Robert said, turning sideways to look at me around the padded headrest of the Town Car. "Want to stop somewhere?"

A vision of the three of us faced off in a restaurant booth quashed my appetite. "No, thanks. I'm more tired than anything."

On the silent half-hour drive, I prayed that Robert E.'s house had a spare bedroom. My neck was still sore from Olivia's depression-era couch. My head felt hollow in that way it does when you're taking a cold, and my throat scratched when I swallowed.

I laid my head back on the leather seat. We drove a long time and soon I was dozing, but I roused as Joey drove the Lincoln beneath a rising garage door. I caught a glimpse of a sprawling, angled structure that could have held five or six of Olivia's little house. At first I thought it was an apartment building.

Joey parked between a tiny, expensive-looking sports car and a bright red pickup with big tires and Marcott Construction stenciled on its side. No worry about a spare bedroom, I decided. My father opened doors for me and carried my bag, which left me nothing to do with my hands. Joey disappeared down a hallway.

"I'll give you a quick tour," my father said. He began a nervous monologue as I followed him through the house.

I felt groggy and surreal as we passed through room after room, up four steps here, down three there. I was a character in some old movie, acting out the part of befuddled waif while the rich stepfather showed me the mansion where he and the wicked step-uncle lived. But the house wasn't properly Gothic; it was all angles and glass, chrome and stone. And everything, *everything,* was white. Somebody had read way too much Fitzgerald.

I heard him say *Georgia marble* and *white pine,* and that he'd designed the house himself. "We've lived here three years," he said, and I knew the we meant him and Joey.

The tour ended in a bedroom four times the size of my old one in Shady River. My father's voice became subdued.

"This is your room," he said. "I had you in mind when I furnished it."

The curtains and bedspread were white eyelet, with mauve-colored throw pillows mounded on the bed. On one wall hung a five-foot painting of girls in hats and gauzy dresses walking barefoot beside a turquoise sea. I stood there in my jeans and wrinkled flannel shirt, gazing at my father's fantasy of me, and thought how disappointed he must be.

At length I realized he was waiting for my reaction. "Wow," I said, with as much enthusiasm as I could muster.

It seemed to be enough. He smiled and crossed the room, opening doors to a private bath and not one but *two* closets. My cheap bag slouched beside the bed like a pound puppy. I hoped it wouldn't leave a stain on the creamy carpet.

What did people put in *two* closets? I wondered.

My father made sure there were fresh towels in the bathroom and toilet paper on the spindle. Then he came back and stood beside me, looking as lost as I felt.

"I'm so glad you're here," he said. "I was afraid I might never see you again." His voice wavered and his dark eyes were liquid behind his glasses. "I hope Ruthie didn't tell you horrible things about me."

My throat hurt clear out to my ears, and I sounded hoarse. "She never talked about you at all," I said. "I thought you deserted us. Then a couple weeks ago, she told me why she left."

A muscle in his jaw twitched, and I knew he was picturing that scene.

"It's true I'm homosexual. Obviously. I didn't know how to tell Ruthie without hurting her. I'd give anything to change the way she found out, but I can't. I'm not a bad person, Bobbie, but I'm not a very brave one."

I closed my eyes and felt the motion of a spring-loaded rocking horse beneath my three-year-old body, remembered sparkling lights on a Christmas tree and my father's smiling face, so much younger.

"Did you know all along? Even when you married her?" *Did you use her to put you through college, knowing you would cast her aside?*

"No." His voice sounded sad. "I didn't know much of anything then. We were so awfully young."

I couldn't look at him. My throat was so tight it was hard to speak. "How did you find out? That you were gay, I mean." I thought of Lenora, the night before I left. Holding her. Wishing I could live inside her skin.

My father leaned back against the white wall and examined the ceiling. "It isn't something you *find out,* so much as you figure it out gradually. In college I was attracted to several people…men…but I hid those feelings. Later, the more time I spent with Joey, the more I knew. Especially when he…um…showed an interest."

On some level of maturity above my years, I thought how difficult this must be for him to discuss with his daughter. But the thought didn't engender much sympathy; he still didn't feel like a father to me. And his answer wasn't much help. I wanted some kind of test, like litmus paper. Pink means one kind of love; blue means another.

"If you still wanted to see your daughter, why didn't you come find me?" I said. "You could have *hired* someone—a detective or somebody."

He sighed. "I don't know. After about a year, we left Atlanta and I buried myself in my work, seven days a week. Tried to start my life over. I was afraid that if I found you, you'd reject me. But I always hoped someday, when you were older, you'd come back." He looked at me with tears in his eyes. "And now you have."

I stood still, my own eyes and nose streaming. He retrieved two tissues from the bedside table and handed them to me.

"Do you think," he said slowly, "that we could have a hug?"

I wiped and blew to give myself time. Then I let him fold me in his arms.

It felt strange, to both of us, I think. I'd never been hugged by a man before. At least, not since I was old enough to remember. His body was angular and bony but he smelled nice, like expensive aftershave.

After a moment, I put my arms around his back and held on tight.

CHAPTER 15

In all the mornings I awoke among the white billows of that oversize bed, I never felt the pea beneath the mattress. That first day, the victim of a wretched head cold, I was definitely no princess.

Robert stayed home with me. He did much of his design work in his home studio anyway, he told me, and maintained another office downtown where he met his clients.

"I don't hide my lifestyle," he said, not meeting my eyes, "but it isn't good business sense to rub people's noses in it. This is still the South."

"Where's Joey?" I asked as my father pulled up a chair for me in his studio.

"Joe goes to work early."

Robert told me Joey owned a mid-size company, having worked his way up from carpenter to foreman to buying the business from retiring partners. He had an office somewhere, too, but spent most of his time driving around in the red pickup to check on crews working at various building sites. Joey had built the house where they lived, from Robert's blueprints.

Robert's studio was spacious and high-ceilinged, equipped with a tall stool and drawing board beside floor-to-ceiling windows that overlooked a private lake. Opposite the windows stood a white table that served as his desk and a bank of built-in, shallow drawers that stored his architectural drawings.

On one wall, artistic pencil sketches of structures he'd designed hung in pairs with color photographs of the finished products. I spent a long time looking at the drawings. I couldn't summon the nerve to tell him about my butterfly art; compared to his, my drawings seemed primitive. Thinking of them, I was caught by an unexpected wave of homesickness.

I thought of the antenor swallowtails, and I missed Lenora and Cincy. Now that I'd found my father and he hadn't sent me away, I should write to let them know I was safe. I meant to write Ruth, too, but that afternoon as I sat at the breakfast-room table with stationery Robert provided, I found I had nothing to say to my mother. I addressed an envelope to Cincy, and the letter inside to Cincy and Lenora both. But I did not list a return address.

In a few days, when my cold was better, Robert took me shopping at an upscale mall. He bought me four outfits, while I made weak protests at the excess. I was desperately tired of my two pairs of ragged jeans, and besides, I'd never been on such a shopping spree before.

"If you decide to stay, we'll get you some more things," he promised.

If that was a bribe, it was also an invitation. I couldn't help smiling.

That first month, Robert stayed home almost every day. Once we went to a museum, and another day we drove the Red Mountain Highway and stood at a turnout overlooking the sea of green hills that was Birmingham. I recognized pines and cedars mixed with deciduous trees that were just turning colors in late October.

"What kinds of butterflies live here?" I asked him.

He didn't know. I told him about my school science project, and he drove to a library where we could look up Southern lepidoptera. The Birmingham library was so huge it was housed in more than one building. I'd never seen so many books.

In November, my father took me to an optometrist and bought me contact lenses—just as Cincy had predicted. I wrote and told her that very night. For two weeks I went around the house blinking while my eyes adjusted, but every time I looked in the mirror, it was worth it. I took the lenses out at night, cleaned them carefully and sterilized them in their little plastic cylinder.

One morning I got up earlier than usual, before Joey left, and overheard him and Robert arguing. Joey accused my father of neglecting his clients. That entire day, Robert spent working at his drawing board and making phone calls. I resented Joey's ability to intimidate him like that. Then again, Robert had spent a lot of time entertaining me instead of working. Even I had wondered how long he could afford to do that.

While Robert worked, I loafed around the house and tried out recipes in the huge kitchen. At lunch Robert and I ate my experiments and rated them on a scale of one to ten. My father had a kind of offbeat sense of humor, and when I was with him, I found I had one, too. We began to be almost comfortable with each other—except when Joey was home. Then Robert was a different person.

I observed closely the interaction between them and decided my father was the wife, Joey the husband, though Robert apparently made more money. They kept separate bedrooms. Though I listened for furtive movements back and forth during the night, I never detected any. Either they were totally discreet or sexually inactive. At least while I was there.

Joey became progressively more irritable the longer I stayed, and

I showed no signs of leaving. An undercurrent of competition had developed between us. Despite the fact that he'd had my father to himself all these years, he wasn't ready to share. I'd been there nearly two months when my father (whom I'd settled on calling Robert) suggested at dinner that we should get me enrolled in school.

I saw Joey's jaw twitch and knew he didn't like the permanent sound of that. "Good idea," I said, to further irritate him.

That evening I heard their voices grow loud behind the closed door of Robert's studio and I crept closer to listen. Joey wanted them to entertain friends at the house the way they used to. My father refused, because of me.

"We never spend time together anymore," Joey said, his voice angry.

Lying awake that night, I tried to take a perverse pleasure in the fact that no matter where I lived, my presence created tension.

At the private school where Robert enrolled me, I was less out of place than I'd expected. The school was academically oriented and full of oddballs. I fit right in. Within a few weeks I was invited to be a junior member of the science team. I didn't know what it was, so I said no thanks. Later I learned they entered spring quiz competitions with other prep schools around the state. I wondered if I'd still be there for the spring semester, and the one after that.

Christmas decorations went up all over the city, but except for an occasional frost, the weather stayed balmy. Rockhaven and the Columbia River Gorge seemed light years away. I kept writing to Cincy and Lenora but still didn't send my address, though I did refer to Birmingham. Robert would have let me phone them if I'd asked. But when I pictured holding the receiver and hearing Lenora's voice, I was filled with an awful longing; I couldn't think what to say.

Sometimes I wondered about Ruth. Did she stay drunk all the time now? Had she lost her job yet? Did she ever miss me?

Two days after Christmas, Joey walked through the living room where I was reading and tossed an envelope in my lap. "Look here, kid. Mail from home." Making it clear that *here* wasn't my home.

I held my breath as I turned the letter over. But the handwriting wasn't Cincy's or Lenora's, or even my mother's. There was no name on the outside, but I recognized the street address in Shady River and heard a roaring in my ears.

Petey Small!

I retreated to my room to open the letter. His scrunchy handwriting brought back the smell of him, working next to me in science lab. The paper shook in my hands.

Pete had learned from Cincy that I'd gone to find my father. Armed with my father's name, he'd called directory assistance for Birmingham and found a dozen Robert or Bob Lees, but the operator wouldn't give out addresses. So he'd quizzed my mother (no matter how I tried I could not imagine this) until he found out about Aunt Olivia in Missouri. Then he'd actually phoned my aunt and sweet-talked her into giving him my father's address!

I was flattered beyond words. I read the details of his sleuthing with a grin that spread wider and wider. Good old Pete always loved a mystery. But who'd have guessed he cared enough to trace me down? My dream from the train came back in vivid detail, and my cheeks burned.

"I haven't told your mom or even Cincy that I have this address," Petey wrote. "If you'd wanted them to have it, I guess you'd have sent it by now. But we're all worried about you, Bobbie. Please write and tell me if you get this, and how you're doing. Jenkins's class is no fun without my partner. Even Jenkins looks at your empty desk like a lost puppy."

I read the letter over and over, wishing it was longer. He'd signed it simply "Pete."

I lay on the bed a long time thinking of Shady River High and

Petey Small. If I was in love with Lenora, would I be fantasizing about Pete? Maybe I was a switch-hitter; I'd heard that about Olivia Newton-John. The idea seemed at once repulsive and romantic.

I wished I could talk to Cincy about it. If I sent her my address, would she write to me? I had my doubts. Across all those miles, I could feel—or imagined—her injured silence. The betrayal in her face that last night had propelled me clear to Birmingham, a guilt trip of continental proportions.

Suddenly I was angry, and sick of guilt. Maybe I'd deserted Cincy, but she had deserted me a long time ago.

A knock on my door sent me bolting to my feet. "Yes?"

My father's voice sounded muffled behind the door. "We're going out to dinner. You ready?"

"Uh...you guys go ahead. I'll fix myself a sandwich."

A pause. "You okay? Joe said you got a letter."

"Yeah. A guy from my old school. I'm fine—I just don't feel like going out tonight. Okay?"

"Sure, honey. I'll see you later."

It was weird being alone in that big house. I wandered the rooms, even stepping inside Joey's bedroom. It was done in hunter green and navy, the only room in the house that wasn't white. It didn't look at all threatening without Joey in it.

CHAPTER 16

I spent more and more time alone in the white house as Robert's life returned toward its norm. He'd been working on a large, lucrative project that required most of his time and attention as the deadline for his drawings drew near. When I came home from school, the door to his study was often closed. I brought library books home from school and lost myself in them after my homework was finished.

Joey came and went silently. I figured he should be happy because Robert was working so much, but he didn't seem happy. A couple of nights he didn't come home at all, and after that there'd be arguing again.

In February I finally sent Lenora and Cincy my mailing address. Lenora wrote back. Reading between the lines of her letters, I got the feeling Cincy was out of control. But Lenora never told me anything specific; she talked mostly about her research and kept me updated on the antenors. Cincy never wrote to me at all.

I wrote to Pete, as well, and heard back from him occasionally.

Now that he knew I was okay, his letters seemed less personal, more chatty. Neither he nor Lenora said a word about Ruth. Maybe because I didn't ask.

Spring came early in Birmingham. As the weather warmed and things began to bloom, I missed the smell of the Columbia Valley. On an impulse one night, I dialed Ruth's number, not knowing whether I would talk or hang up if she answered. I heard a click and then a recording came on. The number had been disconnected. I frowned at the receiver, my body buzzing like a muffled fire alarm.

I wrote Lenora and asked, for the first time, about my mother. The answer came quickly. Ruth had been hospitalized for several days after passing out at the inn. "Cincy stopped in to see her," Lenora wrote, "but Ruth won't talk to me."

I tried to picture Cincy and Ruth in the same frame, and shook my head. It was next to impossible. Lenora said the doctor had sent her to AA, but she didn't know if Ruth had kept going. She still had her job. Maybe she'd just forgotten to pay the phone bill.

For the first time in months, I felt sorry for my mother. If I wrote to her, would she tear up the letter unread? Maybe she'd write back and ask me to come home. I realized the selfishness of wanting her to ask, when I had no intention of living with her again. So all I did was worry about her, and about Cincy.

Why didn't Cincy write me? Finally I asked Lenora straight out, but I didn't get a straight answer. "Don't worry about us, Bobbie," Lenora wrote. "We'll be okay. You deserve to be happy, and I hope you can find that with your father. If you ever want to come back, though, you know you can stay here at Rockhaven."

What *would* make me happy? I asked myself.

And answered: *If I could live with Lenora and everybody else would disappear.* What a bitch I was.

I wasn't exactly comfortable living with my father, but at least he wanted me there. Still, he'd been happy with Joey before I came, and now they were clearly on the rocks. If they broke up on account of me, my father undoubtedly would resent me forever, the way Ruth hated Joey for breaking up her marriage.

That weekend Robert had a dinner meeting with his big client. Joey came home about six Saturday evening. I was sitting at the breakfast-room table doing homework, more out of boredom than necessity.

"Hey, kid," he said. I was sick of being addressed as kid.

"Hey, Uncle Joey." He'd asked me several times to call him Joe.

He looked at me thoughtfully for a moment, while I glared back, and then he smiled. "Want to go out for some pizza?"

It was the friendliest thing he'd said in weeks. He knew I loved pizza; could this be a truce? My heart lurched with hope, but I wouldn't let him see.

"Sure," I said. "If I don't have to change clothes."

"You don't if I don't."

I followed him downstairs to the garage and climbed into the big red truck. Joey never drove the Lincoln unless my father was along.

Peach's Pizza Palace, despite its name, served the best supreme pizza I'd ever eaten. Using a red phone at the table, Joey ordered a large pie, two salads, beer for him and a cola for me. He hung up the phone and folded his hands on the table. The place was loud and gave us a sense of privacy that made me nervous.

"Let's talk it out," he said.

"Talk what out?"

"Don't be coy with me. You're a smart kid. Smart aleck, too, but that's normal for fifteen."

"Thanks a lot."

He fixed me with a direct gaze, his expression neutral. "Are you planning to stay with your dad from now on?"

I shrugged and answered honestly. "I don't know."

"I guess it was pretty bad at home, with Ruth drinking," he said.

I stiffened but didn't answer, concentrating fiercely on a chewed fingernail I was slowly pulling into the quick.

"Stop that." He clamped a beefy hand over mine. "You're going to make it bleed."

I put my hands under the table and forced myself to meet his eyes. My stomach jittered.

"Look," he said. "You resent the hell out of me, and considering the circumstances I guess I can't blame you. But I didn't make your dad gay. He is what he is. We all are."

"Is that right?" I shot back. "What if we don't know what we are? How do I know if I'm going to be normal, or gay like him...and you?"

His lip lifted in the lopsided smile I'd learned to hate. "So you don't think we're normal?"

"Do *you?*"

He shrugged. "Yeah, I do. Whatever's natural for somebody is normal. I don't see that we're committing some big sin."

"Ruining my mother's life doesn't count for anything, then? Because of what you and Robert did, she's a hopeless alcoholic. She doesn't love me and she hates herself. I guess you think that's normal, too."

As my voice rose, Joey's expression changed. Something paternal softened his eyes, some glimmer of feeling I'd never seen there before.

"No, that isn't normal," he said, "and I'm sorry about it. Ruthie and I were close growing up. I always liked her." He picked up a paper napkin and wadded it into a ball.

Then the old Joey was back. "But all that's ancient history and the question is, are you going to let it ruin *your* life?"

"You aren't worried about me. You just want me to go back to Oregon so you can have all of Robert's attention again."

He nodded. "Yeah, well, that would be nice. But the thing is, if I run you off, Robert will hate me for it. If I bide my time, in a few years you'll be eighteen and out on your own. And Robert and I will still be together. We've stuck it out a lot of years, longer than most people. We belong together."

It was the first time I'd confronted the idea that Joey actually loved my father. It made me feel rotten. "I didn't set out to break you two apart."

"Sometimes it's hard to tell that from the way you act," he said. "I understand that you're getting back at us for putting Ruth through hell, but it still pisses me off sometimes. If you're going to stay, I hope we can learn to co-exist."

He paused then, and concentrated on carefully smoothing out the wadded napkin. "But if you decide to go back west, you won't have to worry about money anymore. A smart kid like you should go to college. Robert and I will pay for whatever school you choose. We can send Ruth some money, too, if she'll take it. Get her a house, maybe. Help her get on her feet."

I met his eyes. "You're trying to buy me off." *You lousy son-of-a-bitch jerk.* And he wasn't finished yet.

His mouth twisted to one side. "See, there you go again. Seeing me in the worst possible light." He waited while a pimply faced boy about my age set down an acre of steaming pizza and retreated. "I told you. Stay if you want. But it sounds to me like your mother needs you. A lot worse than you need Robert."

He picked up a shaker. "Parmesan?"

The mozzarella scalded my mouth and turned to glue in my stomach.

That night I dreamed my mother had died. Alone in the house with no one to stop her, she drank herself to death and it was three days before anybody found her. I awoke sitting straight up in the darkness, sweating, my heartbeat pounding in my ears.

* * *

On Monday I had stomach cramps and after lunch Mrs. Johnson excused me from fifth hour. I checked out at the principal's office and walked home. It was less than a mile.

The garage door was closed and I used my key to let myself in the front, hoping nobody was home and I could close the door to my room and lie there without having to explain anything. The house seemed cavernous when I stepped inside. Afternoon sunlight angled down through the high, odd-shaped windows, casting geometric patterns of light and shadow on the floor and walls.

Robert's studio door was closed, which meant he was in there working. I went quietly down the hallway but stopped when I heard male voices rising.

Robert and Joey were both in the studio, and they were arguing. Thinking themselves alone, they made no effort to keep their voices down as they usually did when I was home. Even without standing outside the studio door I could have heard everything.

"Well, she's not *my* daughter," Joey shouted, "and I'm sick of tiptoeing around here because of her. I want us to go out, to have people over, like we used to. There's nothing wrong with having some *fun* once in a while, like we did before you turned into Father Knows Best."

"Listen to yourself! You're acting like an ass. You feel threatened by a fifteen-year-old girl. Grow up, for God's sake."

Joey ignored that. "If she'd get a life it might be different. Why doesn't she go out with friends? She's always here, moping around. Maybe we could set her up with a boyfriend. Or a girl."

Something crashed; Joey cursed.

I opened the door.

Robert's face looked like skimmed milk, his eyes wide behind his glasses. Joey's ruddy face was crimson, but not as crimson as the small crescent of blood on his forehead. At his feet lay my father's ceramic pencil holder. Drawing tools littered the floor. *This must be how their faces looked the day Ruth came home and discovered them together,* I thought, *the day she tried to kill them with kitchen utensils.*

Joey's head gave a small jerk; his smile was a sneer. "Listening outside doors again? It figures." He grabbed a set of keys from the table. "I'm out of here."

I stepped inside the studio to let him pass. Just before he reached the doorway, I said without looking at him, "You don't have to leave. I'm going back to Shady River."

Joey paused ever so slightly. "Frankly, I don't give a damn where you go."

Then he was out the door, but I'd felt his hesitation, heard the fine edge of triumph in his voice. I watched my father's face while we listened to the slam of the door in the kitchen and heard the big engine of the red truck rumble to life.

Robert's eyes seemed fixed on the lingering sound of the garage door grinding shut before the afternoon went still. I saw the tears gather and pain flex his sagging jaw.

"He'll come back," I said.

He nodded. "I know." The large room loomed whitely around us. "You don't have to go back west." But there was no heat in his protest, no conviction.

I waited a moment before answering. "Ruth's been in the hospital. Because of her drinking. She's out now, but she might...need somebody."

He nodded tiredly. "Yes. I suppose she might." He couldn't meet my eyes.

I lifted my chin and kept my spine rigid. Something started to sink inside me, and I had the feeling it would keep on sinking forever without reaching bottom.

Joey, you asshole, my education is going to cost you, I thought.

I had no idea.

CHAPTER 17

As it turned out, my college tuition wasn't what cost Joey and Robert a fortune. It was my psychiatric education at Green Gables Mental Health Facility. When I left Alabama that spring of 1980, not one of us would have guessed where I'd end up less than two months later.

In the gate area at the Birmingham airport, Robert and I stood in uneasy silence. Neither of us could meet the other's eyes. In my hand I clutched a boarding pass for my one-way flight to Portland, Oregon. Robert nursed his cup of coffee. I had refused both food and drink, fearing to lose it all en route.

When the agent finally invited passengers aboard, I took a step backward, denying my father the consolation of a hug.

"Bye. Thanks for all the new clothes. And everything."

He tried to smile. "See you soon."

Neither of us believed it. All morning I'd been remembering what he told me that first night I met him, when I was too tired and scared to know what it meant. *I'm not a bad person,* he had said, *but I'm not a very brave one.*

I made my way down the chilly tunnel of the ramp without look-ing back. It was my first flight ever, and I was surprised the airplane looked so small inside. Robert had booked me a window seat. I closed my eyes for the takeoff, then watched Alabama sink away be-neath the wings. In a few minutes there was nothing below us but clouds.

We landed in a thunderstorm in Kansas City, where I had to change planes. Between the pitch and yaw of our descent and the panic of locating my next flight among a hectic crush of people, I spent my layover in the airport rest room with the dry heaves, promising myself I'd stick to train travel the rest of my life.

Mercifully, the second leg of the flight was smoother. I had phoned Lenora with my arrival time, and I pictured her and Cincy both waiting at the gate, willing it to happen. But I must have doubted, because only Lenora stood at the end of the jetway to gather me in her arms and welcome me home.

It was enough. We hugged a long time, then she held me out at arm's length.

"You look terrific," she said, smiling. "I love that haircut."

Her own dark hair was caught loosely behind her neck and tied with a scarf. She looked tired, and I noticed a few wrinkles around her eyes that hadn't been there before. But her smile was so gen-uine and familiar it made my bones ache.

We laughed at our teary eyes. Then she hooked her arm in mine as we started down the concourse.

Finally I had to ask. "Where's Cincy?"

"At school," Lenora said. "I hope."

"Oh, yeah. I forgot it's a school day." *She couldn't skip to come pick me up?* This didn't sound like the Cincy I knew. And I doubted Lenora would forbid her to come if she'd wanted to. Cincy hadn't written to me one time in the six months I was gone.

I stopped at the first snack stand for a jumbo drink with crushed ice. My stomach couldn't handle any lunch. Lenora tried to pay, as she'd done for my entire childhood, but this time, thanks to my father's guilty conscience, I had a pocketful of money. I was also carrying a check for five thousand dollars made out to my mother. Robert had said he didn't know how else to help her.

I hadn't told Ruth I was coming back.

Lenora and I descended an escalator to the netherworld of baggage claim and stood watching the luggage go round. The silent bags circled past on the conveyor like orphaned children. I wondered what happened to the unclaimed ones that disappeared beneath the rubber ribbons back into the bowels of the airport.

Finally, my luggage appeared. I'd left Shady River with one bag but was returning with two. Robert had bought me a leather suitcase to carry my new clothes. Lenora and I retrieved it and my lumpy satchel and hauled them out to the parking area where her pea-green Volkswagen squatted under a low, gray sky.

"You should get this car listed on the National Register of Historic Vehicles," I said, shoving my small bag into the back seat.

She laughed. "Their records don't go back that far."

She fitted the suitcase into the boot, as she called it, which was up front where the engine should have been. The engine was under there somewhere, though, because it kicked over on only the third try and we were off like a penguin.

The bug shimmied steadily east along the highway toward Shady River. Its engine whined like an electric can opener, discouraging conversation, but I was comfortable just being with Lenora. With Dad and Joey or with Ruth, even with Cincy in the weeks before I left, there was always conflict, always that hot churning in my gut. I was desperately weary of turmoil. With Lenora I felt at peace. For today, at least, I would not analyze that. Gradually my muscles untensed and I watched the scenery slip by the window.

The broad, silent Columbia appeared beside the road. I had

missed its deep and moody blues. Cattail stalks waved in a muddy slough and the willows' new leaves were green with promise. Light rain speckled the windshield and Lenora switched on the wipers. I drowsed to their rhythm, watching the river, and didn't rouse until the car wheezed up the tree-lined driveway to Rockhaven.

Sunshine broke through the clouds, glazing the glass walls of the sunporch with slanted light. My heartbeat quickened. In her letters, Lenora had told me about the second generation of antenor swallowtails, and I could hardly wait to see them.

I carried my big suitcase and Lenora followed with the small one. Inside, I set the bag down in the living room and inhaled Rockhaven's green perfume. The sunporch beckoned me, but I had to see Cincy first.

"Cincy?" I waited, then whistled our three-noted signal.

In a moment I heard an echo—halfhearted, but enough to make me smile. Lenora stayed behind while I ran to the kitchen.

Cincy stood up from the kitchen table when I came in.

"Don't pay the ransom—I've escaped!" I blurted, then froze.

Her eyes looked sunken, her face gaunt below the high cheekbones. But the thing that stopped my breath was the change in her hair. Once raven-colored and shiny as mink, it hung limp and dull, almost as if she'd gone gray. I tried not to look stunned.

She didn't smile.

"Cincy, please don't be mad at me."

Her eyes filled. "How could you leave like that? Without even warning me."

"I was afraid you'd talk me out of it," I said. "And I had to go."

She stood rigid, fists clenched at her sides. My chest felt like a stab wound.

"I had to go, Cincy," I whispered. *For a tangle of reasons I can't even explain.* "I didn't mean to hurt you."

At the slight tremble of her shoulders, I went to her and wrapped my arms around her unyielding body. She was thin as wire. I laid my face on her shoulder and held tight, wanting to absorb her anger and heal the haunted look in her eyes.

"I would never have done that to you," she said. Her tone was hopeless as old bones. I closed my eyes and hung on.

Surely my leaving could not have done this to her. Something else must have happened, and I wasn't there when she needed me. "I'm so sorry. Please don't stay mad at me. I can't stand it."

I felt her thin shudder as she softened and laid her arms around my waist.

She touched my hair, an incomplete forgiveness. "Let go, Sarsaparilla," she said gently. "You're crushing me."

I spent the rest of the afternoon in the dappled sunlight of the greenlab, watching a half-dozen fat antenor caterpillars devour pipevine leaves with oblivious urgency. Three chrysalides hung from twigs inside the glass box I'd set up for the original specimens, and four adults fluttered among the plants in the quarantine section of the greenlab. The artificial weather had confused the timing of their life cycles, but it certainly hadn't dimmed their survival instincts. I couldn't stop smiling as I watched them.

"I feel like their grandmother," I told Lenora, and she laughed.

Cincy stayed with me for half an hour, sitting silently cross-legged on the sunporch floor until she grew bored and drifted away. When I went to check on her, she lay stretched out on her bed, napping. Asleep, her face looked like a malnourished child's.

I found Lenora in the kitchen washing romaine leaves in the sink. I washed up and stood beside her to help, plunging both hands into the cool water. "So which larvae eat Caesar salad?" I said.

She smiled. "People larvae. With marinated chicken breasts and croissants."

"Mmm. Sounds great."

"I'll bet it does, with no lunch."

My hands found another leaf in the water, swished it clean and piled it in the drainer. I lowered my voice. "Is Cincy sick? I know she was upset that I left without telling her, but there's got to be more than that. She looks…wasted."

Lenora was quiet for so long I began to think she wasn't going to answer. And she didn't, until I stopped the motion of my hands in the water and looked at her.

She kept her eyes on the lettuce. "You'll have to ask her about it, Bobbie. We've been at odds a lot and I don't want to make it worse by talking about her problems behind her back."

I nodded, though I didn't understand. "Is she sick?" I asked again.

Lenora took a deep breath. "Not physically. But she had a rough winter and never got back her appetite." Lenora stopped washing lettuce and met my eyes. "Get her to talk about it, Bobbie. Maybe you can help. I can't reach her anymore."

Before I could ask her to define *rough winter,* the phone in the living room rang. Lenora grabbed a towel and hurried to answer. I thought of Robert's house where every bedroom had its own phone, plus another in the kitchen and two separate lines in his studio. I had one of those sudden illuminations when you realize things that should have been obvious before: Lenora had no money. She and Cincy lived only a little farther above the poverty level than Ruth and I always had.

From the kitchen I could hear Lenora's voice on the phone as it changed to a smile. "Yes, she's here. Just a minute."

I thought it must be for Cincy, but Lenora came back into the kitchen. "It's Pete, for you. Cincy must have told him you were coming."

Petey Small. I felt a tiny lurch in my stomach.

I dried my hands and went into the living room, my heartbeat percolating like coffee in a commercial. Before answering, I assumed my school voice.

"Hi, Petey. Welcome back."

His laugh was deeper than it had been when I left. I pictured him leaning against the wall in his parents' kitchen, where I'd visited once or twice.

"Same to you," he said. "So you weren't going to call me, I guess? Even after I wrote you all those charming letters?"

"Was that *you?* Gee, I thought those were from Danny Soames."

I was grinning now, happy to hear his voice, feeling like a science-class buddy again. He considered Danny Soames the scum of the earth, and I'd always accused him of being jealous.

"Yeah, you wish," he said. "Glad to know you're still a wiseass." He paused a beat. "So are you coming back to school tomorrow?"

"I don't know. If I get up my nerve."

"Yeah. Okay." He paused again, then his voice lifted a notch. "Hey, I got my driver's license last month. How about I pick you up this evening and we go for a drive?"

I swallowed a sudden flutter in my throat. *Was he asking me out?* "Sure, why not. I like to live dangerously."

"Thanks a lot. What time will you be through with dinner?"

Not a date, then. Just a drive with a friend. I felt a rush that was part relief, part disappointment. Then again, he hadn't invited Cincy. "Probably seven-thirty."

"Good. See you at seven-thirty."

I said goodbye, feeling giddy as I hung up the phone. Only then did I remember what I had intended to do that evening: go to see my mother. It didn't take much rationalizing to put that encounter off one more day. And tonight when I got back from seeing Pete, I'd try to make Cincy talk to me.

Petey Small stood six feet tall, with sandy-brown hair and a sprinkling of freckles across his nose and cheeks. He was unre-markable-looking, really, except for blue eyes so pale they sometimes hid his active intelligence. I met him at the front door of Rock-haven without waiting for him to knock. It was easy for us to flirt on the phone, but face-to-face, we reverted to acting like buddies, as always. We climbed into Mr. Small's Buick and Pete steered the car down the winding driveway.

Instead of crossing the long bridge into Shady River, he turned onto River Road and headed east along the Washington side. The evening was balmy and smelled like spring, so we rolled down the windows and let the wind do the talking. My hair danced around my head like wild corkscrews, and the good thing about being with Petey was that I didn't have to care. He cranked up the radio and we began to sing aloud with a song we both liked. When the song stopped, he looked over at me and grinned.

"I'm sure glad you're back."

That's all he said. It was enough to make my stomach leap.

I laid my head back on the seat and closed my eyes, opening them when I felt the car slow. Pete turned off on a one-lane sandy road that led down to the river.

He parked beside a grove of budding willows and turned off the engine. "Want to go for a walk?"

"Sure." I let myself out and he waited for me in front of the car. He took my hand to help me jump some muddy ruts in the sand and he didn't let go as he guided us along a flat beach close to the water, toward the last fading light where the sun had disappeared.

I could hear the pulse of the rain-swollen river beside us, and I inhaled deeply of its evening perfume. Petey had brought me to an isolated spot where we weren't likely to be disturbed. I wasn't sure of his intentions, but I began to form intentions of my own.

"It used to be easy for us to talk to each other," he said.

I stopped walking but hung on to his hand. "You brought me out here to talk?" The light had faded now, but the moon was up and in its reflection off the river I could see his face clearly.

"Well, yeah. But it's not supposed to be an insult."

My insides felt furry. I stepped close to him, close enough that he had to know why, and looked up into his face. When he didn't move, I said, "So are you going to kiss me or not?"

It was too dark to see his face redden but I felt its heat when he finally leaned down and put his lips on mine. I slipped my arms around his neck and tried my best to imitate the movie kisses Cincy and I had watched at the Mount Hood Theater when we were kids. At first it felt awkward and silly, but then Petey got into it and everything changed. He put both arms around my waist and pulled me into him. His mouth turned from soft to interested and a moment of terror ran through me, in which I wondered what I had started and whether or not I had nerve enough to finish it.

We finally broke for air and I took one of his hands and slipped it up under my cotton sweater, sucking in my stomach so I wouldn't have a midriff bulge. I kept my face pressed against his shoulder and smelled the clean-laundered fragrance of his shirt, the familiar scent of his skin. I had wondered what this would feel like a thousand times and it didn't feel anything like what I'd imagined.

I felt surprise in Petey's body when his hand touched my bare skin, but he didn't pull his hand away so I pressed it over my right breast, regretting my plain cotton bra and wishing for some lacy underwire thing that pushed me up and made me seem bigger.

Petey whispered into my hair. "Bobbie, do you know what you're doing?"

I wasn't sure if he meant *did I know how to do it,* or *was I sure I wanted to.* The two answers were different so I didn't say anything.

The second kiss was better than the first. Petey's other hand moved down my back to the seat of my jeans and pressed me against him. I was having trouble breathing because my nose was squished against his face, but I hung in there and ran my hand up under his shirt and over the smooth, lean ridges of his backbone and felt him shiver. Something shivery ran through the middle of me, as well. The evening had suddenly turned so warm I wanted to take off my top.

"Bobbie, are you sure?" he said. "This will change everything...."

I mumbled the truth without thinking. "My father's gay and my mom thinks I am and I've got to know."

His body froze and he pulled away from me. His hand came out from under my sweater. "This is an *experiment?*"

"I didn't mean... It's not supposed to be an insult," I stammered. "Don't you want to do it? I thought all guys wanted to."

"I'm not *all guys*," he said. His voice sounded hurt and the moon's reflection glittered in his eyes. "Jesus, Bobbie. Making love is not a freaking science project."

I touched the front of his shirt. "Of course not. I just—"

He stepped away, shaking his head. "It ought to *mean* something."

My face flamed. *I'll bet Cincy never had this happen to her.* I turned away, wanting to run into the cold river and let it wash me away. "Fine. Let's go then."

I trudged back toward the car, tugging my bra back into place. He followed, several paces behind.

We drove the river road back to Rockhaven in silence, my shoulder pressed against the cold comfort of the passenger side door. I gazed out at the twinkling Columbia where the river gods no doubt were laughing their asses off.

I popped the door latch before the car rolled completely to a stop. Petey caught my left elbow and wouldn't let me out.

"Bobbie?" His voice was calm now, gentle. "I like you way too much to be your experiment. That's not fair to either one of us."

I couldn't look at him with tears sliding down my face so I kept my head turned away. "Yeah, sure. I get it. See you around, Pete."

I waited for him to let go of my arm, but instead he pulled me to him and kissed me again. I felt his tongue touch my lip and my insides went crazy. The song on the radio swelled in my head. At that moment I could have thrown away my virginity like a holey shirt. Instead I slid out of the car and ran inside.

Cincy was asleep when I came in. Aware of the strange role reversal, I crawled into her bed as quietly as I could with my jackhammer heartbeat. Her breathing was jerky and shallow, as if she was dreaming. I considered waking her and trying to talk, but she had looked exhausted at dinner, and I let her sleep.

I lay awake and worried about reenrolling at Shady River High the next day, where I'd not only have to face Petey again, but the curious glances of classmates who knew by now where I'd been. Somehow that was simpler than worrying about Cincy's unfathomable misery, or the specter of confrontation with my mother.

CHAPTER 18

Standing in front of the little house on Third Avenue on the wrong side of Shady River, I saw things I'd never noticed before: the peeling paint, a torn screen, the way the carport sagged precariously over one crooked pillar. Maintenance was the landlord's responsibility, of course. But if the tenant never asked, or was behind on the rent...

After school—a strange day in which people who'd rarely spoken to me before said *hi* and *welcome back*—I had reclaimed my red bike from the garage at Rockhaven and ridden back across the bridge and into town. I'd timed my arrival shortly after Ruth was due home from work, before she had time to do much damage with the bottle, in case she was back to drinking. I prayed that wasn't the case, though I didn't know if God recognized prayers from strangers.

At first I thought I was too early. The house looked dark inside. But her old Ford hunched in the shadows of the carport, and in the gathering dusk I recognized a flickering, bluish glow from inside the house; she had the TV on.

Cincy had offered to come with me as a sort of buffer, but I told her I wanted to come alone. Apparently Cincy and Ruth had spent some time talking about me in my absence.

"Go easy on her," Cincy advised me. "Give her some time." That's about all the talking we'd done before we went our separate ways at school.

I tried hard not to resent Cincy's empathy for Ruth, and failed. Unconsciously or not, Cincy was showing me how it felt to be jealous of the relationship between your best friend and your mother. I couldn't blame her. What I didn't understand was why Ruth would talk openly to Cincy when she never did to me.

I stood astride my bike in the street for a long time, stalling. I pictured Ruth in the hospital, ill and humiliated. Would it have been easier for her if I'd been there? I wasn't sure.

I closed my eyes and concentrated on finding my mother sober and willing to forgive me for where I'd been. Perhaps she'd turned a corner, reached that bottom everybody talks about alcoholics having to hit before they can start upward again. I promised myself that if she had, I'd try my hardest to reconcile. I would attend AA with her, if she wanted. Maybe convince her to let Aunt Olivia back into her life, which I thought would be a good thing for them both.

It was dark now and the evening chill soaked through my clothes. I took a deep breath, walked the bike up the driveway and leaned it against the house inside the carport. The battered screen that used to bang shut every time I ran in and out finally had fallen off. It slumped against the house near the back of the carport, the screen pooching outward like a potbelly.

I knocked on the back door. In a moment I heard shuffling inside the house and the vibration of footsteps on the hollow wooden floor. Then the door creaked opened and my mother stood backlit in soft light.

Her hair, cut short now, stood out around her head like lamb's wool. Her face looked puffy and pale.

"Hi," I said. "It's me."

She stood absolutely still. I watched her eyes for some sign of welcome or reproach, or for the shadow they took on after half a bottle. But in the dim light her eyes were too dark to read.

"Are you going to let me in?"

"I don't know," she said slowly. There would be no welcome-home hugs at this house.

We stood in silence while she decided. Finally, she turned away from the door, leaving it open. She was wearing her gray sweat suit with the Chlorox stain on the front. I couldn't remember a time when she didn't have that sweat suit.

I stepped inside. The kitchen felt smaller than when I'd left. "I heard you'd been in the hospital."

She leaned against the stove, crossing her arms. "No big deal, except for the bills."

She didn't invite me to sit. Her body language was clear. I could see her eyes now and my stomach began to burn. "Didn't your health insurance from work cover it?"

Ruth snorted. "They didn't *want* to. Said the policy didn't cover alcoholism. But Sid got tough with them and they finally paid half."

Sid owned the River Inn. "He's been a good boss," I said.

"Yeah. I guess," she said. "He said if it happens again, I'm fired."

"Maybe he thought that would be an incentive. For you to stick with AA." I heard myself playing the role of the responsible one, as I had done with Ruth for years, modeling the behavior I wanted from her. It seemed to be the only way I knew to relate to her.

"You know about that, too, huh?"

"Cincy told me." Actually it had been Lenora, not Cincy, but I knew better than to mention Lenora's name. "Are you still going to the meetings?"

"Sometimes," she said, defensive. "I don't see how it's any of your business."

"You don't? Not because you're my mother?"

She ignored this and changed the subject. "So. Are you back here for good? Or are you going to live with your father?"

"I want to finish school here," I said.

Her hand trembled as she reached for a plastic tumbler from the counter. The familiar aroma of bourbon burned my nose and raised a lump in my throat.

Three six three, Mom drank whis-key.

She took two swallows from the glass, closing her eyes as the fire went down. It seemed to calm her. "Where do you plan to stay?"

I knew this trick; if I said *Here,* she'd refuse me. "With Cincy, I guess. I can't live here if you're still drinking. Not that I was invited."

"I see," she said. "You can't live with a drinker, but you can live with queers. What's the matter, didn't your faggot father *invite* you to stay with him?"

My body felt leaden, exhausted by the futile hope this might go well, that we might talk without lacing every word with malice. "He did, actually. But Joey didn't think much of the idea."

"Ha! I'll bet he didn't." She took another sip from the glass. "Joey thinks about Joey."

Her sneer resembled Joey's lopsided smile so much that the irony nearly felled me. I shook my head to clear the image. "Robert is really sorry that he hurt you. He knows he can't make it up to you, but he'd like to help out, financially." I unfolded the check from my pocket and laid it on the kitchen table.

Ruth stiffened. I saw the heat rise in her face and I went on quickly. "Please take it, Mom. Use it to get out of debt, into a decent house, maybe. Think of it as back child support."

Her eyes turned hard. "I don't want his damned guilt money! He and Joey will burn in hell for their perversion. I talked to Pastor Johnson about it. You better be careful you don't join them."

I nodded. "So now you've got religion."

She drained her glass and glanced around the kitchen with something like panic in her eyes.

"The bottle's on the table," I said coldly.

"You can tell your pervert father I hope he does go to hell, and the sooner the better!" Drops of spittle flew from her lips. She wiped them with the back of her hand.

When I didn't answer, she got louder. "Go on and live with him! After all the years I took care of you and he wasn't around. You're two of a kind." Her nostrils flared. "And don't you make fun of my religion. God's the only one who can save your soul!"

She lunged toward the table but instead of picking up the bottle, she grabbed Robert's check, wadded it into a ball and bounced it off my cheek like a slap.

My eyes flooded; I couldn't move.

She looked at my face, and hers collapsed. I saw her weave as she slumped against the table. "Get out of here," she said miserably. "I'm going to get drunk."

She hooked the neck of the bottle between her fingers and walked away, leaving me alone in her kitchen.

I stood in the semidarkness for ten minutes before I could draw enough breath to make my feet move.

I have relived that evening again and again over the years, and I still wonder: if either of us had known she'd be dead by tomorrow, could we have managed to say *I love you?*

CHAPTER 19

Alone in my mother's kitchen, I memorized the paint-flecked pattern of the yellowed linoleum and the particular musty smell of the house. The refrigerator motor knocked and then shuddered to silence. I remembered awakening to that sound in the night when I was small, sure that something dark and evil was in the house. Maybe it was.

I'd lived here nine years—longer than in any other place. It took a while to say goodbye to those years, and to accept the finality of my mother's rejection.

Get out of here. I'm going to get drunk.

That pretty much said it all.

I thought about our stray cat, Rathbone, who'd slipped out the back door one day and was gone forever.

And so was I.

I straddled my bike and rode away through the quiet neighborhood, feeling cut loose from the earth, like a child's balloon suddenly released, like a dream of flying.

But this wasn't a dream. It was real, and it was scary. The fire in my stomach kept me hunched over the handlebars as I crossed the river bridge. I had a vision of going over the side, bound for deep waters—me and my bike in a long, slow, Evel Knievel arc. Which was impossible, because of the railings.

Halfway up the hill to Rockhaven, I stopped and threw up in the weeds alongside the road. Depleted, I lay on my side in the grass until my knees solidified again. The night sky was alive with fast-moving clouds, the air thick and inky. Above my head, pine branches tossed wildly in a gusty wind. The river had swallowed up the moon.

I walked my bike the rest of the way and parked it in front of the house. The detached garage, which sat at a right angle to the house, stood open and empty. Like Petey, Cincy had turned sixteen and got her driver's license while I was away. I hoped it was she and not Lenora who was gone in the car. I wasn't ready to face Cincy's questions or to hear her defense of Ruth's behavior. I needed to get control of what had happened down there before I talked to anybody.

Sitting on the front step, I watched the flicker of distant lightning. Clouds scudded overhead and clotted in my chest. I sat there until my stomach stopped cramping and I could breathe normally again. Then I dried my face with the tail of my shirt and went inside.

Predictably, Lenora was in the greenlab, her radio tuned softly to old hits from the sixties. The moment she read my face, her expression transformed. I saw anguish there, and love—the kind of look I'd never seen in Ruth's eyes. It took the legs out from under me. I sat down on the floor, fast, to keep from passing out.

Lenora knelt beside me and wrapped me in her arms, rocking me like the child I'd never be again. She didn't talk; she just let me cry, while the wind whipped the trees around our walls of glass. When I stopped, she helped me up and guided me to the chair where she'd been sitting.

"Just rest," she said. "I'll go make us some hot tea."

I closed my eyes and listened to the wind and Elton John's lonely "Rocket Man" on the radio, lost in space. In a few minutes Lenora came back and passed me a hot mug. She handed me a tissue and set the box on the floor. The tea was strong and sweet. I inhaled the vapors, sipped and blew my nose. She sat at my feet, cradling her own cup, and squeezed my knee with one hand.

"Sorry about the blubbering," I said.

"Don't be. If you don't let it out, it will eat you up. I used to worry because you never cried."

"Really?" I laughed a little, struggling not to let the tears take me again. "I love you, Lenora. My mother thinks it's abnormal. She thinks I'm homosexual, like my dad. Until I went out with Petey last night, I thought maybe she was right." Even I heard the doubt in my voice. "I'm sorry. I shouldn't have told you that."

"Never apologize for your feelings, Bobbie." Her voice was clear, not troubled or pitying. "I love you, too, more than my life. Even more, at times—God help me—than my own daughter. That's a truth I'll have to live with, and it may have damaged Cincy forever. But there are many ways to love, and love between women isn't necessarily sexual."

Lenora handed me another tissue. "Your short life has been starved of love," she said. "I knew how much you had to give, and I was greedy. Nobody ever needed me the way you did, or cared about my work. Studying butterflies seems silly to most people, but you saw the beauty and the mystery, and I loved you for that, too."

She squeezed my knee again. "I *am* your mother, and for a brief, fun time," she smiled, "we were scientists together. Most of all, I'll always be your friend. And I promise you, Bobbie, the love we have isn't the sexual kind."

"How do you know that? How does anybody know? Even Dad and Joey couldn't explain it."

"I know it because I know *you*. Lots longer and better than your father or Joey. Even better than Ruth does. I watched you grow up, and I paid attention. I know you *inside out*."

We sat quietly for a minute, and then I told her what had happened with Ruth. "I can never go back there, and I can't live in Birmingham."

"You know you can stay here."

I shook my head. "I don't think Cincy wants me to."

"Right now, Cynthia doesn't know what she wants. And I say you can stay."

My empty stomach gurgled and Lenora smiled. "You sound hungry as a caterpillar. Let's get you something to eat." She stood up and offered me a hand. "How about a hug?"

She waited, letting me accept or reject. I hugged her tightly, the way a girl might hug her mother or her best friend. Another old song came on the radio, one of Lenora's favorites. She began to sway. In a moment we started dancing together, giggling like silly teenagers, letting the tension drain away.

A noise startled us. We glanced toward it, our faces still smiling.

Cincy and Ruth stood in the doorway. The radio and the blustering wind had hidden the sound of their arrival.

Even Lenora was speechless. I felt her body stiffen as she pulled away from me.

Cincy was wearing short shorts and a T-shirt; Ruth was in the same gray sweats as when I'd left her earlier that evening. Her hair frizzed out around her head like sparks and her face looked twisted. She spoke to Cincy, but her eyes never left Lenora and me.

"Are you satisfied now? I never should have let you drag me up here!"

Cincy stared at us, her face as white and expressionless as the moon. She didn't move, but I saw her receding, moving away from us like a series of doors closing.

"Cincy?" I said.

She didn't answer.

Ruth drew herself up and spat on the floor at our feet. "*Like father, like daughter.* You make me sick. All of you!"

She turned and reeled back through the house toward the front door, leaving behind a scent of bourbon.

"Cynthia, Ruth is wrong. It's not like that," Lenora said, and moved toward her.

Cincy backed up a step. "Stay away from me." She turned stiffly and walked away.

For endless seconds, Lenora and I stood frozen. Then Lenora ran after her. "Cynthia!"

I stayed where I was. Past the gusting wind and the roaring in my ears, I heard Lenora's voice as she ran outside, calling Cincy's name. Calling, calling.

A car started and tires spun gravel—Ruth's car, careening away. Then another car door slammed, and I heard the wheeze of the old VW.

With my face pressed into the cool leaves matting the glass walls, I watched Cincy's headlights twist down the hill.

CHAPTER 20

In the blackness of that night I awoke suddenly, unsure at first where I was. Groggy from something Lenora had given me to let me sleep, I sat up in Cincy's bed, where I'd gone so I'd be sure to know if she came home. She hadn't. The luminous numbers on her clock radio read 3:27.

Something was in the house. A breathing, crackling sound that couldn't be the wind.

Smoke. I smelled smoke.

Before I could react, Lenora's face appeared in the doorway, a dim whiteness above striped pajamas.

Her voice was urgent. "Bobbie, wake up!"

"What's happening?"

"The house is on fire! Get outside, quick! I'll call the fire department and meet you out front. Go!"

I jumped into my shoes and ran into the hallway still pulling on my jeans. The hall was full of smoke. I dropped to my knees, coughing, and crawled.

"Lenora! Where are you?"

Flames illuminated the kitchen doorway. I scrambled past it, cut through the dining room on all fours, and felt my way to the front door. It was open—*why?* A draft of air blew in toward the flames. I tumbled out onto the porch, gasping.

In the distance, sirens wailed. I crawled off the porch and collapsed on the lawn. The fire was a living thing in the darkness. I could hear the eerie sigh of the flames. Yellow light flickered through the kitchen windows.

I sat up and yelled. "Lenora? *Lenora!*" My voice was lost against the hissing of the flames. My chest seized in a fit of coughing.

Where was she? Why didn't she come out?

Oh, my God. The butterflies!

I pictured them trapped inside…beating against the glass… bright wings curling into lips of flame. *My antenors.* I struggled to my feet and squinted toward the glass walls of the sunporch. Inside, a shadow moved across the glow from the flames.

"Lenora!"

Break the glass. I picked up a rock from the edge of the driveway and hurled it at the windows. It bounced off.

"Lenora! Get out!"

At the front door, heat hit me like a moving wall. It sucked out my breath and knocked me down. I covered my head with one arm, crouched and plunged into the searing dark.

The air was black and scorching. I couldn't see anything except the flames that raced along the ceiling of the living room. I pushed on toward the sunporch, choking, cowering against the furnacelike heat. Behind me a crash from the kitchen shook the floor. Sparks showered around me. Blinded by smoke, I closed my eyes and tried to run.

Something soft and heavy caught my foot and I sprawled forward. My head struck a table with a sickening sound as I hit the floor.

I groaned and rolled over. The floor scorched my skin. My eyes felt crusted. *Is this how it ends? Am I going to die here?*

"Lenora!"

My scream wavered and died away. Finally my dazed brain focused on what had tripped me—something soft but heavy, something that didn't belong there. Something human.

I crawled backward and found her. The living room drapes went up like a torch and I glimpsed the face beneath me on the floor. It wasn't Lenora.

"Mom?"

I pushed the hair from her smeared face and her eyes flickered open. Ruth tried to speak, coughed instead. I caught the scent of bourbon and something oily—gasoline?

She lifted her hand to my face.

"I tried..." she whispered, choking again, "...to save you. Now it's up to God." Her eyes fluttered shut and her body went slack.

Her mind is gone. Alcoholic delusions.

An overhead beam split and crashed, raining sparks. I covered her body with mine. Racked by another spasm of coughing, I lay helpless, fighting to breathe. A seductive sleepiness pulled me down. I wanted to lie there—just close my eyes and sleep.

But I had to move or we'd burn alive.

I squinted into the darkness. The only clear path lay toward the sunporch. On my knees by Ruth's head, I hooked my arms under her shoulders and began to drag her backward.

There was no air, only smoke to breathe. I heaved her body a foot or two, scrambling crablike toward the doorway, then pulled again. Over and over; the sunporch seemed miles away. Outside, the sirens grew louder and then cut off.

Finally we crossed the threshold to the porch. There was more air here but it felt hot enough to burn.

"Lenora?"

I couldn't see her. Maybe she got out. The awful heaving of the fire filled my head and I heard the walls cracking in the living room. Only one way out. Through the glass.

I stood and grabbed a heavy potted plant in both arms, twisted my torso like a discus thrower, and heaved. I remember the strange coolness of the clay pot just before it left my burned arms, stripping skin. Then the glass wall exploded in a silver shower against the night sky.

The inward rush of air felt like cool water. Flames leaped at the living room doorway, greedy for oxygen.

"Mom! Wake up!"

I tried to lift her, failed. She was dead weight. I sat her up, folded her over my shoulder and staggered to my feet. Faltered, nearly fell.

I braced myself, took a deep breath that seared my lungs and ran headlong through the opening in the glass wall, screaming.

We launched into the cool night air trailing tangled vines, falling, and I heard nothing, not even the sound of my screams.

Falling, falling, and then the sudden impact with earth that snapped my teeth together and took my breath away. I lay entwined with Ruth's body in utter silence, waiting for the pain, feeling nothing.

With great effort, I opened my eyes.

Without my contacts, I saw a blur of red lights flashing in the driveway. A beautiful, silver arc of water connected the lights to the flames on the roof, like an abstract painting. Two yellow slickers with helmets ran toward us in slow motion with no sound.

I felt as if I were breathing under water. The water muffled my ears. My mother's body lay beneath me and on top of me and the two men in yellow slickers were running and I was ready to die now so I rolled back, very slowly, onto the pine needles, and gave myself up to the sucking blackness of the night.

* * *

My memory of the next few weeks is sketchy, except for pain. Beneath the drug-induced blur that blocked out most other sensations, the pain lived with me like a burning oil slick spread over my skin.

Two days after the fire, I woke up in a hospital with my neck and shoulder swathed in bandages and my right arm in a cast. My hair was shaved to a burr. Every breath seared my lungs.

The first face I saw was Petey Small's.

I recognized his voice, but I couldn't remember anything else. I didn't know where I was or why. And I couldn't ask because someone had stuck a tube down my throat.

The walls and ceiling were sky-blue and I thought maybe I was in heaven. But my right arm throbbed mightily inside the cast, and so did my head and my skin. Surely you didn't hurt like this in heaven.

Someone slipped my glasses on my face. Petey's freckles stood out like cinnamon on milk and his eyes looked scared. I tried to smile at him, but my face felt stiff and...*crisp.* Then Petey did the oddest thing. He picked up my unbandaged left hand and held it to his lips. I saw tears in his eyes.

What's the matter with *him?* I thought, and went back to sleep.

And while I slept, the Shady River police, all three of them, investigated the fire at Rockhaven. At first they considered my mother a suspect, because of her recent instability. No one was there to tell them about our final argument, or about her walking in on a scene that convinced her beyond all doubt of a lesbian relationship between me and Lenora. Cincy couldn't tell them because she had disappeared. No one had seen her or the Volkswagen since she drove away from Rockhaven that night.

Ruth was dead, a victim of burns and smoke inhalation. I wasn't quite dead, but I wasn't conscious the day one of the officers traveled to the Portland burn center, where I'd been airlifted the night of the fire, to interview me. He never came back. He didn't have to, because an ambitious young lieutenant got to nosing around and discovered Lenora's debts had been piling up. Grant money for her kind of research had dried up that winter, and she'd floated a loan to tide them over. When that ran out, she'd maxed her credit card. Lenora didn't tell the police about our twisted family histories, only that she'd awakened to find the house in flames.

Checking a little further, the police discovered a fire insurance policy on Rockhaven. They brought Lenora in for questioning. The lieutenant laid out his scenario: She had run up debts she couldn't handle and was further distraught because of problems with her teenaged daughter. (It seemed the police were acquainted with Cincy; they'd brought her home once for underage drinking, and once when they found her wandering the streets of Shady River alone at 2:00 a.m.) In her desperation, the lieutenant theorized, Lenora had set her house on fire to collect the insurance. He never had to address the loose ends of why I was in the house, or Ruth, because Lenora listened to his story, nodded her head and said yes, that's just the way it happened. They helped her write it up and she signed it.

The lieutenant neglected to mention to her that because someone had died in the fire, she could be charged not only with arson and attempting to defraud the insurance company, but with manslaughter, or even second-degree murder.

I knew none of this until much later. For several days, I lay in the hospital bed with an IV attached to my arm, drifting in and out of consciousness. Second-degree burns with respiratory complications—the doctor called it laryngeal edema. I didn't remember the fire or being airlifted from Shady River to Portland.

Whenever I roused, it seemed, Petey was there. Like a nervous parent discussing sex with his child, he answered only those questions it occurred to me to ask.

Through the haze that homogenized my waking and sleeping, I slowly recalled the argument with my mother. Then I remembered riding my bike to Rockhaven in the night, and the scene with Lenora on the sunporch. Cincy and Ruth's shocked faces. But still I had no memory of the fire.

One day Petey held my hand, his face serious. "You don't have to live with him if you don't want to," he assured me. "I talked it over with my parents. We have a spare room, and you can stay with us until you finish school."

I didn't know what the hell he was talking about.

The next time I woke up, the tube was gone from my throat and my father's harried face hung over the bed. He looked ill, his skin viscous as wallpaper paste. He told me that Ruth had died in the fire.

And suddenly I remembered. I felt my feet trip over her body, recalled dragging her to the sunporch and flinging us both into the night. I remembered knowing even then that she was dead. And that she had set Rockhaven on fire to purge the evil of Lenora and me. My mother had tried to kill me.

Acid flooded my stomach. In the midst of his probing, the doctor had discovered I had an ulcer. I couldn't tolerate the pain meds by mouth so they were dripped through the IV that rehydrated me. But the magic fluid didn't do much to dull the knife blade in my middle.

"Are Lenora and Cincy all right?" I asked Robert.

He looked lost and glanced behind him. Petey came to the bedside.

"Cincy took off," he said. "Disappeared." He sounded pissed off about this, as if she'd deserted me. But of course, he didn't know why.

"Lenora? She's not dead, is she?"

"No." Petey hesitated. He glanced at my father, but got no help from him. "She's not dead. Lenora's in jail. For setting the fire."

"What? Why would they think that?" I tried to raise my head, which hurt my whole body.

"For the insurance money."

"That's ridiculous!" I tried to sit up. "I've got to tell them…."

Robert pushed the button for the nurse and gently forced my shoulders back onto the bed. "Take it easy, honey. You're not going anywhere."

Indeed, I couldn't. Anchored to the bed by my injuries, I clutched Robert's hand. "Tell the police I have to talk to them. Please!"

"I will, honey. Lie still now."

I squeezed his hand harder, still trying to sit up. "Lenora didn't do this. I have to tell them."

"Okay, sweetie," he said, nodding to the nurse as she came in the room. "It's okay."

"Settle down now, Bobbie," the nurse said soothingly. "Here. I've got some pain med for you." The hypo worked within sixty seconds.

Day after day I expected the police to show up. I asked Robert to call them again. I don't know if he did or didn't, but they never came.

I questioned Petey, but Robert had forbidden him to talk about Lenora, in order not to upset me. Petey tried to honor Robert's wish, but when I'd been there two weeks he finally gave me the Shady River newspaper with Ruth's obituary, and a Portland paper that carried a story about the fire. I waited until no one was with me to read them.

I read the obit first. In death my mother achieved the respect she'd never earned in life. The accounts mentioned her loyal employment history at the Shady River Inn, but not the alcoholism that nearly cost her that job. They named me as her only survivor—but not the fact that she'd disowned me and then tried to burn me to hell.

I read the newsprint with dry eyes, feeding the grief and guilt to my ulcer. I watched the IV drip into my veins and considered what kind of daughter engendered that much hatred from the person in life who should have loved her most.

Then I read the Portland paper's account of the fire. At the tag end of the story, the final paragraph reported that Lenora Jaines had been charged with arson, attempted insurance fraud and manslaughter after confessing to the Shady River police.

I sat upright in the bed. *Confessing?* Why would she do that? She had to know who set the fire.

I could think of only one explanation. Lenora was trying to protect me from knowing my mother had tried to kill me. She was afraid the knowledge would push me over the edge. I felt sick to my stomach, powerless, pinned to the bed like a collected moth.

The next day, they transported me from the burn center to the one-floor hospital in Shady River under the care of my hometown GP. Robert had flown back to Birmingham to take care of business, promising he'd be back in a few days. I had my doubts. He'd been more and more distracted as my hospital stay dragged on. Petey's parents had finally required him to go back to school, so I was alone when they loaded me into the ambulance for the ride. The horizontal trip left me car sick and exhausted, but at least I was free of the IVs.

After the nurse in Shady River settled me onto the stiff white sheets and left the room, I looked around at the mint-green walls and age-darkened crucifix hanging by the door. I wondered if this was the same room where Ruth had once lain near death from alcohol poisoning. Maybe even the same bed. Was this where she'd finally gone mad?

I eased myself from the bed, found a phone book in a drawer and got an outside line on the bedside phone.

"Police station," a male voice said.

I kept my voice low. "I need to speak with Lenora Jaines. Is she in jail there?"

"Who's calling, please?"

"A friend. Is she there?"

"Just a minute." I could hear his muffled voice talking to someone else, then a shuffling, and he was back.

"You'll have to talk to her attorney. I can give you his name and number, if you like."

"Yes. Hold on a minute."

There was no paper in the bedside stand but someone had left a ballpoint pen that said Northwest Mutual Life on it. I scribbled the lawyer's name and number in the margins of the yellow pages. Leonard Shavers. I called his office but his secretary said he wasn't in.

"Can you please give him my name and tell him it's important I talk to him about Lenora Jaines?"

"Certainly," she said. "Spell that for me, please?" I spelled Bobbie Lee, read the number off the old-fashioned black telephone, and told her where I was. Exhausted and hurting, I crawled back in bed and went immediately to sleep.

Late that afternoon Leonard Shavers, attorney-at-law, came to see me. He'd been appointed by the court to represent Lenora. Shavers was past sixty, balding and shaped like a top.

"Lenora didn't do it," I blurted before he'd even settled into the straight-backed chair.

He eyed me sympathetically. "There isn't much I can do for her," he said. "She admitted setting the fire for the insurance money. She was in debt with no way to pay it back, and upset about her daughter. We pleaded emotional duress and asked for mercy in sentencing—"

"*Sentencing?* What do you mean? They can't send her to prison!"

He seemed taken aback. "Well, someone did die in the fire, you know. Even if it was accidental—"

"Accidental? Are you all crazy?"

The lawyer's eyes went wide behind his glasses and he leaned away from me.

"My mother set the fire," I said, enunciating as if he were hard of hearing. "I was there!" My chest burned from breathing too fast and I fought to keep from crying.

For a moment Shavers paid attention. "Did you see her do it?"

"Of course I didn't see her do it, or I'd have stopped her. But she was *there,* in the middle of the night."

My voice had risen and a nurse stuck her head into the room, frowning. I sank back on the bed for fear she'd send the lawyer away. But this wasn't the Portland hospital with its strict rules and efficiency. The nurse only scowled and closed the door.

I lowered my voice. "My mother was very angry with me. And with Lenora. She tried to kill us!"

Leonard Shavers sat back in his chair. "Lenora was afraid you might think that." He sighed, shook his head. "That's not what happened, Miss Lee. Lenora told me so herself. You must not think your mother tried to kill you." His voice was gentle, condescending, but I could hear behind it the echo of Lenora's words. She sent him to convince me, I thought. She's going to jail to keep me—and the world—from knowing I am such a freak that my own mother wanted me dead.

My body had become so heavy I couldn't lift my hand to brush the tears away. "Please," I said. "You've got to stop her. *Please* don't let her go to jail."

But I knew Lenora. If she'd set her mind, this mousy excuse for a lawyer couldn't change it. I had to tell the police myself, or the judge—somebody who would do something. And I had to get out of this hospital to do it. I turned my face away from Leonard Shavers until he left the room.

Every stubby hair regrowing on my head zinged with pain. They'd been weaning me off the heavy drugs, giving me Tylenol by mouth and Zantac for the ulcer. The pain made me feel alive again. I lay still, embracing it, feeling the blood throb in my arms.

Waiting, I listened to the muffled voices in the hallway and heard a supper cart rattle down the hall. The nauseating aroma of Swiss steak wafted through the partly open door. Later, when the nurse came in with my bedtime meds, she scolded me for not eating, so I kept the Jell-O and milk. She took the rest away.

After dark, when the floor quieted and the nurse had made her last rounds for the night, I climbed down from the bed and searched the tiny cabinet for clothes. There were none, of course. What I'd had on the night of the fire would have been ruined. I pulled on the robe and slippers Robert had bought me in Portland and tucked a spare blanket under my arm. I wasn't sure how cool the night outside might be.

My slippers scuffed softly as I walked down the dim, quiet hallway, past the high countertop of the abandoned nurses' station, and out the double glass doors into the night.

CHAPTER 21

Outside the antiseptic-scented hospital, only the damp smell of the river seemed familiar in the darkness. I walked down the sidewalk past the parking lot, but I couldn't recognize the streets. At the corner I stopped to get my bearings. My head felt like a helium balloon, as if my whole body might rise up and float away.

To my left I saw streetlights in the distance. I turned toward them and started walking. Partway down the block, shivering, I made a cape out of the blanket I was carrying. It was hard to do with a cast on one arm. Finally I got it wrapped around me and walked on.

I must look like an escapee from a mental institution, I thought, and began to giggle. Laughing hurt me all over, but once I'd started, I couldn't stop. I kept on until I got the hiccoughs and tears slid down my cheeks. In the hospital bed I hadn't needed a sling for my arm, but now the weight of the cast, which bent at the elbow, made me wish for one. The struggle to support the cast and keep the blanket from falling off exhausted me.

The downtown area of Shady River appeared ahead of me and

suddenly I recognized everything. It was a comfort, like having your directions turned around and then something clicks and you can tell that south is south.

I knew where I was going, too. I turned north a block to the street behind the main drag, where giant hemlock trees hung over the sidewalk and hid me from the streetlights. The stores along Main were probably closed, but I couldn't take any chances.

A block before I reached my mother's house on Third Avenue, I stopped to rest. Sitting on the curb, I pulled the blanket around me and leaned my head between my knees, breathing through my mouth. Everything looked swimmy. Good thing I hadn't eaten that Swiss steak at the hospital; I'd have lost it for sure. I took deep breaths until my legs felt solid again, then I stood up and walked on.

The little house looked dark and deserted. But then it had pretty much always looked that way. Robert had promised to come back from Birmingham this week, but even if Joey let him, he wouldn't stay here. This came much too close to squalor for my sensitive father. He'd get the nicest room at the Shady River Inn, or more likely at one of the chain motels on the highway.

My white hospital blanket glowed eerily in the darkness. I slipped into the shade under the carport and tried the back door. It was locked, but I found the spare key still inside a rusted orange juice can next to the house.

Inside, I tried to turn on the small light over the kitchen stove. Nothing happened, so I tried another and then another. The power was off. The house smelled musty and cold, but I was warm under my blanket, except for my feet. Ruth's presence haunted the house. There were dirty dishes in the sink.

I went down the dark hallway to my bedroom. In the thin light sifting through the curtains, the room looked just the way I'd left it nearly eight months ago. I felt around in a drawer and found a pair of socks, sat on the bed to pull them on one-handed. Exhausted, I lay back on the pillow and wrapped one edge of the spread over me.

It was no good, though; much too lonely, and strange shadows danced on the ceiling. I went down the hall to my mother's room. In the doorway I hesitated a moment, trying to get my mind around the fact that she was gone forever. The newspaper accounts hadn't said anything about burial. I wondered what they'd done with her body. Maybe Robert had it cremated, the ashes sent back to Aunt Olivia. I liked that idea. Olivia would take care of her.

I lay down on my mother's unmade bed and turned my face into the pillow that still held her scent. On the wall hung a picture that hadn't been there before, and even in the dim room I could tell it was my drawing of *Mourning Cloaks on Poplar*. I pulled the bedspread over my legs and cried myself to sleep.

A rapping like machine-gun fire awoke me.

I opened my eyes to early daylight. Cocooned in my blanket, I lay absolutely still, but my heartbeat shook me in the bed. I jumped when someone hammered on the front door again.

"Bobbie Lee? Are you in there?"

It was a male voice I didn't recognize. I stopped breathing.

I heard him come around to the back door and try the knob. I had relocked it when I came in, a miracle, and I remembered leaving the key on the kitchen table.

The back door rattled and so did my pulse. He called my name again, beating on a windowpane until I thought the glass would break. I held my breath and waited.

Then the knocking stopped. In a moment I heard a car start up and drive away.

I concentrated on breathing. When my legs stopped shaking, I got up and sneaked through the house to the front window. The street was quiet and empty. Who could have been looking for me? Would the hospital have called the police?

From the Presbyterian church several blocks over, deep bells peeled out a hymn. *It must be Sunday. It might even be my birthday.* I knew it was May, because Petey had brought a calendar to my room in Portland, to keep me in touch with reality, he said.

I went to my bedroom and struggled into an old pair of jeans that were too tight before I went east. They fit me now. The house felt chilly, but I couldn't get a sweatshirt over my cast. I found two old flannel shirts and put them on, one over the other, and my ancient sneakers from the back of the closet, shaking them out in case of spiders. I left the laces undone.

In the bathroom, I was glad to find the toilet would flush, the water still running. My arm inside the cast ached, and so did my stomach. I looked in the kitchen cabinets for something to soak up the acid and found a box of dry cereal. I sat at the kitchen table, tired from the effort of getting dressed, and ate cereal straight from the box.

I had to make a plan.

I would walk to the police station and ask to see the chief. I'd tell him my story and demand to see Lenora, throw a temper fit if I had to. I knew the jail adjoined the police station, so that's where she must be. The thought that I might see Lenora in only a few hours gave me a rush of hope. Unfortunately, it also released more acid into my stomach.

I drank a glass of water from the kitchen tap, then splashed some on my face. The dry cereal was swelling. I drew another glassful— and then the thought occurred to me that if the water wasn't turned off, maybe the phone wasn't, either.

I took the receiver from the wall phone and sure enough, there was a dial tone. Mom had kept emergency numbers on an index card taped to the wall. I dialed the number for the police department.

It rang and rang while my heartbeat skittered and thumped. Maybe the officer on duty had gone for doughnuts. I leaned against the wall and counted; after twenty-three rings, a man answered. His voice sounded like the guy at the front door that morning, and my throat closed up.

But that was paranoid. I swallowed and tried to sound like an adult. "May I speak to the chief of police, please?"

"Chief's not in on Sunday."

I'd already forgotten that detail.

"Can I help?" he said.

I hesitated. If he was the one looking for me, I couldn't tell him who I was. But I had to find out about Lenora. "I'm a friend of Lenora Jaines and I wanted to visit her today."

"Sorry. She isn't here. They transferred her to Stevenson."

My chest constricted. "Stevenson? What for?"

"It's the county seat. She'll be sentenced in district court, if she hasn't been already."

"But…isn't there going to be a trial?" I heard my voice rise and I fought for control.

The officer paused. "Who is this?"

"She didn't do it!" I said. "She didn't set the fire!"

"Is this Bobbie Lee?"

"No," I said, too quickly. "Just a friend." My head pounded.

The cop's voice changed. Fake nice. "Miss Lee, we've been looking for you. People are worried. Your friend Pete, and Doc Halsey. Tell me where you are, and I'll come pick you up."

I hung up. Lunged to the sink and heaved up my waterlogged Wheaties.

When the spasm passed, I ran lots of water and wiped my sweating face with a wet dish towel.

They can't do this. They can't take Lenora away from me, too.

I had no money, no way to get to Stevenson. If I called anybody for help, they'd put me back in the hospital. I bit into the dish towel to keep from screaming. Then I wadded it up and threw it at the phone as hard as I could, and fled out the back door.

Half a block down the street, my knees gave out. As I fell, I turned my body to protect my broken arm and hit the ground on my left side, hard. I lay still, absorbing the pain, trying to breathe. Then rolled on my back and closed my eyes, my face sweating.

This was not real; it couldn't be happening. I couldn't live without *any* of them—without Lenora, without Cincy, without even the mother who'd wanted me dead. It wasn't fair.

Suddenly it came clear to me that this was my punishment. Everything that had happened was my fault; I had ruined all four of our lives.

If it weren't for me, Lenora wouldn't be going to prison.

If it weren't for me, Ruth wouldn't be dead.

If it weren't for me, Cincy wouldn't have run away.

I was a curse, the bad seed of a warped father and a wretched, insane mother. My stomach roiled.

I got to my feet and stumbled toward the river. Now my whole body felt sweaty. The ground trembled weirdly beneath my feet— had I imagined it? No. My horrible selfishness was shaking the earth. Vertigo spun my head.

I deserved what I got—but not the *world.* If I moved fast maybe I could stop it, save the earth from destruction. I had to hurry. My feet wouldn't run, but I kept slogging, leaning forward so my feet had to catch up. At the entrance to the river bridge, yellow-and-black barricades blocked the road. I looked across the river and saw the spire of Rockhaven's naked chimney on the hillside, a sentinel above the charred slash that traced downward to the bridge.

The fire had gotten away from them. It had burned down the hill and eaten up the wooden floor of the bridge on the opposite side. Coming after me.

Now it had found me; I felt the burning in my bones.

I slipped between the barricades and stumbled onto the bridge. The wooden floor was undamaged on this side and my sneakers made a muffled thudding on the heavy, oiled planks. I kept going to where the flooring was burned away, exposing the iron girders and concrete pylons that rose up from the riverbed. Beneath my feet the water was a hazy, gray reflection of the morning sky. Its surface looked flat and still, but I knew that below that deceptive mirror the river gods ran fast and deep.

I stepped onto one of the girders and walked it like a balance beam, my loose shoes shifting on my feet, my left hand reaching out reflexively for the railing along the edge. Over the deepest part of the channel I stopped and looked down.

I wasn't high enough.

Holding on to the side rail, I tipped my head back and traced the pattern of metal struts that webbed upward against the sky, up and up and over the bridge. I closed my eyes and felt the world revolve.

I placed one foot on the struts and started climbing. Using my cast to hook around a crossbar, I pulled myself up with my other arm, found more footholds, and ascended. It was slow going. Far away I felt the pain in my legs and arms, but here I was numb.

A sound like distant thunder—or something exploding—sent a tremor through the bridge. I had to hurry. One foot slipped off the beam and I stopped, clinging. Couldn't let it be an accident; it had to be an act of will. I turned my face toward the charred remains of Rockhaven. The house had burned completely; nothing left but rubble and the blackened chimney spire. Little eddies of ash swirled like the ghosts of butterflies.

The magic of the sunporch was gone forever; my antenors, gone. Lenora, Cincy, Ruth, gone.

Behind the hills where the morning haze was clearing, a strange gray cloud loomed above the horizon, mushroom-shaped, like the ones I'd seen in pictures of Hiroshima. Was the whole world on fire?

God, forgive me. I never meant to destroy the people I loved.

I braced my legs inside a triangular bridge span and ducked underneath it, shifting my feet one at a time until I was clinging to the outside, my back against cold metal. I looked down. A tickling sensation arched my feet over the bars and flashed up my legs like an electric current.

I closed my eyes and felt the tears on my face dry to salt. No more tears now. Too late for that.

Facing into the clean, west wind, I clung to the world with one hand, still afraid to do what must be done. The ominous cloud behind Rockhaven boiled larger and I heard the river call my name.

I leaned out and let go.

Chapter 22

Columbia River Gorge, 1990

That was ten years ago, and I'm still falling. Today as I drive the two-lane road that parallels the Columbia from Plymouth to Portland, the memory of that morning comes on me strong. My hands grip the steering wheel; the smell of river water is imprinted in my sweat.

Breathe. Relax and breathe.

Petey Small pulled me from the river that day. Perhaps it was his voice, not the river gods, that I heard as I fell. Pete was an athlete, a strong swimmer. He'd been out looking for me that morning, and he thought I might go to Rockhaven. Pete saw me go into the river and dived in after me, keeping both of us afloat until a fishing boat came alongside and pulled us aboard.

I have no memory of his heroism. The last I remember is the cold shock of hitting the water. I drew the story out of Petey bit by bit when he visited me in the asylum. They didn't call it an asylum at Green Gables, of course; they called it a mental health facility, but that sounds so sterile. I called it the Nut Orchard, because that sounded friendlier, more personal.

Pete came to see me three times, each visit farther from the last. Then we wrote letters, and gradually we stopped. But I'll never forget the debt I owe Petey Small, not just for saving my life, but for his constant vigil in the Portland burn center.

The disaster-shaped cloud on the horizon that Sunday morning turned out to be Mount St. Helens, which had chosen the same day I did to self-destruct. That explained the earth shaking beneath my feet—but not quite to the doctors' satisfaction. I was incoherent when they pulled me from the arms of the river, and local medical opinions declared me a danger to myself.

GG was rather posh as institutions go. Robert readily spent the money; not only did the facility have an excellent reputation, it was two thousand miles from Birmingham. I didn't mind it there, really. The nurses were ribald and kind. They shared cigarettes with me when they were on break—I wasn't allowed a lighter of my own—and they treated me more like a friend than a patient. Compared to some of the other residents, I was a pillar of sanity.

Aunt Olivia wrote to me, too. Robert gave her the address. She couldn't afford the cross-country trip to come visit, but I treasured those lovely, food-scented letters full of spelling mistakes. She sent me hand-embroidered pillowcases when I got married. We still write to each other several times a year.

My stay at Green Gables feels like a previous life dimly remembered during hypnosis. Even those idyllic months when David and I first found each other seem hazy and unreal. Probably the medication I was taking clouded those memories, or maybe the shorted-out synapses of my brain. Whatever the cause, I regret that loss of clarity, because those early days with David were the happiest of my adult life.

After we married, David attended classes all day to finish his degree. I puttered in our tiny apartment on the edge of campus, sewing yellow curtains for our windows, experimenting with shrimp soufflé for dinner. Being free from the supervision at Green Gables was a heady, nervous thrill, and I loved my two morning classes at the university.

Most of all, though, I was horny. Both the idea and the physical act of sex with my new husband possessed me totally; it felt so liberating, so *wholesome*. I considered David spectacularly normal, and I couldn't believe he was attracted to me. Certain it wouldn't last, I feasted on his saneness, his beautiful masculine body, and the incredible fact that he actually loved me, at least for a while. I'd have followed him into hell. Luckily, he only took me to Canada.

Thinking of David now, I smile and shift my stiff muscles on the car seat. I've been gone from home four days, and these memories of our first weeks together create an ache inside me. I miss him. Perhaps it's true that we don't value what we have until we almost lose it. I wonder what will become of the two of us.

The trees along the highway open out and I can see the river on my left and the countryside to my right. In contrast to the years at Green Gables, this river valley where I spent my childhood is as real and familiar as the scars that streak my neck and arms. I roll down the window and inhale the scented air. I'm nearing Shady River. In less than an hour I'll see Cincy for the first time since I've been married. In her rare phone calls over the years, our conversations are all politeness and undercurrent. I hang up feeling that I know less about her life than I did before.

Shady River straddles the main highway, but Main Street is one block over. I turn two corners to drive down it. Mr. Tucker's variety store is gone, though the building still stands. A red-lettered sign in the window shouts a sale on used furniture. Only the bank building and the Shady River Inn remain unchanged.

At the single stoplight, I turn south again toward the river. The old bridge is gone. Instead of replacing it, they've built a new one three miles downriver. Made entirely of steel, no doubt, unburnable.

I park on the crumbling edge of blacktop where the bridge used to be and get out of my car. Shading my eyes, I stand on the riverbank and let the smell of the Columbia wash over me. Nothing is left of the old bridge except the two concrete pylons closest to the bank on each side. I imagine the effort and the huge machines it must have taken to remove the steel girders and the center pylons. On the hillside across the channel, no trace remains of the fire that destroyed Rockhaven, but its chimney spire still stands, in memoriam.

A sudden chill sends me back to the car. Driving toward the new bridge, I wonder if Cincy will have arrived ahead of me, or if she'll show up at all.

Gravel crunches beneath the tires as I wind my way up the abandoned road to Rockhaven. Grass sprouts between the tire tracks and a humid breeze sings through the pines. Tomorrow, or perhaps today, is the first day of spring.

Trees and brush shoulder together along the roadside, obscuring the wreckage of the house until the final turn. A dark blue car with a California plate sits on the mat of pine needles that used to be the driveway. I grip the wheel and ease up on the accelerator.

I had hoped for some time alone to pray over the ashes, to compose myself before seeing Cincy again. Now she's here, and my chest closes in on my rabbiting heart.

I park my car beside hers, a small foreign model. Thin lines of rust outline its weathered dents like wrinkles on a face. Cincy left in one beat-up old car and has come back in another. I wonder how the venerable VW finally met its demise.

Cincy is not in sight. I get out, close the car door quietly and stand before the charred remnants of my childhood. The forest has re-claimed its own. Blackened rafters decay beneath thick un-dergrowth and dormant vines climb the side of the chimney spire. A buddleia has gone wild in the living room, its gray-green leaf buds swelling in the afternoon sunshine. Gardeners call it butterfly bush.

God, how I'd loved that house.

My eyes trace the outlines of each room and see two little girls, cross-legged on an oversoft bed, stringing shell necklaces and shar-ing the secrets of their fatherless lives. Where the fallen sunporch once extended over the hillside, I see a lonely preteen in thick glasses, immersed in a magical world where unlovely creatures be-came winged wonders of color and light.

I was only a child. Even when I went off the river bridge, I was only a child. I say it aloud, forgiving myself. Something shifts inside my chest like a gate clicking shut.

My eyes are wet when I turn away from the site and tilt my face toward the wooded hillside that rises behind it. I cup my hands around my mouth and call, "Cincy? I'm here!"

In the stillness that answers, the sizzle of tires drifts up from the road that winds along the river. Somewhere a wren trills out his mating song, and crows caw in the woods. A vein of worry inches through my chest.

"Cin-*cee!*"

Then I hear it. From the slope above, a three-noted whistle jerks me back a dozen years and takes my breath away. Laughing, I force my dry mouth into a whistle, but the airy squeak doesn't even si-lence the wren. I lick my lips and loosen my tongue to try again. Somehow this seems vitally important: *I must return the call.* I pucker up, concentrating all my breath behind the effort.

My whistle rings loud and clear up the slope, and in a moment I hear Cincy's again and see a flash of blue jacket, waving through the treetops on the hill. I know the exact boulder where she's standing. I can picture its shape, feel its warmth on the backs of my legs. I wave vigorously, grinning so hard my face hurts, and clamber up the hill as fast as possible in my inappropriate shoes.

To my slow eyes, nothing appears to be blooming this early in the season, but the hillside above the river is alive with insects who know better. The sun warms me as I work my way upward. In a few minutes, I break into the clearing I was headed for.

Cincy is sitting on a slab of gray granite shaped like the prow of a ship, her feet dangling. The moment I see her I forget the troubling reasons that brought me here; the ten years between us is wiped away.

The pitch of her voice is even deeper than I remembered. In fact, it sounds much like her mother's. "Hey, Sarsaparilla."

"Hey, Rapunzel," I answer, laughing.

She's wearing a T-shirt and jeans with sneakers. When she smiles, her beautiful face lights up. I'd almost forgotten how striking she is. Suddenly I'm thirteen years old again, a girl prowling the hillside with my best friend. I stumble right up and throw my arms around her.

She wasn't ready for this, but I ignore the slight stiffening of her spine and squeeze tighter. In a moment she laughs and hugs me back. When we turn loose, our eyes are liquid.

"I've never seen you in short hair before," I say, touching the shaggy black fringe around her face. "It looks good." But she's too thin, and her skin looks translucent and pale. The wonderful cheekbones seem severe above her hollow cheeks.

"So does yours," she says. "You were ahead of the styles all those years and we didn't know it." My reddish-brown hair, which I used to fight to straighten, now kinks down to my shoulders, held out of my eyes with a clamp.

I hoist myself onto the rock slab beside Cincy and look out across the valley. From here the road is hidden by thickets of fir and pine, but the slate-blue river stretches out beyond, flat and glassy in the slanted light of late afternoon.

"I can't believe we're here," she says.

"Me neither."

In unison we lie back on the rock outcropping like two railroad tracks facing the sky. The sun-warmed granite feels secure against my back and the pleasant hum of the hillside seeps into my bones. I close my eyes and turn my face to the light. One Saturday in spring when we were fourteen, we lay naked on this rock beneath an unseasonably warm sun. Cincy wanted an all-over tan, and I wanted whatever Cincy wanted. The memory makes me smile. Behind my eyelids, the molten world hums with the sound of bees. I wish I could lie here forever without confronting the things we must talk about.

Cincy sits up and retrieves her bundled jacket from the ground. She unrolls it in her lap and two small bottles gleam in the sunshine. She hands me one. "Three six nine, the moose drinks wine."

I accept, grinning. It's one of those little bottles like they serve on airplanes, a chardonnay. I'm not supposed to drink with the medication I'm taking, but what the hell. The glass feels cool and foggy in my hands as I twist off the cap.

Light glints greenly through the bottles. I feel the delicious slow burn move down my throat and warm my stomach. I used to hate the sweet red wine Ruth drank, but this tastes clear and crisp and I am thirsty. In the deepening blue overhead, a nighthawk searches for prey, sweeping higher and higher on pointed wings. Its piercing cry echoes down to us.

"So how are you?" I say finally, instead of *Thanks for coming, where have you been all these years, why did you abandon Lenora and me?*

"I'm okay." Her voice is a shrug. "How about you? Staying out of the Nut Orchard?"

"Uh-huh. David's been a good influence."

"Yeah," she says. "David's a good guy."

Her comment brings me a sudden vision of David haunting the empty house in the mountains, and I hear again the ringing of his unanswered phone.

"You had something to tell me," Cincy says. I can tell she wants it over with, whatever I've come to say.

Where do I start? Mark Twain said if you must swallow two frogs, swallow the big one first. But my courage flags, and I start with the small one.

"Your father is back."

She turns toward me, her face blank. "What? Whose father?"

"Harley Jaines. He came to my house. Then I saw him again outside the prison when I went to see Lenora."

"Harley Jaines?" Her tone is disbelieving, the name strange on her tongue. I imagine her wondering why they let me loose from the orchard.

I try to explain. "He isn't dead. He was missing in action and *presumed* dead. Not dead."

The color drains from her face. "What the fuck..."

"That's why I wanted to tell you in person."

She stares at me, her mouth slightly open. "How do you know it's really him? It could be some screwed-up war buddy, pretending—"

"He looks like that photograph you kept on your dresser. Older, of course, and heavier. Besides, Lenora knows him."

She shakes her head, speechless.

"He wants to see you. He asked me to tell you that."

"I'll be damned." She laughs without humor. "My old daddy, home from the war."

"He's retained a new lawyer for Lenora. She has a parole hearing coming up, but he's going to push for a pardon and try to get her released." I wait a few beats before going on. "He's pressuring me to testify at the hearing. Tell a judge that Lenora didn't set the fire."

We're both quiet. "And?" she says finally. "Are you going to?"

"I don't know. When I saw Lenora yesterday, she ordered me to stay out of it."

Cincy drains her wine and puts the bottle in her jacket pocket.

"Why won't you visit her?" I ask.

She lies back on the rock again. "I should have brought more wine."

"Was it jealousy? You thought she loved me more than you?"

"She did. And to make it worse, you loved Lenora more than me."

My pulse lunges. I have no response for this.

"*Jealousy* is too weak a word," Cincy says, and heat creeps into her voice. "I was destroyed. You were mine since I first found you in the second grade. My best friend. My soul mate." She turns her head to look at me. "You know—the way *you* feel about Lenora."

Above us, the nighthawk screams and swoops toward earth. The wine burns my stomach.

"The night I saw you and Lenora dancing," Cincy says, "I knew you'd chosen each other."

A strangled sound escapes my throat but Cincy pushes on, the words obviously stored up for years.

"I had just sworn to Ruth it wasn't true, convinced her to come talk to you. And then we found you like that."

"It *wasn't* true," I say hoarsely. "I loved her, yes. She was much more of a mother to me than Ruth ever was. But we were never lovers."

"You would have been, though, if she'd wanted it. You'd have walked through fire for her. *Did* walk through fire. You went back into that inferno to get her."

Something rises in my mind like a sea monster floating slowly from the depths. Something I don't want to know, or have always known. I push it away. "Did you ever tell Lenora how you felt?"

"No. But she knew. I blamed her when you left for Birmingham, and we fought all the time." Her voice sags. "Dating all those guys and having sex was a way of getting back at you both. I even seduced the track coach."

"*Mr. Hastings?* He must have been forty!"

"He was single—"

"That's statutory rape!"

"—and he was really nice to me, and we spent a lot of time talking. We were friends." She sighs. "And for his kindness I seduced him and got pregnant. I knew it would ruin his career if anybody found out, so I told Mom I didn't know whose it was. She took me to get an abortion. That's why I looked like shit when you came home."

My breath clots and I can't stop the hand that moves to protect my stomach.

"So I blamed Lenora for that, too," Cincy says. "It's what teenage girls do, I guess, blame everything on their mothers. Look at you and Ruth."

When she sees my face, she stops. "Bobbie?"

I struggle to keep my voice normal. "I'm sorry, Cincy. I never knew."

But I should have known. I should have talked to her the night I went out with Petey Small. Though it's too late, I try to atone by telling her the secret I haven't told Lenora, or even David. "You always were ahead of me. Now I'm the one that's pregnant."

"Really?" She fixes me with an amazed smile. "That's great! You were born to be a mother."

I look at her as if she's sprouted fins. "How can you say that! Look at my family history. Look at my screwed-up life. I've been in the Nut Orchard, for God's sake!"

"Yeah, but you weren't crazy. You just jumped off a bridge." She shrugs. "It was a pretty logical response, under the circumstances. We drove you to it."

I shake my head. "I don't have a maternal bone in my body."

"*That's* total bullshit. You mothered me all through school."

"Me? No, *you* mothered me…."

"You always knew what was right and what was wrong. You were my conscience—when I'd listen. Look at how you mothered those *worms*. And remember that little kid on the train you wrote me about?" Cincy smiles. "You wanted to adopt him for your brother, take him with you. You took care of Ruth, too, as much as you could."

"I can't be responsible for a *baby,* Cincy. What if I ruined her life? I'm too scared."

"That proves your fitness, right there. Only good mothers worry about being good mothers. Besides, you don't have to do it alone like our moms did. You've got David."

My face must look stricken because Cincy says, "Uh-oh. Is it not David's baby?"

"Of *course* it's David's."

"Well, then, what? Isn't he happy about it?"

I find it hard to swallow. "He doesn't know. And I'm not sure he'll be there when I go home."

Cincy shakes her head, her face sad. "Jeez. We're alike in *one* way, Sarsaparilla. Our childhood equipped us to deal with weirdness and trauma, but if something good happens, we don't have a clue."

For a long while we sit in silence. The shadows have grown long and the air cool. Dusk settles on the hill and the sounds of the woods change to night sounds. Crickets chirp; a foghorn echoes on the river.

"You've got to tell David," Cincy says. "It's his baby, too. You're not like me when I was sixteen and screwed up. Mom did what she thought best for me and she was probably right. But David loves you, doesn't he? And he's decent and smart and employed. You're not in this alone. Even if, God forbid, your marriage doesn't last, the kid would still have two parents who love her."

I let that stand for a moment. "So do you."

Cincy scoffs. "Yeah, right."

"Are you going to see Harley Jaines?"

"Why should I? Where's he been all these years?"

"You could ask him."

"If I cared." It's the teenage Cincy, flippant and callous. That's how I know she wants to meet her father but she's scared. When Cincy gets scared, she does crazy things. The sea monster rises to the surface again, echoing her words: *You went back into that inferno to get her.*

The knot I have swallowed for ten years begins to unravel. This is the big frog, the real reason I made this long drive. Not to tell her about Harley Jaines or Lenora's hearing. But to confront the black center of the madness that I've kept buried for so long.

"Cincy, how did you know I went back into Rockhaven while it was burning? That's not something you could have read in the paper."

"No. I saw you."

"You were there?"

"Yes." She looks at me in the semidarkness, waiting. I can see she has waited ten years for me to ask.

"Jesus, Cincy. Ruth didn't set the fire, did she. You did."

When her face turns toward the moonlight, her cheeks glisten. "Yes. I set the fire. Surely you've known that for a long time."

I shake my head.

"I never meant for anyone to die," she says. "I swear. I thought I'd lost the two people I loved most, and instead of jumping off a bridge, I lashed out. I don't expect you to forgive me."

I brace both hands on the granite rock to anchor a weaving sensation in my head. "I might forgive your setting the fire—you felt betrayed, it was an impulsive act. I get that. But how in God's name could you let Lenora go to prison for something you'd done? And stay there *ten years!*"

She turns toward me, her face a wreck. "Don't you see that the truth would be worse for her than prison? Her own daughter set her house on fire and ran, nearly killed her—and you. Do you want her to know that her daughter's a monster?"

I have no answers.

"That's why I can't visit her," Cincy says. "I can't risk telling her the truth. She thinks she's there to protect you. She'll get out soon and go have a life somewhere."

Her voice pleads for understanding, for the forgiveness she doesn't expect. And I know she needs this, especially from me. I can see the millstone of guilt she's carried all these years; it sits on her thin frame like a visible curse. Part of me wants to weep for the misery we all inflicted on one another in the name of love.

But another part of me wants to strangle her and leave her body in the woods. *How could she set Rockhaven on fire? How could she let Lenora stay in prison?*

Once again I cannot give Cincy what she needs. I've got to get away from her—and away from here.

The path down the hillside is draped in moon shadow. I fight my way through brush and trees, my breath ragged, my arms flailing at the darkness.

CHAPTER 23

My room at the Shady River Inn has a squeaky brass bedstead and frilly, Victorian decor, but the plumbing looks much the same as when Ruth worked here years ago. While the shower gathers steam, I take out my contacts and pour two sleeping tablets into my unsteady palm. But just before popping them into my mouth, my hand stops.

What effect might these pills have on an embryo? Once I've thought of this I can't swallow. I put the pills back in the bottle and snap the cap. Without stopping to consider the hour or the possibility of endless, unanswered ringing, I walk to the phone and call David collect.

The machine picks up after the fifth ring. The operator is sorry; my party doesn't answer.

Where is he?

A hot shower soothes my knotted shoulders but still I lie awake in the puffy bed, images flickering through my brain like a slide show run too fast. I see flames in the darkness, feel Ruth's body catch my foot as I stumble. Picture Cincy skulking outside the house, both excited and horrified by what she'd done.

Why doesn't David answer the phone?

Cincy looked so thin, her coloring somehow off. Is she ill? Would she have told me?

My stomach jitters; this could be a very long night. I wish for the sleeping pills' guaranteed oblivion, but try a mantra instead: *Relax your toes, relax. Relax your feet, relax your ankles, and your calves, relax. Relax your knees, relax your thighs, relax your hips, relax.* Somewhere on the fifth trip over each body part, I drift away.

The sun is already high when I awake, streamers of light angling between the motel drapes. If the night was full of dreams, I don't remember them. I resolve to wean myself from the sleeping pills. I've spent too much of my life medicated.

In the inn's breakfast room, I fill small flowered dishes with fruit, yogurt, a bagel, and go back for French toast with syrup. The orange juice is freshly squeezed and the coffee is aromatic and slightly flavored with something I can't name. I take an extra cup for the road.

It's midmorning by the time I pay my bill and unlock my car. While the motor warms up and the wipers swipe dew from the windshield, I think of my mother, who used to make the beds and clean the bathrooms in this hotel, and of the unjustified blame I've heaped on her memory for ten years. I think of Cincy and wonder if she started driving back to California last night. Maybe she slept in her car. I'm still angry about what she's done. But she may be right that the truth could hurt Lenora more than her wasted years.

I don't know what I'll tell Harley Jaines when he inevitably hunts me down to ask if Cincy will see him, and whether or not I'll show up at Lenora's hearing. This morning I know only one thing for sure: I am headed home to David.

It's a good day for driving—clear skies, just hazy enough to keep the morning sun from piercing my eyes as I drive east along the Columbia. I drive faster than usual, my hands confident on the wheel, making good time. Still, it's too far for one day's drive and I'll have to spend one more night on the road. Shortly after noon I stop for a sandwich and try to phone David at the museum. The receptionist is cheerful and connects me with his extension. He picks up on the second ring.

"David Dutreau." His business voice.

After so many failed tries, I am unprepared when he answers. I stand in the phone booth with the rush of traffic outside and try to make my voice work. "David, it's me."

"Roberta?" He sounds relieved and this raises my hopes. "Where are you?"

"South of Spokane someplace, on my way home. I've tried and tried to call you at home."

He pauses before answering. "I've taken a room in town. There wasn't much point in driving all that way every night to an empty house." His voice sounds different now. Sad, and tired.

"I see," I say slowly. "Well, I'll be there tomorrow, around five, I think."

Another pause. "I wasn't sure you were coming home."

"Why not?" I hear only his sigh through the receiver. "Will you be coming home?"

"I don't know. But please call me when you get there, so I know you're safe."

"David? Just how mad at me are you?"

I hear him exhale into the receiver. "I'm not angry anymore. It goes a lot deeper than that."

My breath freezes. "You're leaving me, aren't you?"

"Look, I don't want to discuss this on the phone. But we have some decisions to make. Or you have. I've made mine."

"What is yours?"

I picture him pressing his thumb between his eyebrows the way he does when he's tired or perplexed. He lowers his voice. "I can't talk about this now."

"I'm sorry, sweetheart, I..."

"Don't start apologizing. It's your answer for everything. Apologies won't fix things."

My knuckles whiten around the edge of the tattered phone book inside the booth. "Where are you staying?"

"At the Rosemont Motor Inn near the museum. Wait a minute, I have the phone number here somewhere...555-7373. I'm in room twelve."

I picture a generic motel room, David's shaving kit lined up neatly with the little bottles of shampoo beside the sink. Stale coffee rises in my throat.

"Please call me when you get home," he says.

"I love you, David. Whatever happens, I want you to know that."

When he answers, I hear the hurt in his voice. "Do you realize I can count on the fingers of one hand the times you've said that to me?"

And then the connection is broken.

I stand in the phone booth with my forehead against the cool glass and probe the chasm that has just opened before me. I realize how much I want him to stay, and that it's not just because I'd be lost without him, but because he'd be lost without me. David needs me—not just someone, but me.

It's a powerful feeling, to be needed—like being part of a real family. For a moment I can picture three of us, mother and father and child. My legs are unsteady as I step out of the booth and lean against the car.

If I tell him I'm pregnant, he'll stay. I know this. But he'll stay out of obligation, and I'll never know whether he'd have left me except for our child. Any chance to reconcile for the right reasons would be doomed.

Every mile that uncurls before me routs the chasm deeper. There's too much time to think and no way to stop. I consider taking one of my tranquilizers with the last swallow of my cold coffee, then think of the tiny, curled thing inside my womb and let my hands tremble on the wheel.

At dark I stop at a roadside motel somewhere in Idaho. For dinner I eat ice cream to calm my jittery stomach, but I keep my promise not to take the sleeping pills. I'm rewarded with a restless night, fits of dozing pocked by stressful dreams.

The next morning, waiting in line at the U.S./Canadian border, I consider turning the car around, disappearing into America with nothing but my credit card and three changes of clothes. That's what Cincy did; she just ran, without the credit card or clothes. She had nothing. And look how it turned out for her—drugs, a succession of unsuitable lovers, guilt that festered like a cancer. Much as we might want to be, we aren't like the butterflies that came and went at Rockhaven. For people, there are always consequences.

For hours the road snakes through and around mountains. This time the dramatic scenery slides by unnoticed, eclipsed by the images inside my head. It's growing dark when I pass through the last small town before Calgary, and the road has turned frost-white beneath the headlights. I watch, gripping the wheel, for the road that leads up the mountain to our empty house, but when I see the turnoff my arms stiffen and refuse to turn.

I zoom past, heading toward Calgary. To the Rosemont Motor Inn.

Though I can't picture the motel, I know approximately where it's located. In thirty minutes, I'm turning in the drive. I coast down the line of rooms that open on to the parking lot, looking for number twelve. David's car is not in front of it, nor anywhere in the darkened lot. He probably stopped somewhere for dinner.

I park the Honda on the outside edge of the lot near the street, straighten my hair and lipstick as best I can with the interior light, then head for the motel office. A small, mostly bald man stands behind the desk. No one else is in sight. He smiles when I approach. "Good evening, ma'am."

I give him my friendliest smile. "Good evening. I'm sorry to bother you with this, but I need to get into our room and my husband has the key. Dutreau, room twelve. I wonder if you could please let me in, or issue us another key?"

"Of course. May I see some identification? Hotel policy, you know."

"Certainly." I fumble in my purse and extract my driver's license.

He glances at it, checks the register, then reaches beneath the desk. "Here you are, Mrs. Dutreau." He hands me a plastic card.

"Thanks very much." I smile again and leave quickly, walking down the sidewalk next to the doors that are marked with black painted numbers. I slip the card into the slot above the doorknob and, when a tiny green light flashes, push my way inside.

The room is neat and looks unoccupied. I stop, afraid he has gone, but then I see his shirts and slacks hanging in the closet alcove. His running shoes sit underneath. I touch the shirts, inhale David's scent and close my eyes until my chest stops aching. I use the bathroom, then kick off my shoes and sink into a padded armchair to wait.

I'm asleep when David comes in. When he switches on a lamp in the darkened room, I jerk awake, disoriented.

He stands facing me, looking shocked—not the reaction I'd hoped for. "You're here," he says.

I take a deep breath and sit up straight. "If you're going to leave me, I didn't want to have this scene at home where one of us might have to think about it later every time we walk through the kitchen."

David nods as if he understands. He looks exhausted. I wish we could just go to sleep, holding each other, and talk this out in the morning. But the straight way he holds his spine as he crosses the room to empty his pockets on the nightstand tells me this can't happen.

He sits in the other chair, facing me across a small table that doubles as a desk. He doesn't ask how I'm feeling, or have I eaten. His face is expressionless, past hurt. Maybe past caring.

My voice sounds strained. "You said you'd made a decision. I'd like to hear it."

He looks at his hands, then at me. "I committed to our marriage from the beginning, but you never did. I can't live that way anymore. I shouldn't have to, and I won't." It's a practiced speech and he exhales once he gets it out.

"You're right. You shouldn't have to."

But he's not finished. "I think we should separate until you decide what's important to you. You don't live with me, as it is. You live in the past somewhere."

"I know."

My lack of argument pushes his irritation over the edge. "If you *know,* why don't you snap out of it? Do you *want* to? Do you know how lonely I am in that house? Maybe you don't care."

I take a deep breath and try to say what really matters. "I *do* care. I can't stand to think I might lose you. Can I put everything that happened with Lenora and Cincy out of my mind? Probably not. But I know I've got to put it in perspective—stop reliving it and move on. I was trying to do that, until Harley Jaines showed up."

David shakes his head. "He just brought things to the surface. You've stayed in that house like a captive for nearly four years." He pauses. "When is the hearing in Spokane?"

"I don't know. I'm not going."

"Are you sure?"

I take a deep breath, wondering how to say it simply. "Nothing I could say at the hearing will help Lenora."

He looks at me a long moment. "So you're hiding again."

"What?"

"Maybe you *should* go. Maybe that's what it takes to put an end to it."

"No." I repeat, "Nothing I could say will help Lenora."

In the dim, silent room, the heater hums to life and blots out the sound of traffic from the street. I wait. It seems I've waited forever. David sits slumped in the chair, his head hanging down.

"David? Do you love me?"

"You know I do," he says, almost a mumble. "Lots of people who love each other can't live together."

He's thinking of his parents, how his brother's death ruined them and starved him of the nurturing he needed. They left him alone with his grief and his guilt. He needs me to help him feel whole again, and I've let him down.

"What do you want, really?" I ask. "Would you rather live without me? Would that be easier for you?"

His head lifts and I see tears in his eyes, too. "Damn it, Roberta, nothing's easy. Don't make me sound selfish because I want a real marriage instead of pretending."

"I didn't mean to. What I mean is—" I take a deep breath "—I don't want us to separate. I'm afraid if we do, we'll never go back together." My voice breaks. "I don't want you to leave me."

David can't stand to see me cry. A forlorn sound escapes his throat and he is driven from his chair to kneel beside me. He takes me in his arms.

I hold him fiercely, wanting to melt into his skin so we could never be pulled apart. I think again of the baby; I could tell him now and bind him to me.

And that would be so wrong.

I hold him tightly and dream of a day I can tell him he's about to be a father. I picture us walking the trail behind our house in the snowless, alpine spring, stopping in a meadow to give him the news, making love among the wildflowers.

My hands knead his tense shoulders, move down his back; he doesn't let go. I slide from my chair to press closer to him, slip my fingers into his hair and gently move his face toward mine, kissing his eyes, his temples, feeling the hunger grow in him as it does in me. He lets me slide the jacket from his shoulders, lets me cover his mouth with my lips while I pull his shirttail loose, run my hands beneath it and feel the muscles tense beneath his skin. My chest thickens with wanting him, and I thank whatever gods there be when finally his hands begin to move up my back.

I feel him shiver and let resistance go. He holds me so tightly I can barely breathe, don't want to, and his kiss deepens until everything else goes away but the smell of him, the feel of his wonderful body. I pour into him; there is no me, no David, only a single loving force under its own control, building its own rhythm.

We don't bother moving to the bed; we move into each other. Sex has always been this way for us. But this is more than sex. This is healing; this is loving. He can't leave me after this. And I can't let him.

The next morning when I awake, David is gone.

Chapter 24

The closet alcove stands empty; David's shaving kit is gone from the bathroom. It's midmorning, but with the heavy drapes drawn, the room is still semidark. I stand in the center of the room, naked and shivering, trying to understand what has happened. If he's only gone to work, why would he take all his things?

Then I see the note on the nightstand. I snatch it up, turn on the lamp.

"Making love doesn't change what's wrong between us. I'm going to stay at Mitchell's place for a while. His number is in our lister at home. Call me when you've made your decision. David."

He has left me, after all.

I sink to the floor and wrap my arms tightly around my knees, holding myself together. Rocking back and forth, I stare at the fallen slip of paper until my arms ache and my teeth begin to chatter.

David is gone.

I crawl to my suitcase and pull on my warmest clothes and two pairs of socks. I am cold to the bone.

The desk clerk confirms that David has paid the bill. When I place my key on the desk and pick up the bag that sits beside me, the clerk reads my face and looks at me with pity in his eyes. I turn away.

Outdoors in the sharp, cold morning, the sun is wildly bright. My breath comes out in steamy puffs. So this is it—my marriage is over. My love for David was not enough to save it, my pledge to work at leaving the past behind was too little, too late.

In a moment of strange clarity, I assess my situation: I am alone and pregnant, emotionally unstable, and virtually unequipped for gainful employment. A wrinkle of hysteria rises to the surface. I am poised on a bridge span above a deep and silent river, and I am falling.

"No." I blink my eyes and step back from the brink.

A hand touches my arm. I look up to see a stranger standing at my elbow and I'm surprised to find myself in the motel parking lot, wearing my heavy coat, holding a suitcase.

The stranger is dressed in business clothes, a valise in his hand. "Are you all right?" His voice sounds kind.

I can feel the blankness in my eyes. "I think so. Yes. Thank you."

My car sits straight ahead of me, frost-covered in the morning sunlight. I walk toward it stiffly, leaving the stranger there with a quizzical look on his face. I unlock the door and get inside.

Breathe and blow.

The engine springs to life and I steer carefully onto the street, aware that it's dangerous to drive when I'm this distracted. I scan the intersection twice, left and right, before crossing.

David knows I love him, and that I am trying to put myself together. If that's not enough, there's nothing more I can do. Other people lose husbands or wives, and they move on. Surely my life is worth living even without him.

I have choices. I could keep the baby—have someone to love—although right now that seems like a supremely selfish act. I put off that decision until later. Not today.

Right now I'll just drive home. One mile at a time. In those familiar surroundings, I will decide what to do, how to live. Where to hunt for a job. I could call Robert for a loan, if I had to. He and Joey would send money to keep me a safe distance from Alabama. I haven't seen my father since he visited me at Green Gables nearly a decade ago. When I told him to go away and leave me alone, I'd never seen anybody so relieved.

Maybe I'll call Dr. Bannar, ask if I can work at the hospital. But no—if I go back there, I'll be dependent again. I'm sick of being dependent. I think of Bobbie Lee at fifteen, catching a train to find a new life. For the first time in years, I recognize that girl as me. Until now she has seemed like a separate person; we even had different names—Bobbie Lee, Roberta Dutreau.

I turn up the mountain road toward home. It feels like years since I left, though it's been less than a week. An early spring sun has shrunk the mounds of snow beside the entrance to the driveway. I park the Honda in the detached garage and walk past the picnic table to the back door. A lone mountain jay flutters away from the empty bird feeder, scolding. Poor things. I must put out seeds for them. They're as hungry as I am—it's past noon and I haven't eaten since yesterday lunch.

In the kitchen I grab two granola bars and devour the first as I carry my bag upstairs. The house smells deserted. I open the bedroom curtains and let sunlight flood the quiet room. The message machine by the phone blinks spastically. I count the blinks—at least a dozen. David hasn't been home in days. I push the playback button and let the tape rewind while I unpack my bag and eat the other granola bar.

My own voice comes on the tape, tired and tense when I tried to reach David. There are a couple of hang-ups, possibly sales calls, or David calling home to see if I've arrived.

And Harley Jaines. His bass voice overpowers the scratchy quality of the tape. I stop midmotion to listen.

"Mrs. Dutreau, please call me at this number as soon as you can." He reads the phone number twice. Our machine doesn't give date and time, so I can't tell when he called.

Next a lady from some charity wants us to make a donation; then the nurse at the family-planning clinic comes on the line. She sounds cheery and says tactfully that they're just following up to see how I'm feeling.

Then Harley Jaines again: "Mrs. Dutreau. It's important that I talk with you right away. The hearing is set for Friday at 9:00 a.m., at the Spokane courthouse. This is Wednesday evening. If I don't get a call from you tomorrow morning, I'll plan to come pick you up." His tone is sternly polite, a veiled threat.

I scramble the desktop for a calendar, trying to figure out what day this is. Thursday. I exhale relief. I can still call him and avoid his visit. I'll tell him straight out that I will not testify at the hearing. What can he do, break my neck? Do I care?

There's one more message, which must have been left this morning. David's voice sounds tired. "Bobbie, I drained the pump before I left the house, so it wouldn't freeze up while nobody was there. You'll have to turn it back on, and then turn the water on to the house, if you're going to stay there."

If I'm going to stay here? Where else would I go?

His voice pauses and I hear the whir of the blank tape passing. "I.... Call me if you can't get the water on."

Not a word about last night, about leaving me while I slept. My face burns. I slam the empty suitcase into the closet. *I can turn on the damned water without your help, David. I've done it before.*

First I dial Harley Jaines's number and am grateful when I get a recording. I leave my terse message: Do not come out here; leave me the hell alone.

Downstairs I swig orange juice and pour out the milk, which has gone bad. In the utility room, I pull on my fleece-lined boots and my parka and gloves. The morning has warmed and icicles drip from the eaves, but I'll still have to wade through snow to get to the pump house, and the metal handle of the water lever would freeze my bare hands. I'm glad for this chore to do, something physical, an act of self-sufficiency.

I scoop up a bucket of birdseed and take it along, filling the feeders and scattering extra on the ground around the picnic table. By the time I walk to the pump house and look back, birds are swarming the seeds already. I smile, not quite so alone.

Maybe I *could* live here by myself. But then, where would David go? It's his house, after all.

I'll think about that later. Right now, I need water so I can flush the john.

I pry open the pump house door and step inside, find the pull-cord to the bare bulb overhead and stoop to my work. A small electric coil heats the shack just enough so the pump won't freeze up on cold Canadian nights, and David has left this on. I turn on the power to the pump and listen to its whir and gurgle. Then I place both gloved hands on the curved steel bar that turns the water on and off and shove, putting my weight behind it.

The darned handle's stuck. I heave at it again, give it a kick. Still it won't budge. The thought of calling David to drive out here and push this handle is unacceptable; he'd think it was an excuse. This simple task becomes a test of my fitness to live without a caretaker. I refuse to let it defeat me.

The pump house is no larger than a closet, with no elbow room. I wedge myself onto the concrete floor between the wall and the pump, brace my back against a beam and both feet against the handle. I take a deep breath and push the lever as hard as I can, swearing for added strength.

When the handle goes, my feet slip. I sprawl on my back on the cold floor, legs entangled in the hardware of the pump. I have to inch my torso out the doorway and crawl out onto the snow like a cater-pillar.

"Bobbie?"

The deep voice jolts me so badly I nearly wet my clothes. I jerk myself into a sitting position and look up into the stolid face of Harley Jaines.

In person, he's not so formal as he was on the phone—he uses my nickname. And as I stagger to my feet, resentful that he's star-tled me, it is Bobbie Lee, not Roberta, who faces him.

He stands in the patchy snow twenty feet away, hatless, dark and bulky even in his light jacket. And he's not alone. The man with him wears a khaki jacket with dark blue pants and a police-style hat. I recognize the uniform—Royal Canadian Mounted Police.

I scowl at Harley Jaines. "What are you doing here? I called your number and left a message." My voice sounds shrill in the moun-tain silence.

"We're out of time." He nods to the tall man beside him. "This is Constable Sanbourn."

The Mountie touches his cap. "Ma'am. I'm sorry to surprise you this way, but I've been ordered to serve you this subpoena." He steps forward, pulling an envelope from an inside pocket. He is very tall.

I back up as he holds the envelope out to me. "A subpoena? What for?"

"The Washington State judicial system wants you to appear in court in Spokane on the twenty-eighth of March. To testify at an evidentiary hearing for a woman prisoner down there."

"What...?"

He pushes the envelope forward again, insistent, and I put out my hand without looking at it.

"The state has agreed to reopen Lenora's case," Harley Jaines says. "This is a hearing to consider whether or not there's sufficient new evidence to give Lenora the trial she should have had ten years ago."

"What new evidence is that?"

Both of them stare at me. I stare back.

"You're the new evidence," Harley Jaines says. "You can tell them what really happened."

My parka is suddenly too hot; my heartbeat pounds against my cheeks. "No, I can't. I didn't see who set the fire."

"We have evidence of what you tried to tell the police and Lenora's attorney at the time. And we found out your mother set fire to the house where you used to live in Atlanta. Along with your testimony, there's plenty to get a trial."

"Lenora doesn't want this. It's all your doing."

Harley Jaines meets my eyes, but evades the accusation. "We're going to get at the truth. One way or another."

"You'll have to do it without me. I'm not going."

The constable scuffs the toe of his boot in the snow and then looks at Harley Jaines. "That's all I can do," he says. "I have no authority to arrest her on a Washington State subpoena."

Harley nods, and I see his jaw harden. The Mountie touches the brim of his hat again and nods in my direction, then crunches back across the yard toward the driveway. A crazy moment of triumph surges to my head. Could it be that easy?

It takes me a moment to realize that the mountie is leaving me alone with Harley Jaines. I call after him but it's too late. His cruiser springs to life and rolls down the driveway.

Harley and I face off in silence. He is calm, expressionless, his eyes black as ravens. I remember what Lenora told me about his working undercover for the government in Southeast Asia. *They disappeared him.*

He shoves his fists into his jacket pockets and I wonder how many men he has killed with those hands. I wrap my arms around my abdomen.

"I thought you and Lenora were close," he says. "Why don't you want to help her?"

I think of Lenora, ordering me to stay out of it and get on with my life; and of Cincy, her haunted eyes. "I didn't see anyone set the fire. I can't help her."

There's no hint of understanding now in Harley Jaines's eyes. They narrow as he squints against the sunlight. "I think you can. I'm not leaving here without you."

A rush like silent wings runs through me. I'm acutely aware of our isolation here, my powerlessness in the face of superior physical strength.

"We can do this the easy way or the hard way," he says.

"Dead or alive?" My sarcasm doesn't quite cover the tremor in my voice.

He says nothing, his eyes locked on my face. I flash on an image of him shoving me bodily into his car, or perhaps drugging me. I'd be less trouble that way. *Just go with him. What else can you do? He can drag you into the courtroom, but he can't make you testify.*

But what if the judge can? What will I say?

"I see. Well, then." I swallow, pretending to be calm. "I'll drive my own car. The hearing is Monday?"

"It's tomorrow morning. That's why we're going now. Together."

I can't think what to do. I stare at him, waiting.

"We'll drive straight through tonight. I have a place in Spokane where you can rest and clean up before we go to the courthouse." When I don't respond, he says, "You'll probably want to pack a few things."

I start walking toward the house and he follows. He's right behind me at the back door, gripping the door frame so I can't shut and lock it. I turn and look at him, close enough to feel his body heat. His expression chills me.

He follows me upstairs and watches as I put a change of clothes and some toiletries in an overnight bag. "Take a pillow for the car," he says. "You might as well get some sleep."

I lay the pillow beside the closed suitcase, take clean slacks and a shirt from the closet and start toward the bathroom. He moves to follow.

"I have to pee!"

He steps ahead of me and glances into the bathroom. The window isn't operable, so he steps aside.

His presence looms outside the door while I use the bathroom and change clothes. The toilet flushes; I've succeeded in turning on the water. Leaning over the sink, I splash icy water on my face and blot it with a towel. My head feels light. In the mirror my skin looks bleached. His fist rattles the door and makes me jump.

I exit the bathroom without looking at him and pick up my pillow. He takes the bag and shadows me downstairs. At the last minute, standing in the kitchen with the lights already turned off, I decide to leave a note—some record of what's happened to me. I scribble a few words on the telephone pad and toss it on the kitchen table, but who would find it? David won't be home tonight.

Harley Jaines locks the door behind us while I walk ahead of him out of the house, clutching the pillow to my chest. He puts my bag and pillow in the back and opens the passenger-side door, waits while I climb inside. Then he leans across me and fastens my seat belt as if I'm a child. His scent imprints itself on my memory—no cologne, just the slight trace of soap and his unique male smell.

I forget to breathe. The ringing in my ears is louder than the engine when he starts the car. *Breathe and blow.* It wouldn't do to pass out now.

As we lurch away, I look back at the house from the window of Harley Jaines's black vehicle.

I forgot to turn the water off. If there's a hard freeze, the pipes might burst.

David will have to deal with that. I feel as if I'll never see this place again.

CHAPTER 25

In the car with Harley Jaines, I sit stiffly on the front seat as we wind down the mountain road toward the highway. We do not speak. At the junction where I had turned west six days ago, choosing the scenic route to Spokane, Harley Jaines turns east toward Calgary.

In half an hour we're in the city. Traffic has begun to thicken toward the evening rush hour but he drives fast, braiding a path among the slower cars. He connects with the freeway that drops south out of the city and soon the suburbs are behind us. We spear through flatlands with the mountains to our right. Gradually my chest loosens and a feeling of inevitability takes over. I can't escape; there's no point sitting here wound up like a spring. My fists unclench, and I begin to wonder about this man who has basically kidnapped me.

Something about his profile reminds me of Cincy. I try to pinpoint the resemblance. The nose? The heavy eyebrows? Maybe it's the way his shoulders lean slightly forward, like an unspoken challenge. Another similarity: Harley Jaines does not spend his free time obsessing about his car. The windshield is smeared with road scum and insect innards, and the floorboard grits beneath my shoes. Cincy's car looked much the same.

Two hours pass with nothing but road noise and the whistle of wind through an inch of open window. I have plenty of time to imagine the hearing in Spokane, what the courtroom will look like. I picture myself on a witness stand, a stern voice demanding, *Do you know who set the fire that killed your mother?*

If I refuse to answer, will the judge keep Lenora locked away?

If I refuse, will the judge lock *me* away?

The divided highway ends and we turn west toward the Rockies. I spread my feet on the sandy floorboard to absorb the curves. Harley Jaines glances over at me. He switches on the radio, a country-and-western station, and adjusts the volume low.

"You hungry?" he says.

"Yes." But mostly I'm thirsty.

The highway is strung with small towns. He chooses one and pulls through the drive-in window of a fast-food restaurant. Without consulting me, he orders hamburgers and colas to go and we roll on, chewing up the miles.

We cross out of Alberta into British Columbia. I feel disoriented, lost in space. My head drops back against the seat, wanting sleep. After a while I rouse and see darkened roadsides beyond the reach of the headlights. My bladder is full to bursting. "I need a rest room stop."

Harley Jaines pulls off the road at a café where semitrailer rigs are parked like slanted dominoes in an acre-wide lot. According to the road sign just past the driveway, we have connected with the highway to Cranbrook, which I drove through before. At least I know where we are.

When I come out of the ladies' room, he's waiting with foam cups of coffee, which I decline. "Want to get in the back so you can sleep?"

He opens the back door and I climb in, drop my purse on the floorboard and prop the pillow against the opposite armrest. "There's a blanket behind the seat," he says. He controls the door locks from the driver's seat.

Some time later, I awake and watch the flicker of passing headlights on the ceiling of the car. He has opened his window a crack for fresh air and he's humming with the radio—*All my exes live in Texas.*

What about your ex-lives, Harley Jaines? Where do they live?

We're slowing down, and I realize we must be nearing the U.S. border. I unkink my legs and sit up, my head still thick with sleep. It's the same crossing I drove through a week before, one that's open twenty-four hours a day. Harley Jaines pulls forward and stops beside an officer who wears a military haircut. The officer's eyes flicker from the ID Harley Jaines offers to his face, and back again. He shines his flashlight around the inside of the vehicle, then asks to see my ID. Harley Jaines waits with his foot on the brake, the motor running. I think of shouting that I've been kidnapped, but suddenly the officer gives a short salute, Harley Jaines returns the gesture, and we zoom through the checkpoint and across the border.

Someplace in Idaho, I awaken as the car rocks to a stop. I sit up and recognize the town as Sandpoint, an hour or so north of Coeur d'Alene. The dashboard clock reads 1:00 a.m., which I assume is Pacific time.

"Let's get some breakfast," Harley Jaines says.

I climb out, my legs stiff and painful. My hair sticks up and my mouth tastes like pond scum.

Inside the all-night restaurant, I slump opposite Harley Jaines in a gold-vinyl booth. Despite the hour, he looks wide-awake.

The middle-aged waitress with a face as tired as God pours coffee into Harley Jaines's upturned mug. I decline coffee and scan the menu. The aroma of sausage and pancakes roils my stomach, but apparently it smells good to him because that's what he orders, with eggs sunny-side up. I suppress a shudder, order dry toast, tea and orange juice. Harley Jaines looks at me as if I'm crazy.

When the waitress has gone, we lean back in the booth and eye each other.

"Did you talk to Cynthia?" he says.

My first impulse is to deny anything he asks. But what's the point? "Yes."

"You told her I'm here? And want to see her?"

"Yes."

He waits while the waitress refills his coffee and sets down the makings for my tea. I pour hot water over the tea bag and let it steep.

"What did she say?"

"She said, 'I'll be damned. My old daddy, home from the war.'"

It's a direct quote, but it sounds like a flip answer and I wait for him to react. He merely nods and stirs his coffee. His silence gets on my nerves.

"Why did you wait so long to find Lenora?"

He doesn't look up or show surprise at my sudden question. "I didn't think she'd want to see me."

"Because you abandoned her?"

"Yes. And because of things that happened over there."

I wonder what, exactly, he did in the jungles of Cambodia, why he couldn't come home. But the answers might be too heavy to know.

"I wasn't the same man she knew before I went to 'Nam," he says. "She didn't want me to go. Thought the war was wrong."

"Was it?"

When he meets my eyes, his are so dark they stop my teacup midway to my lips. "All war is wrong."

When the food arrives, my stomach jitters. Harley Jaines's plate is a sea of grease. I manage to get down one point of toast and some orange juice before he cuts into a fried egg and yellow goo spurts out.

I sprint for the bathroom.

I'm hanging over the commode in the first stall, having lost my toast and orange juice, when Harley Jaines comes into the ladies' room. He wets a paper towel, folds it into a square and hands it to me. I bathe my sweating face.

"I guess you're pretty scared about this," he says to my back. "Either that or you're pregnant."

My head jerks up and I look at him. He is leaning against the row of lavatories, his face impassive.

He can't know. He's only making conversation.

A woman appears at the open door of the ladies' room and takes in the both of us before she scowls and turns away. I go to the sink and rinse out my mouth.

"I'll go pay for breakfast," he says. "As soon as you're okay, we'll get going."

In the parking lot, I opt for the front seat, too woozy to ride in back. Standing in the circle of light from a street lamp beside the car, he waits for me to buckle up, then hands me two packets of soda crackers.

"Here. These help the morning sickness sometimes."

I meet his dark eyes and see something there I haven't noticed before. Not a softness, exactly, but some capacity I wouldn't have guessed. "Thanks."

He hands me a lidded cup, as well. "It's 7UP."

He gets in and starts the car. I tear open a cellophane packet and take a bite of salty cracker. "How did you know?"

Harley Jaines pulls out of the parking lot and onto the main road before he answers. And when he does, the voice is even heavier than usual.

"I've lived a long time."

* * *

It's nearly 3:00 a.m. when we arrive at Harley Jaines's apartment on the same side of town as the women's prison. I stand in the doorway, sluggish from dozing in the car, while he enters and turns on lights. Everything about the apartment looks temporary, undoubtedly furnished. The fixtures are cheap but clean; the carpet looks like gray artificial turf. From where I stand, I can see no personal effects. He motions me inside.

"Is this where you live?"

"No. I stay here when I'm visiting Lenora. You can use the bedroom, I'll crash on the couch. I'll wake you in a few hours. We need to be at the courthouse by eight."

When I don't move, he glances away. "There's a lock on the bedroom door."

I don't bother to use it. Lying on top of the rip-cord bedspread, I pull the edge over me, roll into a fetal position and stare into the darkness. In a matter of hours, a judge will ask me what happened the night of the fire. Last week it would have been easy to blame the fire on my mother. Now I cannot. Will not. Even in the time-honored arena of blaming mothers, there's a line that should not be crossed.

I think of the last words my mother said to me. *I tried to save you,* she whispered, and I thought she meant from the mortal sin I'd inherited from my father. But in fact she'd tried to save my life, despite what she thought I shared with Lenora. A mother's love is the only explanation; Ruth must have loved me, after all.

I think of Cincy ten years ago, a confused teenager, just like me. She'd been through an abortion, and she believed the two people she loved most had betrayed her. Instead of jumping off a bridge, she reacted with anger. How can I blame her? Maybe she wasn't rational enough to think about the consequences, to realize we might die in the fire. Or maybe she was.

I don't know if the truth would free Lenora or do irreparable harm. But I do know one thing: if I go to court and name Cincy as the arsonist, Lenora will hate me for it.

I'm still awake when Harley Jaines's knock rattles the door. While I clean up and change clothes, he makes coffee and wheat toast with pieces of crust torn away, probably where the bread had gone moldy. We don't talk. I slather two slices with huckleberry jam and feed the sugar to my jumping pulse. The orange juice Harley Jaines pours from a can tastes like metal.

We drive through the heart of Spokane and turn west on Broadway. A strange castlelike building looms ahead of us like something displaced from Disneyland. Its French Renaissance turrets spike upward into an overcast sky.

"Look at that," I say, pointing listlessly.

"That's where we're going," he says. "That's the county courthouse."

He finds a parking place along the street. Huge maples stretch newly leafed branches above the courthouse lawn. The morning air feels cool and damp. On the sidewalk, I entertain a quick vision of bolting across the lawn and fleeing into the unfamiliar streets beyond. But I never was a fast runner. I take a deep breath and step through the door Harley Jaines holds open for me.

People in business clothes move through the quiet marble hallways. A woman behind an information desk directs us toward a wide staircase and we climb to the third floor. At one end of the hallway a man in an expensive gray suit is pacing the floor. When he sees us, he strides forward.

"You made it," he says to Harley Jaines, glancing at me with a slight nod. He pauses as if waiting for an introduction; none is forthcoming. I assume he is the attorney Harley Jaines hired.

"There's a witness lounge where you can wait," the man says. His shoes click on the marble floor as he ushers us to the opposite end of the hall and opens a door, standing aside.

The room holds a sofa and chair, a coffee table spread with well-thumbed magazines. A lamp beside the sofa has collected years of dust in its shade.

"I'll come get you when we're ready." The attorney disappears.

Harley Jaines and I look at each other. "I'll wait in the hall," he says. I know he's standing guard outside the door.

The room is quiet except for distant footsteps and voices. I pace the floor and wonder if Lenora is waiting in another such room somewhere in the building, and if they keep her handcuffed like a real criminal.

Lenora wants me to keep quiet and leave the past alone.

Harley Jaines wants me to say that my mother set the fire.

Ruth won't be there to defend herself.

And neither will Cincy.

CHAPTER 26

I've never been in a courtroom before. It is smaller than I'd pictured but imposing enough, with wood-paneled walls and rows of leather armchairs in the empty jury box. Half a dozen people are loosely assembled in the spectator pews when the attorney escorts Harley Jaines and me into the room. We sit there, as well, while the attorney goes to a table in front of the railing. My fingers twist and untwist the strap of my purse.

On the wall behind the judge's bench hangs a bas-relief Seal of the Superior Court of Spokane County. Ferns cascade from hanging pots in front of north-facing windows. The loamy scent of potting soil blends with the used air of the courtroom, and for a moment I'm reminded of the sunporch at Rockhaven. I hazard a guess that this is the domain of a woman judge. My mind's eye sees a flickering parade of defendants and plaintiffs whose lives were changed in this room.

There's movement behind us and somehow I know that Lenora is here. Before I can turn my head, a side door at the front opens and a bailiff announces, "All rise."

I have guessed right about the judge. A slim woman with short, brownish-gray hair, she sweeps into the room and gestures to the polished oak table where the attorney stands. "Take your seats, everybody," she says, in the voice of someone accustomed to being obeyed.

The table runs perpendicular to the judge's bench, unlike the ones I've seen on TV, and there are chairs on both sides. Instead of sitting above us, the judge comes to the head of the table and waits impatiently for everyone to be seated. Her eyes are light blue and hard as glass.

Lenora's attorney, still standing, looks at me. "Ms. Dutreau, we need you up here, please." Reluctantly, I leave my pew and walk forward.

Lenora will not meet my eyes as she is ushered to a seat across the table from me. The attorney sits beside her. Devoid of makeup, her face looks gray against her loose prison uniform. A police officer joins us at the table, and another man, whom I assume to be from the prison because of the hefty file he places in front of him.

Finally Lenora looks at me. "Bobbie, don't do this," she whispers.

I look at her urgent expression, her wonderful wrecked face, and am overcome with sorrow. How can I leave her to serve more years in prison?

The judge frowns and clears her throat. "This is not a trial," she announces. "This is a hearing to determine if new evidence exists that would warrant a trial for Lenora Jaines—" she consults a paper in front of her "—on the charges from 1980 of arson and second-degree manslaughter—apparently a plea bargain, or she'd have faced a murder charge."

She clears her throat again and puts the paper down. "I want to hear first from you, Ms. Jaines."

"Your Honor..." Lenora's attorney begins.

"I said, I'll hear from *Ms. Jaines*."

The attorney casts a worried glance at Harley Jaines in the spectator pews.

"Ms. Jaines," the judge says, "you confessed to setting this fire and accidentally causing the death of Ruth Lee, who supposedly came into the burning house to rescue her daughter. Is this correct?"

"Yes," Lenora says.

"And do you now recant that confession?"

"No, Your Honor."

The judge looks irritated. "Then why are we here?"

The attorney jumps in. "To learn the truth, Your Honor. Mr. Jaines has retained me on Lenora's behalf because he has uncovered evidence that Lenora did not in fact set the fire, but confessed to protect someone. That person is here today."

The judge glances at her notes. "And that would be you, Ms. Dutreau." She pronounces my name correctly. Her sharp eyes examine my face.

"Yes, ma'am." I clear my throat.

"I understand that you had to be subpoenaed to attend this hearing."

"Yes, ma'am." *I had to be kidnapped.*

"Your Honor, may I?" the attorney asks.

She sighs. "Go ahead."

"Ms. Jaines's former attorney, one Leonard Shavers, wrote in his notes that Ms. Dutreau—then Roberta Lee, the deceased's daughter—had told him in her hospital room that the deceased, Ruth Lee, actually set the fire. And that Ms. Jaines was protecting Roberta Lee, who was fifteen at the time, from that knowledge. Ms. Jaines and Roberta Lee had a very close relationship, one that apparently aroused a fierce jealousy in Roberta's mother, who was a known alcoholic."

"I've read the brief, Counselor," the judge says, her face impassive. "You're telling me your client confessed and went to prison so the girl, Roberta Lee, wouldn't realize her mother tried to kill her?"

"Yes, Your Honor."

"That seems a bit far-fetched."

"Ms. Jaines loved Roberta Lee as if she were her own daughter." The irony of this phrase impales me. I glance at Lenora and for a moment our eyes meet. She looks away.

"And where is this attorney, Leonard Shavers?"

The attorney looks disappointed. "Unfortunately, he suffered a heart attack and died two weeks ago, Your Honor. The judge in Skamania County who heard the case ten years ago is also deceased. We asked for the transfer to Spokane County as a matter of convenience since Ms. Jaines was incarcerated here. But you have a copy of Leonard Shavers's notes in your record."

"Yes, and they're pretty sketchy. He didn't give much credence to what Miss Lee had to say."

"We've also asked Sergeant Davis here to testify," the attorney says.

The judge nods to him. "Sergeant?"

The officer I didn't recognize leans forward, resting his forearms on the table. He sits tall in his chair and his arms are muscular. "I was on duty the morning of May 18, 1980, at Shady River Police Station. I remember it clearly because that was the morning Mount St. Helens blew up."

I stare at him, another ghost from the past.

"I got a call," the sergeant continues, "very early for a Sunday morning, from someone who sounded like a teenage girl. She didn't identify herself but said she was a friend of Lenora Jaines's and wanted to come see her. When I told her Ms. Jaines had been transferred to the county seat at Stevenson, she freaked out. Started yelling that Ms. Jaines was innocent, that she didn't set the fire.

"We'd been looking for Bobbie Lee—everybody called her Bob-

bie instead of Roberta then—since she'd turned up missing from
the hospital the night before. I suspected it was Bobbie on the
phone, so I tried to calm her down and find out where she was, but
she hung up. An hour or so later, some fishermen pulled her out
of the river, along with the young man who'd kept her from drown-
ing." The officer shrugs and stops speaking.

"Was that phone call from you, Ms. Dutreau?" the judge asks.

"Yes, ma'am."

"I appreciate your fine manners," she says dryly, "but can you add
anything to these proceedings except *yes, ma'am?*"

I clear my throat, which is dry as sand. "What do you want me to
say?"

"Let me remind you that you're in a court of law, and though
we're doing this informally, you are compelled to tell the truth,"
she warns. "I can have you sworn in if we need to. Do we?"

"No, Your Honor."

"Do you know who set that fire, Ms. Dutreau?"

I look directly at the judge, avoiding Lenora's eyes and the specter
of Harley Jaines in the seats behind us. "Yes."

"Was it Lenora Jaines?"

"No, ma'am. It was not."

I feel the breath escape from Lenora's attorney. Lenora shakes
her head.

"Who did set the fire, Ms. Dutreau?"

I fasten my gaze on a gold button at the neck of the judge's robe.
There's a moment of silence while Her Honor waits. My mother's
face—her whole dismal life and terrible death—flash before me.
I think of Cincy at sixteen, even more disturbed than I was, though
I was too self-involved to see.

I think of my broken marriage, my pregnancy, the years of therapy with Dr. Bannar that are about to go up in smoke.

"I did, Your Honor."

Lenora looks horrified. "That's a lie!"

"Quiet," the judge snaps. The bailiff looms behind her.

The judge's ice-blue eyes search my face. "Why would you do such a thing, and then let someone you loved go to prison for it?"

"I set it because I wanted to die. The same reason I jumped off the bridge. I didn't want Lenora to go to prison, but they did it so fast I couldn't stop them. I was in the hospital."

"Your Honor, please, this is not right," Lenora says, her face pleading.

The judge considers me for a moment. "You told Leonard Shavers that your mother set the fire."

"I was fifteen, and desperately angry with her. Besides, my mother was already dead. I thought it couldn't hurt her." To me, my voice sounds flat and tired; I wonder if it sounds credible to the judge.

Lenora's attorney looks stunned. "Ms. Dutreau had a mental breakdown, Your Honor. She was institutionalized for several years."

I can't tell if he intends to support what I've said or to discredit me. I glance at the judge to read her expression, but her eyes have fastened on something else, someone entering the courtroom. Every head at the table turns to follow her gaze.

Cincy is standing at the railing.

I hear Lenora's breath suck in and my heart lurches.

"I need to speak, Your Honor," Cincy says. "I'm Cynthia Jaines."

Cincy's face is stark below the dark fringe of her hair. Her clothes seem too large.

Behind her, Harley Jaines leans forward in his seat, his face intense as he sees his grown daughter for the first time.

"Were you present the night of the fire?" the judge asks Cincy.

"Yes."

"Come forward, then."

Cincy comes to the table but does not sit. She stands behind an empty chair, gripping its back with bony fingers. "Bobbie didn't set the fire."

"I doubt she did, either," says the judge. "But why would she say so?"

"She has no choice. It's the only thing she can say without blaming it on her dead mother or betraying her childhood friend." Cincy's dark eyes meet mine and she tries to smile.

"And that friend would be you?" the judge asks.

"Yes," she says. "I'm the one who really set the fire."

"You did?" The judge heaves an exaggerated sigh and leans back in her chair. "Wonderful. *Everybody* is Spartacus."

Her Honor frowns at Cincy. "Why should I believe *you,* when I have all these other choices?" She sweeps a hand around the table.

Cincy's fingers are white on the chair back, and her eyes flicker to Lenora's. Lenora's face has lost its practiced prison composure and for a moment betrays the deepest loneliness I've ever seen.

Suddenly I realize *she knows.*

My God, she has always known.

Cincy fixes her gaze on the courtroom wall and begins to recite the details that are necessary to convince the judge. "I went to Ruth's house that night to find Bobbie, and instead I found Ruth drinking and bawling. She told me she'd been awful to Bobbie, that she'd sent her away and would never see her again. I tried to convince her there was no sexual relationship between Bobbie and my mother or me. I begged her to go to Rockhaven with me, to reconcile with Bobbie. Finally she agreed but insisted on driving herself so she could leave when she wanted."

Cincy swallows, looks down at her hands, then back at the judge. I am torn between wanting to hear her side of the story and wishing she had kept her secret forever.

"When Ruth and I walked in," Cincy says, "I saw Bobbie and my

mother together on the sunporch. They were…dancing. I thought
they'd betrayed me. That everything I'd said to Ruth for Bobbie's
sake was a lie." Her voice breaks, but her face shows no emotion.
"I couldn't let myself feel that much hurt. Instead I hated them both,
and I hated Ruth, too, for being there."

Cincy takes a deep breath. "Ruth drove off and I followed. I could
hardly see the road. She stopped her car on the other side of the
river bridge and I stopped, too, but I didn't get out. Ruth came to
the window, ready to say *I told you so* until she saw how crazy I was.
I started ranting and yelling and she tried to calm me down. I
jammed the car in gear and took off.

"I drove as fast as I could along the river road until I had a plan.
Then I shot a U-turn and came back to Rockhaven." Cincy squints
toward the distant memory. "I hid the VW way down from the
house and walked up the hill and waited in the trees. When the
lights were out except for the little one Mom always left on for me,
I made myself wait some more. Then I got the gas can we kept in
the garage and sneaked into the kitchen. I sloshed gasoline all over.
Struck a handful of kitchen matches at once. I threw them and
ran."

She crosses her arms on her chest and rubs them, shivering. Her
voice drops to a whisper. "I had no idea the place would go up so
fast. I barely got out the door. I hid in the trees, and in a minute
Ruth's car came racing up the hill. She jumped out and ran inside—
I guess she'd seen the flames. I thought she would warn them, get
them out.

"I wanted to run but I couldn't move. I heard sirens across the
river. Then I saw Bobbie crawl out the front door and I started crying, *thank God, thank God, she's safe.*" Cincy looks at me. "But you went
back in. And I knew you'd gone in to get Lenora.

"Then the roof fell. The first fire truck got there and I ran
through the trees down to the car, terrified I'd be caught. As soon

as the second truck had gone up the hill, I tore out onto the river road and kept driving. I was so scared. I felt like a monster for what I'd done."

Cincy's voice turns harder. "When I got to Portland I took the highway south and drove all night till I ran out of gas. I let some guy at a filling station screw me for twenty bucks and a fill-up, and kept on driving until I got to California. I didn't know Ruth had died, or what happened to Bobbie or my mother, until months later. I just hid."

The courtroom is silent. Nobody moves.

I remember what Cincy said about my suicide attempt: *We drove you to it.* Just as surely, we drove Cincy to it. Of the four of us, I was luckiest. I'd only gone insane.

Lenora buries her face in her hands and her shoulders shudder.

"Bobbie kept quiet all these years not just to protect her mother," Cincy says, "but to protect Lenora from knowing what I'd done. Can you imagine?" she asks the judge. "All I wanted was for them to love me as much as they loved each other."

Lenora rises from her chair. Her attorney puts his hand on her arm but she shakes it off. When she speaks her voice sounds hoarse.

"You're wrong, Cincy. I went to prison because I knew it was you."

Their eyes connect.

"You *knew?*" Cincy whispers.

In the silence that follows, a thrumming sound rises in my ears. Cincy must hear it, too, because she doesn't hear Harley Jaines leave his seat in the pews behind her and come toward us. Even the judge sits mesmerized as his imposing figure steps through the opening in the railing and comes to stand behind Cincy.

His hand is gentle on her shoulder. She turns and looks up at his face. I can't see Cincy's expression, but I can see his and my throat closes up.

This is a man who has done terrible things, and who understands how those things can ruin you.

Harley Jaines lets his daughter look at him, lets her recognize herself in those dark eyes and angular cheekbones. Then he wraps her in his arms.

I swallow hard to silence the keening inside my head as Harley Jaines leads Cincy down the aisle and out of the courtroom.

CHAPTER 27

The courtroom is silent after Cincy and Harley Jaines have gone. Lenora watches the door where they disappeared, her eyes hollow. Finally her attorney asks the judge for her conditioned release, and the judge addresses the only person at the table who hasn't spoken through the whole proceeding, the man I had pegged as a prison official. Apparently he's from the district attorney's office, instead.

"If the state has no objection," the judge says, "I will release Lenora Jaines to the supervision of her attorney, pending an official release. I see no reason she should spend any more time in custody."

"No objections, Your Honor."

"Does the State plan to pursue further charges in this ten-year-old matter?"

The prosecutor gets the message. "No, Your Honor."

The judge nods. "We stand adjourned." She rises, pulling us all to our feet. She picks up her files and leaves the room. Her step seems slower than before, her demeanor less brisk. I wonder how she can watch such human dramas every day without letting them eat her up. My own limbs feel like water.

When Lenora meets my eyes, the hardness I saw at the prison has melted from her face. "I'm sorry, Bobbie. I couldn't tell you."

"I know." I reach across the table and squeeze her hands. "What will you do now?"

She looks blank for a moment, as the realization that she is free sinks in. "Harley has a place by the ocean."

The attorney leans toward her and touches her arm. "We have some paperwork to take care of, Lenora."

She nods and lets him lead her away. She doesn't look back.

In the hallway outside the courtroom, I search the faces that pass me by and realize I'm foolishly looking for David—as if now that this is over he might magically appear and take me home. Instead I find Harley Jaines coming out of the witness lounge where I'd waited before. Lines of fatigue mark his stoic face.

"Is Cincy okay?" I ask.

He shakes his head. "I don't know. I'm trying to get her to come home with us."

Home with us, he says. Him and Lenora. The idea cuts me a little.

"I need to get my overnight bag out of your car."

Harley Jaines frowns. "How will you get home?"

I shrug. "Maybe I'll fly. I have a credit card." *But no one to pick me up from the Calgary airport.*

"I have to wait here for Lenora and the lawyer," he says, and hands me his keys.

I look at him. "Maybe I'll just drive off in your car."

I've never seen him smile before. It changes his face completely, his teeth straight and white, his dark eyes crinkled at the corners. He is the handsome soldier in the photo that used to sit on Cincy's dresser. "Never happen," he says.

As I turn to walk away, he adds, "Thanks for what you did. For Lenora and Cynthia both."

I fetch my bag and return Harley Jaines's keys, then tap on the door of the witness lounge before entering. Cincy is slumped on the sofa, elbows braced on open knees, her head hanging down like someone fighting light-headedness. I drop my bag on the floor and sink into a chair facing her.

"I don't blame you for hating me," she says to my shoes.

She doesn't even realize she has rescued me again.

I lay my head back against the chair. "I was really angry at first. But I'm no judge of anybody's past. Not even Harley Jaines's." I take a deep breath and blow it out. "You came here today, and that took a lot of guts."

She shakes her head. "No. I'm just clearing my conscience in case there's a God."

At first I think this is another of her flippant responses, but something in her tone warns me. "What do you mean?" She doesn't look at me, and doesn't answer. "Cincy, what is it? Are you sick?"

"I didn't intend to tell you."

"And you thought you could get by with that?"

She's quiet a moment, then says, "I have cancer," and finally looks up. "They took one breast, but it's already spread and I've been taking chemo. Which explains this lovely hairstyle."

I feel my mouth open but I don't know what to say. "Oh, Cincy. That...*sucks.*"

Cincy laughs. "You said it, Sarsaparilla." When my eyes fill, she says, "Don't you dare cry."

I take a deep breath, blink vigorously. "What's the prognosis?"

"My friend Rick—he's an R.N. at the hospital where I go for treatments—keeps urging me to fight it. He has more faith in medicine than I do. I'm supposed to start another round of chemo next week."

"God, Cincy. Did you tell Harley?"

"No. I only told the prosecuting attorney, so he wouldn't arrest me before I could get out of here and go home." She gives me a warning look. "I don't want Lenora to know. I've tortured her enough."

Cincy lays her head back, her spine conforming to the sag of the sofa. "She has a chance to start a new life. The best thing I can do for both of us is go back to California. I've been working for an insurance company, so I have good coverage. And I have Rick."

We sit in silence for half a minute, while I think of what Cincy's facing and consider her odds. "Can I come, too?" I ask.

She thinks I'm joking and tries to laugh. "You need to be with David. Did you tell him about the baby yet?"

"David left me."

We look at each other, two lost souls linked at childhood. "Let me go home with you, Cincy. We have a lot of catching up to do."

When we leave the courthouse, the hallways are empty. We see nothing of Lenora or Harley Jaines.

CHAPTER 28

On the long road south to Redding, California, Cincy and I take turns at the wheel. The pace is leisurely; Cincy is on indefinite medical leave from her job, and I have nowhere else to be.

Her old car shimmies like a cheap hotel bed when the speedometer hits fifty-five. We talk only about silly things that make us laugh, and we play the radio. While I'm at the wheel, Cincy naps, and during those quiet stretches I try hard not to think of Lenora searching the courthouse for Cincy, wondering where we've gone. But Lenora's still the strongest person I know, and she has Harley.

David, however, is not so tough. He'll worry when I don't come back. He's not the type to shut off caring like a water faucet, and I've no desire to make him suffer. When I get to Cincy's place, I'll call and tell him where I am.

At Portland, we cross the Columbia and the Willamette Rivers and shimmy on down Interstate 5 through the Willamette Valley. Halfway home, with me at the wheel, Cincy reads me the rules.

"There'll be no talking about death," she says, "or about the bad stuff that happened when we were kids. And no fussing about me and how I'm feeling. We're only going to have fun. Drive to the beach, horseback-ride in the mountains. Hit the malls."

"Sounds exhausting."

"Well, gut up, girl. I'll give you two days to rest, then we're off." The sockets around her eyes are dark gray.

She rests her head against the seat back and closes her eyes. After a few miles, when I think she's asleep, she says, "I'm not going to take any more chemo. It can't cure me, just make me feel like hell for the time I've got."

I nod slowly, taking this in. "Okay."

She opens her eyes and smiles at me. "Very good, Sarsaparilla." She lays her head back again. "I can't wait for you to meet Rick. He's very cool, and he's more than just my nurse."

We stop for the night in Eugene, Oregon. At an ATM machine, I withdraw two hundred dollars in U.S. currency, using David's and my joint credit card. The bill will go to David. I suppose if he refuses to pay it, my card will stop working. At a discount store that stays open late, I use the card again to buy underwear, contact lens solution and a mystery novel with a cat and roses on the cover.

We arrive in Redding at midafternoon the next day and pull into a complex of one-story duplexes in the north part of town. "This is it. Lucky number thirteen," Cincy says.

Her apartment is light and small, with walls the color of sunlight and an eclectic mix of secondhand furniture that she's refinished or repainted. It reminds me of David's and my first apartment on campus, except that hers has an extra bedroom. The bedroom's barely bigger than a walk-in closet, however, and there's no furniture in it. She's been using it for storage. For now, I'll bed down on the couch.

We set our bags in a corner and Cincy gives me a walking tour of the neighborhood to stretch the kinks from our legs after so many hours in the car. Then she calls Rick and invites him to go to dinner with us. He has class that night, however, which Cincy has forgotten. She promises we'll drop by the hospital tomorrow.

"He's preparing for the MCAT," she tells me, "so he can apply to medical school."

At a local trattoria, Cincy orders the pasta special, which we agree to split, and a small carafe of red wine. She pours me only half a glass.

"After this," she says by way of a toast, "no more alcohol for you. It's not good for the baby."

I had almost succeeded in forgetting I am pregnant. Cincy's eyes nail me. She waits with her glass raised.

"Okay," I say, knowing what she wants, knowing that if I say the words, it's a promise. "No more alcohol, and no more sleeping pills. I've already started backing off the depression medicine. Dr. Bannar warned me not to quit that stuff cold turkey."

Cincy smiles and clinks my glass. For that moment, she looks young again, healthy. "Good for you. My goal is to hang around long enough to see your baby born."

I sip the wine and think, *I have no goals at all.*

Leaving the restaurant, I see a Help Wanted sign by the cash register and ask for an application. Cincy frowns.

"I *have* to get a job, you know," I tell her. "At some point David's bound to cut off this credit card."

That night I lie awake on her art deco sofa, memorizing the clicks and hums of my new surroundings. The extra pillow from Cincy's bed smells faintly chemical.

I'm going to keep my baby. I'll be a single mom. The idea scares me to death.

Cincy sleeps late the next morning, and at midday, we venture out to buy me a Hollywood bed with a decent mattress. I put it on my credit card again.

When we get to the hospital where Rick works as an R.N., he's in the chemo lab with a patient. We linger in a waiting room furnished with California impressionist prints and white leather furniture. Several nurses say hi to Cincy as they pass. One comments on her haircut, another says something bawdy about her love life. They do not ask how she's feeling.

"This is where I took my treatments," she tells me. "They're good people."

In a few minutes, a slim black man in blue scrubs comes into the room, grinning. "Hi, Scooter. Glad you're back."

Cincy gets up and hugs him, smiling.

"Rick, this is Bobbie."

Rick's grip is firm, his arm strong. "Hi, Bobbie. Nice to meet you at last." He is light-skinned, with a smooth-shaved head and one tiny gold earring. I like his smile.

"Same here. I hope we're not disturbing your work."

He waves it off. "I'm due a break. I'll buy you ladies a drink in the cafeteria."

Holding Cincy's hand, he ushers us through the maze of hallways and elevators to the basement. The lunch crowd is mostly gone and the place is quiet. Rick brings three colas to a corner table.

"So. What do you girls have planned?" He doesn't ask about Lenora, or why I'm here or how Cincy feels, and I wonder if she's read him the rules, too. But I watch his eyes evaluate her sallow color, her condition, as Cincy jabbers about our morning of shopping. His face betrays no conclusions nor loses its smile. I wish I knew what he's thinking, and begin to plot a way to talk to him alone. He can tell me what to do for Cincy, how to take care of her when things get worse.

"Have you been to northern California before?" Rick asks me.

"No, I haven't. But I like it already."

Rick has a good bedside manner. He makes eye contact and he

listens when I answer. "The weekend after the MCAT," he says to Cincy, "let's take Bobbie out to Capetown."

"Great! We found this really quiet, wild beach," she tells me. "It's beautiful. Too cold to swim, but we can beachcomb. And there's a terrific little café that only the locals know about, with an outdoor deck." In Rick's presence, Cincy seems transformed. Her face looks genuinely happy.

"Meanwhile, can I take you girls out to dinner tonight?" Rick says. "What do you like, Bobbie? Seafood? Chinese?"

"I'll eat anything I don't have to cook."

He and Cincy laugh. "Just like Scooter," he says. "Why can't I meet a woman who likes to cook?"

At dinner that night, Cincy tells Rick I'm pregnant. I feel my face flush.

"Barely two months," I say, trying for a casual attitude. "Not quite time to pick out names yet." Which of course leads to a spirited debate on what to name the baby.

"Let's see," Cincy says, "there's Gwendolyn, Rapunzel, Sarsaparilla…." Then she has to explain our laughter to Rick.

He suggests Shaunda and Lorraine, which we quickly veto. "What about *boy* names?" he asks.

Cincy and I look at each other, then, in unison, we shake our heads. "Naaaah. It's a girl." And more laughter.

We linger an hour after dinner before Rick has to go home and study. Cincy looks tired when we say good-night at Rick's car. She lets me drive.

"He's a great guy," I tell her.

"Yep, he is. Which reminds me. Did you call David yet?"

I leave a brief message for David on the machine at home, then try to get his friend Mitchell Sampson's number from information. There's no listing.

The next week I write to David in care of the museum. I tell him about the credit card charges, and ask him to ship me a box of things so I won't have to buy so much. My list includes clothes, my makeup, a few prized books and my needlework. I tell him about Lenora, and about Cincy's cancer. Despite her plan for all the things we'll do, her strength slips daily and I anticipate long quiet hours ahead.

As I fold the letter into its envelope, Cincy asks, "Did you tell him?"

I know what she means, and sigh. "No, and I've already explained why." I seal and stamp the letter. "I've agreed to your rules, now here's mine. You must respect my decision not to tell David I'm pregnant. No nagging me, and no telling him on your own." The tone of my voice leaves no room for debate.

"All right, all right," Cincy grumbles. "But you're wrong, wrong, wrong."

Mr. Zazzio, proprietor of the Olive Pit trattoria, phones me to come in for an interview. He is short and plump and smells pleasantly of garlic and olive oil. His black mustache is flecked with gray and curls up at the ends, giving the impression of a constant smile. We talk at a table by the window before the store opens for lunch. Cincy has been a regular customer here. He knows her by name and knows she's been ill.

He leans forward, his short arms folded on the wooden tabletop. "Why you want to work for me?" he asks earnestly, and for a moment I can't think how to answer.

"I need a job," I say, "and I like the way this place smells."

Mr. Z bursts into hearty laughter. "I think you and me get along just fine. Come to the kitchen and meet Mrs. Z."

Mrs. Z smiles at me but is too busy to shake hands. She has flour smudges on her forearms and cheek, but her checkered apron is spotless. A fragrant pot of tomato sauce bubbles on the stove. As we leave the kitchen, she calls something in Italian to Mr. Z.

"She says you're too skinny and need to eat more pasta," he whispers.

I am delighted to learn the position isn't for a waitress, as I'd assumed, but for a baker. "I don't know much about baking," I admit, "but I'd love to learn."

Mr. Z waves away my doubts. "I train you myself. You have to get here at 6:00 a.m. sharp, but you get off at noon."

It's perfect; Cincy sleeps late in the mornings, and I would be free in the afternoons and evenings. I smile. "I've always been a morning person."

He slaps his hand on the table. "You're hired. Come in Monday at six o'clock." Then he laughs again and before I leave he folds me in a hefty Italian hug. This must be what it's like to have a grandfather.

Just when I begin to think David isn't going to send my things, the box arrives. It's huge and still sitting in the entryway when I get home from work because it's too heavy for Cincy to lift. Together we wrestle it onto the Formica tabletop and I slit the packing tape.

The comfort of finding my familiar sweaters and jeans surprises me. Without intention, I lift each one to my face as I extract them from the box; they smell like home. My books are there, along with two plastic bags of makeup in bottles and tubes, and he has removed the wooden dowels from my needlework tote and enclosed the whole lot in the box. I am thrilled and grateful for his thoughtfulness. I picture David packing the box and my nose burns. I wonder how he's doing, whether it hurt him to pack my things.

Underneath everything else, wrapped in tissue, I find the stack of butterfly pillowtops I made for Lenora. My breath stops as I uncover the brightly colored linen squares and lift them from the box. David must have thought I meant for him to send these, too, when I asked for my needlework.

Cincy picks up a painted lady and holds it up. "These are beautiful! Did you make these?"

I nod. "From my own drawings." My voice feels tight.

Cincy spreads them one at a time on the sofa back—the mourning cloak, a white admiral, my antenors. "I know this one! The blue *Morpho!*" she says. "They're gorgeous."

I extract my work-in-progress from the tote bag. "Anise swallowtail," I tell her, holding it up. "It's not quite finished."

"We can make them into pillows and toss them all over the apartment," she says, grinning.

Sure. Why not.

"Believe it or not, I have an old sewing machine a former landlady gave me," she says.

Together we calculate how much fabric to buy for the pillow backs, and how many bags of stuffing. It will be a project, something for Cincy to do in the long afternoons when she's too tired to go out.

"I'm surprised you didn't embroider any *worms*," she teases.

I raise my eyebrows. "It's not too late."

She makes a face.

Six mornings a week in Mr. Z's stainless-steel kitchen, I knead yeast and flour into fragrant Italian bread dough and shape it into slender loaves, long ones for the dinner crowd, small ones for sandwiches. I learn to make homemade pasta, and pizza dough from scratch. The first few weeks I feel mildly nauseated by the smell of garlic so early in the day, but the morning sickness is short-lived and soon I've gained five pounds from eating my own creations. I take bread home to Cincy, too, but she gains no weight.

Each morning I awaken to birdsong in the trees outside my open bedroom window. I like getting up at first light and going out when the streets are quiet, the air cool and dry. After the time changes for daylight savings, the sun is barely up when I slip out the front door and lock it behind me. Cincy insists I drive her car to work because she never goes out before noon anyway. Indeed, some days she stays in bed until I get home. For entertainment, we stroll the malls, but she tires too quickly for horseback riding in the hills.

Rick scores high on his MCAT and we celebrate over dinner. But with his work schedule and mine, it is May before the three of us can take our planned trip to the ocean. Mr. Z gives me Saturday off and we make the three-hour drive across the mountains and along the Trinity River to the sea. Rick and Cincy talk of a place south of Eureka where the coast is wild and rugged, not yet built up. Rick says there's a chance we'll see orca whales passing through.

The day is clear and exceptionally warm. We leave our car in the parking lot of the Pelican's Roost café and hike a sandy footpath to a cliff that overlooks the ocean. Cincy has to stop and rest along the way, but the view is worth the effort. White-edged waves roll and pound onto jagged black rocks. Sea lions bask in comical positions above the slap and spray, their fur drying to a lighter brown in the sunshine. Between rock outcroppings along the shore, the sand looks almost white in the sunshine.

Rick points out a path that winds downward to the beach and we descend.

The sea lions ignore us as we roll up our pant legs and walk the surf line, carrying our shoes, flinching at the icy fingers of water that sprawl on the sand. When Cincy gets tired, she and Rick find a rock in the sun and I walk on alone, inhaling the smell of the sea.

A hundred yards down the shoreline I pick my way over a small mountain of boulders and emerge on a stretch of secluded white beach that opens flatly to shallow turquoise water. The waves are gentle here, the beach cocooned by granite-colored cliffs. Weathered cypress trees dot the rocks and cluster on the clifftop. The place is wild and beautiful, and I stop on the beach to take it in.

Ancient rocks tower above me; surf foam laps at my feet. I close my eyes, welcoming the warmth of the sun on my face, and feel extraordinarily lucky to be here in this moment, whole and sane, on this spectacular earth.

Turning into the wind, I lift my arms in celebration. And that's when I feel it. Something moves inside me, the first distinctive flutter of life—like the kick of a tiny, determined foot.

At midafternoon, the three of us are sprawled like sea lions in padded lounge chairs on the second-story deck of the Pelican's Roost, overlooking the Pacific. The sun dries our pant legs and glints off our sunglasses. Rick and Cincy drink beer from brown bottles and I sip a fruity, frozen rum drink without the rum.

Cincy looks exhausted but happy. We drowse for an hour, then Rick becomes restless and descends the rock embankment again to beachcomb for shells. Cincy and I rest languidly on the padded chairs, watching his figure grow smaller in the distance, listening to the surf and the cry of the gulls.

Cincy will not live to see my baby. I've known this for some time now. Cincy knows, too.

"I'm ready to talk about dying now," she says.

All the breath goes out of me. I wait, inadequate to the task.

"Do you ever wonder what comes after? If there's really an afterlife, or just nothing, black and endless."

A cool sea wind stirs our hair. "Some people believe our spirits come back again and again," I say.

"That's a nice thought," she says. "I like it better than the idea of heaven and hell. That never did make sense to me."

"Hmm."

"The idea of nothingness sounds scary, but when you think about it, it isn't so bad. If your consciousness just snuffs out, you won't know it. You don't exist. No pain, no thoughts, no dreams." She snaps her fingers. "Nothing. The people you leave behind have it worse."

My mouth goes dry, but my throat's too tight too swallow the drink in my hand. "Maybe so. The ones who love you won't forget. They'll miss you terribly."

"I don't want that. Well, I want to be remembered, sure, but I don't want you and Rick to be sad. There's no point. We live, we die. It happens to everybody."

I cannot speak.

"Two things I want to tell you, then I'll shut up," she says. "First, I want to be cremated. Can't stand the thought of being buried in the ground. And second, when you think it's close, it's okay to call Lenora."

CHAPTER 29

At a pay phone in the hospital lobby, I make the call. I dial the number I have memorized, drop a row of coins into the slot and wait for connections to happen. Today Oregon seems a long way from here. Outside the tall windows beside the phone, the California sun has warmed to a perfect temperature and the air is fragrant with the scent of citrus blossoms. Nobody should die here in June.

Lenora answers on the second ring.

"Lenora, it's Bobbie."

I phoned her a month ago, shortly after Cincy's and my conversation at the beach, to warn her. To give her time to adjust to the knowledge that Cincy is dying. Lenora wanted to come then, but I told her no. That's not what Cincy wanted.

Now her voice is low-keyed and controlled, but underneath I hear the stiff vibration of pain.

"How is she?"

"She collapsed in the shower this morning. I brought her to the hospital, and she's resting. Nothing broken, thank goodness." The next sentence is harder to say. "They've started her on morphine."

"Oh, God," Lenora says, and for a moment the line is quiet. "It's going to be fast, isn't it."

"If she's lucky."

Lenora doesn't need to know that Cincy lay helpless in the running water for an hour before I got home because she was too weak to crawl out of the tub. Or that the pain shows in her eyes almost constantly; that she's losing her nouns, a sign the cancer has reached her brain. These realities will be apparent soon enough.

"I'll get there as soon as I can," Lenora says.

I give her directions to St. Anthony's Hospital and also to Cincy's apartment. "I'm not sure which place we'll be. She wants to go home, and Rick can give the injections."

With little else to say, we sign off. I'm glad she's coming, and I dread her arrival.

Down the hall, I push gently on the door to Cincy's room, but there's no need for quiet. Cincy lies in a deep, druggy sleep, her face slack and putty-colored. I touch her short, black hair where it feathers out on the pillow around her head. It's almost dry now; she was washing it when she fell.

I sit on a chair beside the bed, lay my face on the cool white sheets and weep. I need to get it done before she wakes, before I take her home, before Lenora comes.

I spend the night in the chair beside her bed. Rick arrives early the next morning to be there when Cincy's doctor makes rounds. Cincy won't eat her breakfast, and when the doctor comes, she insists that he remove the IV.

"I want to go home," she says. She has left written directions refusing any "extreme or unnatural measures" to preserve her life. Rick supports her decision, his jaw tight.

The doctor is tall with graying temples, a face that's seen everything, yet somehow his eyes remain young. "I understand," he says. "And you have good friends who can help you do that. I'd like to keep you here today, until you get some strength back, then release you tomorrow morning. How's that?"

"Okay," she says. Her skin looks yellow against the white sheets. She has a large purple bruise on her forearm where it struck the bathtub when she fell.

"To get stronger, if you don't want the IV, you're going to have to eat," the doctor says. "You can have anything that sounds good. Pizza? Ice cream?"

"Ice cream."

"Julie will fix you up." He glances at the nurse and she smiles. "Leave the oxygen tube in place," he tells Julie, "but she's not to be put on a respirator."

The nurse gives her another injection, promising ice cream when she awakens. Cincy sinks into sleep.

Rick goes to work, three floors below in the therapy unit. The waiting room down the hall from Cincy is empty, so I slump onto the vinyl sofa. On the overhead TV that is never turned off, a man with no arms plays guitar with his feet.

When I awake, the waiting room clock reads 1:30. My neck is painfully stiff, my spine knotted. I struggle to sit up.

In the chair across from me, Harley Jaines sits like a granite Buddha, hands resting on his spread knees. My mind still leaden with sleep, at first I think I've dreamed him. What is he doing here?

But of course he would come. Cincy is his daughter. Somehow that's hard to remember. Seeing me awake, he nods.

"Is Lenora with her?" I ask.

"Yes. We've been here about an hour."

I rub my eyes and forehead, my stiff neck. "You haven't been in yet?"

"No. They needed some time alone." He sounds uncertain that Cincy will want to see him.

I run my fingers through my tangled hair and replace the clamp that's supposed to hold it out of my eyes. "They've had an hour," I say to Harley Jaines. "Come on."

When we enter the room, Lenora is feeding Cincy ice cream. Cincy opens her mouth like a baby bird. Both their faces are printed with emotional exhaustion, but with something else, too—something like relief. Lenora looks up and smiles, and I know things are all right between them.

"Look who's here," Cincy says. "It's my whole…." She can't think of the words.

"Damn family," I say.

"Yeah." Then she smiles, with ice cream on her lips.

The next morning, we take her home. Rick supervises. He is cheerful and efficient, and Cincy responds to him the way she always does. Lenora hovers in the background, watching them, while Harley brings Cincy's car to the front entrance. I will drive us home; Lenora and Harley will follow.

Cincy's smile is weak, her eyes glazed. She doesn't seem to be in any pain but she's short of breath. Rick moves her easily from the bed to the wheelchair, and downstairs, into the car. When she's belted in, he kisses the back of her hand. "I'll come by as soon as my shift is over. You okay, Scooter?"

"Good," she says. The word sounds slurred.

At the apartment, Harley Jaines carries her inside and settles her on the bed. Cincy is tired and ready to sleep. Lenora fusses over her bedding a few moments and we leave the door open a crack in case she calls.

Then Lenora and Harley and I are together in the small living room with nothing to do. Harley paces.

"Why don't you go out and get us some sandwiches for lunch," Lenora says to him. He nods, grateful for escape.

When he's gone, Lenora wanders the apartment, looking at her daughter's things without touching them, until she comes to the sewing machine I've set up on the kitchen table. She picks up the pillow sham of the mourning cloaks. Cincy has finished the backing on six of them.

I stand at the doorway and watch as Lenora runs her fingers over the stitched butterfly. She lays it aside and looks at the others one by one until she comes to the antenor. She bites her lip.

"Cincy doesn't know I made them for you."

She looks at me with gentle disbelief. "Of course she knows."

Lenora folds me in a hug. We have no words to name the years that came between us, and no need of them. Those years have disappeared.

Using a grapefruit, Rick shows me how to give morphine injections. My head feels skittish as I hold the plump fruit and insert the needle, imagining Cincy's thin flesh. "Lenora would probably be better at this."

"I don't know Lenora," he says quietly. "I trust you."

We are in the kitchen alone. It is evening; Lenora and Harley have gone to their motel room. I set my jaw and keep trying until I get it right.

"Okay. Now try it on me," Rick says, and pushes up his sleeve. "Just insert the needle. Don't push the plunger."

His arm is smooth and brown and muscular, nothing like Cincy's, but still I quail before pushing the needle beneath his skin.

"Don't be tentative," he advises. "It's better if she feels the stick than if you have to do it over."

I nod and push the needle in, pulling it back out quickly.

"Good," he says. "That's good. Keep practicing on the grapefruit, and tonight before I go, I'll help you do it for real. One of these times she's going to need it when I'm not here."

I feel sick in my stomach.

The next day Harley disappears for two hours and comes back with a folding wheelchair, which he opens in the living room.

I shake my head, thinking she'll never get in it. He catches my look but ignores it, rolling the chair into her room. I follow. Cincy is awake.

"It's beautiful outdoors," Harley says. "Want to go for a walk?"

Cincy eyes the chair a moment, then looks up at him. "Sure," she says. "I could use some fresh air."

Even now, I still can't predict what Cincy will do.

Father and daughter go off down the sidewalk in the June sunshine while Lenora and I stand and watch.

That's the only time I see Lenora cry.

Harley and Cincy's afternoon walks become a daily routine. Sometimes they're gone more than an hour, and Cincy tells us they've been to the park watching the kids swing, or that they sat by the pond and fed bread crusts to the ducks. Sometimes she can't remember where they've been.

Rick visits every day. He and Harley circle each other warily but politely.

Cincy is receding. We help her to the kitchen table for meals but she has no interest. She forgets the names of foods, and sometimes our names. Her kidneys begin to shut down.

Lenora stays all night now, sleeping on the sofa though I offer my bed. Harley goes to their motel room overnight and disappears for long periods during the day, but he never misses Cincy's afternoon ride.

One evening when Lenora and I are alone with her, Cincy becomes restless and agitated. Her eyes dart around the room and her speech isn't coherent. Lenora and I sit beside her bed, holding her hands. Finally she settles and comes back to us from wherever she was. She recognizes us again and appears to be comfortable, relaxed.

"My two favorite women," she whispers quite clearly, and closes her eyes. Then she is gone.

CHAPTER 30

Harley Jaines drives back to Oregon alone. He has taken a job with a company that ships lumber from a port in Tillamook Bay, Lenora tells me. He works in the yard, driving machinery that moves tons of lumber. Considering his background, this surprises me.

"He likes being outdoors," Lenora says, "and he's no good at being idle."

She stays on to help me sort Cincy's things and clear out the apartment. When we're finished, we will drive Cincy's old car north to Tillamook. Cincy deeded the car to me, and left a few thousand dollars she had in a bank account to Rick, to help with medical school.

"I can't take this," Rick says, his eyes miserable when I hand him a cashier's check.

"Yes, you can," I say, folding his hand around the check. "Cincy told me you had put yourself through college and nursing school, and that you'd be doing the same with med school. This won't help much, but she wanted you to have it."

"God, I miss her," he says.

Because he can't hug Cincy, he hugs me, and hurries away with his grief locked inside. I wish I could help him, but nobody can.

Lenora and I donate Cincy's furniture and dishes to a local senior center, pack the car with the personal effects we've chosen and leave the rest of her things for Goodwill, including her clothes and the ancient sewing machine that doesn't work right. I visit Mr. and Mrs. Z's trattoria to say goodbye and receive floury hugs. Mrs. Z piles fresh bread and hard cheese into my arms, for the road.

Lenora and I drive away from Redding on the last Monday morning in June. Cincy's ashes travel with us on the back seat, the urn packed in a special box furnished by the mortuary. The last few days have exhausted our grief, at least for now, and we talk easily while the miles slip away. She tells me stories from the prison; I talk about David and our failed marriage. Like Cincy, Lenora insists it is unfair not to tell David about the baby.

"He's the one who left me," I point out, but she's not convinced.

I have agreed to stay with her until I decide where to go and what to do about finding a job. I wonder how Harley Jaines will feel about this, but I've made no other plans. For months I've been living one day at a time. Now I feel aimless, drifting, as if I'm waiting for something but I don't know what.

Lenora and Harley's house sits on a bluff overlooking a wildlife refuge and the ocean. We arrive in late afternoon and unload the contents of the car temporarily into a garage beneath the house. Harley gets home just as we've finished.

"Nice timing," Lenora teases, and kisses his cheek. He doesn't seem surprised to see me.

Lenora asks Harley to show me around while she makes something for dinner. Harley Jaines and I walk the grounds with our jackets zipped to the neck, six feet of space separating us.

"It was private property before the park came and surrounded it," he explains. "The old couple who built it couldn't keep it up anymore and I stumbled on it just when they'd decided to sell. It was blind luck."

And expensive, I'm certain; it definitely has location. Either Harley Jaines has money, or he has a huge mortgage.

The house isn't fancy or large, just two bedrooms and two baths. The dining area sits at one end of an open kitchen. But the house is secluded by woods and the view from the outdoor deck is spectacular. After dinner, Lenora and I sit there to watch the night come down. The only lights are the moon and a zillion stars.

"I like this house because it's too small for the past to live in," Lenora says. Still, history clings to them. By day Harley works at the docks and at night he walks the beach alone. Lenora, too, has her solitary ways. I watch the two of them when they're unaware, so separate and silent, yet they're easy together and there's never a cross word between them.

The window in my guest bedroom faces the woods behind the house. Harley has put out a salt lick that attracts deer, and Lenora has erected a bird feeder and planted a butterfly garden. Over the next week, we spend a lot of time there, pulling weeds or sitting silently to watch for winged visitors. We finish the butterfly pillows and toss them on the beds and the window seat in the living room. Every time I see them I think of Cincy.

I've been there less than two weeks when David arrives. I return from a walk in the woods to find his car in the driveway, he and Lenora sitting in the wooden chairs on the deck.

Undoubtedly Lenora has called him and told him I'm pregnant. Unlike Cincy, she feels no compunction about interfering in my life. She scheduled me an appointment with an obstetrician as soon as we arrived here, and she's told me several times I should call David. I knew eventually she would call. But I didn't know if he would come.

Now that he's here, I know this is what I've been waiting for all along.

David is watching me approach when I first see him. As I climb the steps to the deck, Lenora gets up and goes indoors.

He looks young in his faded jeans and open windbreaker, his blond hair in need of a trim. I'm overcome by the remembered scent of him, the feel of his arms in my dreams.

"Hello," he says. His eyes move from my face to my hair, to my abdomen. I'm five and a half months along, enough to show.

I sit in the chair still warm from Lenora's presence and meet his eyes. "I'm glad you came."

"Lenora told me about the baby." His expression is anxious, but there's no anger in his eyes.

"I expected she would. Did she also say why I hadn't told you before?"

"Yes."

I turn my eyes toward the ocean. "It seems a silly reason now, after all that's happened." Then I look at him and ask, "If I weren't pregnant, would you have come?"

His eyes are blue and open as a cloudless sky. David never lies.

"I've been waiting and waiting for you to call," he says. "I never should have left you like that. I felt I was losing you and I didn't know what to do."

"I know."

The sea breeze blows our hair. I hear the distant cry of gulls and the lonely wash of the waves.

"Bobbie," he says, and I look back to him, trying to remember whether or not he's ever called me by my nickname before. I don't think so.

"I miss you," he says, spreading his hands. "Every day."

"I miss you, too."

He leans forward, his face intense. "Come home. Not just for the baby, for me. And for you."

I look in his eyes and know he needs me to give what I wasn't able to give before. Am I capable of that? I want to. I want to give him body and spirit, the rest of my life. I want to give him his child.

"It's a boy," I tell him and smile. "We're going to have a son."

CHAPTER 31

Shady River, Oregon

Late for migration, a monarch butterfly rows its jagged path upwind across the placid Columbia. I stand at the center of the new river bridge and watch the butterfly's progress until it shrinks out of sight. It is September, and the breeze feels like a drink of cool water, crisp and welcome. Some time during the second trimester, my body transformed from cold-natured to hot. My hand rests on my rounded belly, which protrudes beyond the reach of my jacket buttons.

I was astounded when the technician first told me it would be a boy. I'd never considered anything except a daughter. I know nothing about little boys, and that feels absolutely right to me, as if I've been given a clean slate. A chance to make my own mistakes.

We're going to name him Peter Benjamin. Peter for Petey Small, who thought my life was worth saving. And Benjamin for Benny, a little boy on a train who was for a few hours my brother. David likes the name, too. Every time I walk past him, his hand reaches out to feel his son kick.

Lenora stands on the bridge beside me, lost in her own thoughts. We are looking down into familiar waters. A car rumbles past behind us, vibrating the metal floor beneath our feet. Finally Lenora lifts the pewter urn and slowly pours Cincy's ashes into the light wind.

To the river gods we entrust this friend, this daughter, this sister. Free her spirit. Let her rest.

White debris clings to the surface of the water, then slowly disappears. When the residue is gone, Lenora tosses the urn into the river. It disappears with a jarring *plunk.* She never was a sentimental sort.

Our mission finished, we walk back to the Oregon side of the bridge, enjoying the autumn sunshine on our shoulders. David and Harley stand beside the cars, talking. For two men who couldn't be more different, they are oddly comfortable together. Harley's shadowy silences still make me uneasy. I believe he took Cincy's death hardest of us all.

David watches my face as we approach, the habitual frown line etched between his eyebrows. I wonder if it will ever leave him, even after the baby is born.

"You okay?" he says.

"Fine." I smile to convince him. He worries about me far too much, but I appreciate it, even when it drives me crazy.

I hug Lenora goodbye and wave to Harley.

"Phone us as soon as you start labor," she calls from their car window as they drive away.

"We promise," David calls back, waving.

He opens my door and waits while I wedge into the passenger side. Then he climbs behind the wheel. It's a slow season at the museum, so we're taking a vacation, a last fling of freedom before the baby comes. Although it makes him nervous, we deliberately haven't planned a route or made reservations. We're going where the road leads us. Flexibility training, David says. As parents, we'll need it.

We drive along the winding river road with the windows down, our hair whipping in the wind. One hand smugly on my stomach, I experience a moment of careless and expansive happiness. David glances over at me and smiles. For one golden instant, the frown line is gone.

More and more as the days go by, I am coming to believe that David and I will stay together, till death do us part, despite the tiny pockets of ourselves we still keep private. By the time we're Lenora and Harley's age, perhaps those pockets will be full of each other.